COMPELLED

SHAWNTELLE
MADISON

Cari,
Love has no
limits.

Shawntelle Mad

This novel is a work of fiction. Names, characters, places, and incidents are the product of the author's imagination or are used fictitiously. Any resemblance to actual events, locales, or persons living or dead is purely coincidental.

ACKNOWLEDGMENTS

Wow, what a ride! It's been nearly two years since Coveted was released and now Natalya's journey has reached this point. It's amazing to think back to when I got the call from my agent Jim McCarthy about the offer from Betsy Mitchell with Del Rey books. The first two books had the best editors in the world. Thank you, Tricia Narwani and also Mike Braff.

I have so many people to thank for helping me with this book. To Sarah Bromley and Wayne Purdin for offering a hand to help me craft the best book. Thank you! To my Magic & Mayhem Writer sisters for their support. Thanks Amanda Bonilla, Amanda Carlson, Nadia Lee, and Sandy Williams!

Additional thanks Amanda Bonilla for reading a few scenes for me. You rock, sister.

The opening of this book has been read by so many people including Missouri RWA's CORE critique group and my critique partners Amanda Berry and Jeannie Lin. Thanks, ladies!

Additional thanks to Tommi Veijalainen for help with the Finnish language.

To anyone I didn't mention, thank you for being there to support me. I'm grateful to have you in my life.

Prologue

Years of suffering and solitude can change in an instant. For me, everything changed on a wintry New Year's Eve night. As the new year's sun rose, I wasn't Natalya Stravinsky anymore, the ostracized werewolf from the South Toms River Pack.

I was something much more: I was the pack's alpha female. Such a thing weighed heavily on my shoulders as I drove home with my new husband, Thorn, and struck me again the next morning when I woke up with my beloved at my side. The season would change soon, and with it, the snow would melt, yet I'd still be the same on the inside.

Or was I? Thorn didn't make me feel that way. Nestled side by side in our new home together, we held each other all night. Every now and then, I reached out to touch his golden hair. He'd snore, not so much as twitching while I took him in my arms. After experiencing the fight of my life last night, I should've slept like a hibernating bear. Yet, I was restless, burdened.

I drew my nose to his chest and inhaled. His

wonderful scent whispered poetry to my soul, and any pain I had wilted away. Here was my best friend, all mine, until he succumbed to what was bleeding his life away. As to when he would die, I didn't know. All I knew was that Thorn didn't have decades, or maybe even years left. With his arms wrapped around me and mine over his shoulders, no one could take him away from me — for now.

I held onto that. I'd waited this long for him.

I will covet the time we have together until the very end.

Chapter 1

Two months later

"You suck at being an alpha female. A trip to the proctologist for a rectal exam is a lot more intimidating than you are."

My head whipped up to frown at Aggie. My best friend, who had relocated from New York City, had moved into my old place. She had lived here for the past two months, but I still stopped by to check up on things. Agatha McClure didn't call my visits checking, though.

"Women don't go to proctologists," I snapped.

"Some of the chicks I've seen in Manhattan probably do."

I rolled my eyes. "I'm doing just fine, Aggie."

"In which alternate universe?" The loud crunches from eating her bowl of Cap'n Crunch grated my nerves, but I ignored it. "Or do we need to talk about what happened yesterday at Barney's?"

I offered a half-shrug. Damn her and her sharp memory. Besides her cereal, her morning turkey club sandwich looked good too. I settled for oatmeal instead.

"During your *little* visit to my workplace, you got told off by a preschooler." She stopped to give me the eye.

"That kid puts one over on everybody." And me in public, apparently.

"Not grown-ass werewolves." She finished her bowl and added a second serving. When she snagged some milk from the fridge, I noticed she'd gotten two milk jugs from Costco. *Way to support your eating habit, Aggie.* At least everything was still lined up nicely. She was still catering to my little obsessive-compulsive disorder, even though I no longer lived here. "This has to end now before you're challenged."

"Nobody's gonna challenge me."

"At the rate you're going, a whole kindergarten classroom full of werewolves can take you down."

"I'm better now. Even Thorn said so the other day."

She stopped mid-chew and flipped her ponytail over her shoulder. Her red hair was in the messiest of hairstyles. "You do have a smidgen or two of self-confidence, but not enough for me not to be concerned with your well-being."

"You don't have to be."

"Might as well do this now instead of later." She took her fresh bowl of cereal — still considered crunchy in my view for the next five minutes — and put it in the fridge. Then she sat across from me and stared.

"What?" I blurted.

Aggie leaned a bit forward. "If I hear you contemplate letting people screw around with you, I get to kick your ass and then the folks who put you down get a crack at you. Got it?"

The urge to take the plate with her sandwich away came to mind, but I quashed the idea. She still had a death-grip on the sucker. "Understood."

"Look me in the eye when you say that."

Damn, she'd caught me again. I slowly took in her face from her mouth up to her eyes. They were bright blue. Sharp. Unrelenting. Uneasiness settled into me, curling my stomach.

"Don't you dare hesitate." Aggie let go of the sandwich, gripping the table with one hand and the other grabbed my chin to hold me steady. "You can do this. Don't back down."

"I'm not hesitating."

"Yes, you are. On the outside, I see the confidence. But in here," she tapped my chest, "I see a wall you've built. You believe the wall is high enough for you to trick the world into believing you're an alpha female, but I see right through it."

My lips formed a straight line. Cussing her out right now would feel so good. She probably sensed my rising anger, but she didn't act on it.

"As of right now. This minute. This second." She let go of me and sat back. "If you doubt yourself in front of me again, I will rearrange your bedroom."

"You wouldn't dare."

Her eyebrows lowered. "Try me."

Aggie's warning stuck in my head for the rest of the morning. Even more so during my quick "inspection." My little breakfast visits had an ulterior motive: I wanted to make sure the place was as clean as I had kept it. After I had some oatmeal, I washed off my plate — while checking around the sink and cupboards.

Naturally, after such a large meal, I needed to wash my hands in the bathroom. That room was pleasantly well kept, minus a sweater on the floor, but I wouldn't dock points for that. Aggie had even scrubbed behind

5

the toilet, too.

"You're going to be late for work." Aggie leaned against the bathroom doorframe. "Or should I give you some gloves and a bottle of tub cleaner?"

"Just washing up." I wiped my hands on the towel again. A fresh one my nose told me.

"Bullshit. Get your ass to work, Nat. I got things covered here."

As I made my way out the door, I asked her if she wanted to meet for lunch at Archie's.

"I got the evening shift tonight at work. How about tomorrow?" She didn't mention how we'd missed out on a lot of nights together. Besides Thorn coming back into my life, things had changed for Aggie, too. She had a relationship. A pretty good one, since his scent was all over the place.

"I have dinner with my parents. We'll get caught up eventually, then," I said softly.

I left the house and kept my chin up. This was for the best. I needed to stand on my own and reluctantly slide into the expected role I'd earned. I'd told Thorn I wasn't ready to be the alpha female, yet others didn't see things that way.

On a snowy night two months ago, I'd fought another pack member, Erica Holden, for the position of alpha female over the South Toms River Pack and I'd won. Barely. Everyone who was present had seen another side of me.

As I pulled up to work outside of the Bend of the River Flea Market, or The Bends as the locals called it, I resolved to at least attempt to take Aggie's words to heart.

I closed my eyes. The minute I stepped outside the car door, I'd try for a new start: No more doubts. No more self-effacing behavior. No more whining. I'd wear my big girl's panties with pride. I was the alpha female now.

Running the pack as the alpha female didn't stop me from working at The Bends. The store offered the best deals among the flea markets along the Garden State Parkway. Bill, my boss, was a pretty good businessman in the antiques game, but, like any goblin, he created more problems than profit.

Instead of entering through the back, my usual route, I chose to go through the dock. See? I could divert from habit if I wanted to do it. I preferred the back door during warmer weather especially. The outdoor area was covered with a long, steel awning to protect shoppers who browsed our wares on the rows of tables out here. Even the hardcore shoppers didn't like to come out here in March. The weather tended to fluctuate between freezing cold and damn-I-still-needed-a-jacket cold.

Once inside, I dropped off my purse in the business office, my home away from home. Even though I'd briefly quit a few months ago, Bill welcomed me back. It didn't take me long to straighten out the messes the staff had created while I was gone.

The customer service bell rang from the service floor, so I sprang into action, leaving the office through the double wooden doors. Just the feeling of working lightened any anxiety I had. Some might scoff at the kind of work that I did, especially since I used to work in NYC for a publishing company as a copy editor, but I found my job rewarding and relaxing. To be honest, before Thorn had returned many months ago, this place had been a crutch, a calming habit I maintained on even my darkest days. Every morning, The Bends would be here, waiting for me, and I'd go through the motions like a junkie enjoying her fix.

Not all customers gave me that oh-so-warm-and-gooey feeling though. This morning, I had a shape-shifter leaning against the service desk with a frown that practically filled his face.

The confidence in my step was artificial, but I approached the desk with a smile. This was a customer, after all. Differentiating a human from a shifter came by smell — when they wanted to be detected. Shifters usually took the scent of the form they assumed.

Which meant this fellow didn't give a damn who saw him. Usually shape-shifters didn't like to hang around places where spellcasters shopped, and for a good reason.

That was when I noticed the obvious. My eyes beat my nose in this regard. Not a single early morning shopper included a spellcaster. No witches, wizards, or even warlocks. One of our consistent customers, an elderly wind witch named Mrs. Weiss, hadn't made an appearance either. She usually hovered near the wand display, in a fog of vanilla perfume, browsing the goods for the longest of time.

"Hey, my mom's looking for a 1940s highlighter trunk she saw on the Internet. Is it still available?" The leather from his biker pants rubbed against the glass.

"Yes, we still have it. Do you want to buy it and pick it up at the loading dock?"

He nodded. "If the air stays clear for a while, that sounds good."

My right eyebrow rose. "How long has the air been clear?"

He grinned, revealing a set of perfectly straight teeth — a perk for shape-shifters. "A few days, now that the war has begun."

I about choked on the sharp inhale that coursed down my throat. "Excuse me?"

"You folks out here in Jersey are always the last to hear about the stuff going on in the big cities." He shrugged. "The shifters always smell trouble coming first. Especially since those rat bastards come looking for us when they need power."

People like the chap in front of me were prized possessions to spellcasters. I'd learned from a close wizard friend about how the power generated by shape-shifters and werewolves like myself could be harnessed by spellcasters, whether we wanted to be used or not.

My nerves rose to alarming levels, forcing me to grip the counter. "Where are they fighting? Who's involved?"

I waited for an answer, but he chose that moment to clam up. "Just be careful out there," was all he said.

Since he wouldn't give me any more information, I decided to wrap up the sale. "I'll have someone bring your trunk to the dock as soon as we make arrangements for payment."

After the customer paid for the trunk, I glanced around the room again, perhaps hoping my observation earlier had been a mistake. We always had at least one spellcaster roaming around.

"Something wrong, Nat?" Bill peeked at the register. He wasn't referring to my well-being.

"Nothing important. A customer bought a trunk."

"Just what I wanted to hear. More junk has got a home." He sighed and adjusted his round wire-frame glasses. Bill used a glamour to hide his true appearance, but right now, he had an uncanny resemblance to the cartoon character Dilbert. "Did you ever find that goblin who you *stole* the knife from?"

I rolled my eyes. A few months ago, when I was in Atlantic City, trying to help my father, I met a strange goblin who tried to attack me with a mysterious blade that changed based on the kind of enemy I faced. I ended up the new owner when I couldn't find the guy to return it.

I'd even showed the goblin blade to Bill, hoping he'd say it belonged to his long lost brother or something. No dice.

"I didn't steal it. When the guy moves back into his repair shop, I'll send it express mail so he can have it back in his happy little hands." I gave him a curt smile and then returned to the back office to get some work done. The man I needed to see was emptying trashcans. The Bends's janitor also hauled goods as needed around the store. His scent, a haze of myrrh and frankincense, hit my nose first before anything else. The guy was covered in it, since he stuffed his zombies like burritos with the stuff.

"Hey, Nat." He glanced up, the dark circles under his eyes quite prominent under the skylights in the business office. Slowly, he added the trash into a container on wheels.

"Morning." I quickly went to the computer and logged in. Just smelling him brought back memories of a date night I've wanted to suppress for the rest of my life, a dinner where one of his zombie minions made an appearance to show me a thing or two about his master's proper treatment.

Also, a piece of a zombie, dunno what, fell in my food.

Yep, it went down as creepy as you'd imagine.

I printed the paperwork for the trunk and turned to hand it to the necromancer. I gasped to find him right behind me.

"Hey, how's it going?" I mumbled.

With him so close, my nose twitched. His floral scent was pretty overpowering.

"I've been doing great," he said. He had some cute blue eyes, but the dead thing just didn't work for me.

"There's a customer who—"

"Matter of fact, I've been seeing someone."

Oh, really. Now that came out of nowhere.

He continued. "I met her a week ago, picking flowers in the graveyard."

"How nice." *What kind of nice girl hung out in a graveyard?*

A small smile broke out on his face. "She was picking the dead weeds along the head stones. I thought she was so angelic, gathering all her flowers into a broken wicker basket."

Uh, that kind of girl.

"She sounds nice," I said. "I bet you two make quite the pair. So if you could — "

"Her name is Marlene and she's quite handy with a sewing needle. Whenever somebody has a body part that falls off, Marlene is right there to — "

"Whoa. Okay, there." I waved my hands in front of his face. "How about we work on stuff for The Bends." With a dry laugh, I shoved the paperwork into his full hands. "There's this trunk a customer needs — "

He drew the piece of paper I handed him to his nose. "Are you wearing a different perfume?"

My mouth dropped open, but I quickly closed it again. "Uh, no. Why?"

"From where I'm standing your aura is the same, yet your scent is weird. The things you touch leave a mark I can smell. The computer, this piece of paper. There is something different about you."

"When did you notice this?"

"I guess around New Year's. I've been too busy to really approach you about it."

Had something bad happened to me? Was it an alpha female's scent maybe? Or perhaps I had some kind of magic clinging to me I didn't know about. Worry tried to seep into my mind like black ink, but I pushed it away. "Do I smell bad or something?"

"It's very faint. I've never smelled this on a

werewolf before, either. I can check into it if you like?"

"No need." The last thing I needed was more up-close-and-personal time with a dude who touched rotting dead folks.

I left him with the paperwork and headed back to the main floor to keep myself busy. With the strange lack of witches and wizards in the area as well as my alpha female issues, I had too many things to worry about.

Just one more might bring down everything I've built up.

Chapter 2

A few days later, on my day off, I eagerly headed to my aunt Olga's apartment. It was sunny, promising to be a great day of visiting with family.

The minute I approached the door, I caught a whiff of baby lotion and heard the gurgles of an infant. I had a bag in hand, containing yet another recent purchase, a gift. An older blonde woman opened the door and quickly got out of the way as I bounded inside.

"Heh. Good to see you too, Nat," my aunt Olga said in Russian. I'd have time to give her a proper greeting later. She wouldn't go anywhere.

An elderly woman, my grandma Lasovskaya, gently patted my three-month-old niece's tummy in a small portable crib.

"Sveta," I whispered with a grin to the baby.

The tiny girl with a bit of blonde peach-like fuzz hair on the top of her head squirmed at the sound of my voice.

"Hey, *princessa*. It's your *tyotia*," I said.

Seeing Sveta made all the worries pressing against my shoulders disappear. Even though she was still young, she was my family's hope for the future.

"Are you hungry, Natalya?" Grandma asked.

"I can make extra food for you and Mama," Aunt Olga offered. My aunt acted as caretaker for my grandma during the day.

I leaned down and kissed both of Grandma's cheeks. Her wrinkled skin was warm and soft. "Not right now, but thanks."

Grandma chuckled and handed me the baby. "You're not here to see me, huh?"

A sigh escaped my lips as I cuddled the baby close to my chest. Sveta's wayward fist found her mouth, and she suckled on it. Such a simple act filled me with happiness. I didn't get quality time like this due to work. Once in a while, Karey, Sveta's mom, needed a sitter when her normal one backed out, which came as a surprise to me, since Sveta had so many aunts on Karey's side, even if they were all bat-shit crazy. Last year, my brother married Karey, a wood nymph he'd knocked up. Like a gang of mobsters, the wood nymph's numbers ran deep and they fiercely protected their own.

Crazy aunts or not, I had the baby all to myself and she eventually fell asleep in my arms.

Grandma looked on with a grin. "So how long until I get to hold one of yours?"

If I had been drinking, I would've done a spit take. "Not any time soon, Grandma. We just got married. Thorn and I need to adjust to my new status."

Grandma chaffed. "That's a poor excuse. Your grandpa Pyotr didn't wait long to get me in the family way."

"Oh, Mama," Olga said with a laugh.

Grandma never held back when it came to having new babies in the family. Once Alex married Karey, she switched targets. I hadn't married a good Russian boy like my parents expected, but the local pack leader was just as good. Just thinking about Thorn made me smile. Now they hoped for me to produce a litter or two. As if I didn't have enough to worry about. Like how many full moons Thorn had left.

Aunt Olga finished preparing Grandma's lunch and left her food on a tray. She offered me a serving of chicken soup, but I refused. Nobody could get me to move with this baby in my arms.

In the middle of a bite, Grandma turned to me. "I heard from an old friend a few days ago."

"From Russia?" I asked.

"Yes. It was Tamara."

The name brought a flash of memories from this winter. I'd made a journey north to help my father with a werewolf obligation called a moon debt. Somehow, thanks to the help from close friends, I succeeded, but one of the obstacles in my way had been Tamara. A sinister older woman with a cunning smile came to mind.

"Why would she contact you?" I asked. "I thought she worked for a pack leader in Maine."

"She reached out to me about old magic. She didn't go into details as to why she'd returned to our homeland. Only that during her time in Russia, she'd gotten close to uncovering a spell to remove curses from objects."

My stomach felt like it dropped onto the floor and rolled away. A few months ago, I didn't know werewolves could cast spells. Our people called it old magic and these days the laws governing werewolves, the Code, prohibited any werewolf from using it.

"And what else did she say?" I asked.

Think of big girl panties with obnoxious pink flowers. I took a deep breath. Was this the news I craved hearing, news that would save my husband?

Grandma patted my knee. "It's not what you think, Natalya. I believe it isn't."

My chest tightened. I glanced at Sveta, my heart breaking as I wondered if she'd ever know her uncle. Would he die before she even took her first steps?

"Tamara wants me to go check her work, and I'm too old to consider such a request. The last five centuries have been hard on me." Grandma had seen so much since emigrating from nineteenth-century Russia.

I nodded, staring at the minuscule lines on Aunt Olga's coffee table. "So what do you think, Grandma?"

"It's probably a rumor of some kind. She said the wizards have been working to remove curses from their weapons. The spellcasters are fighting among themselves, and, somehow, the warlocks have found a way to tilt the balance. They've found a way to curse wizard weapons and render them useless."

So that was why there wasn't as much stock at work for the past couple of days. Did that mean none of our spellcaster customers would ever come back?

Grandma continued with a sigh. "I've got too many years on me to play with old magic."

"What about Thorn?" I blurted.

"I know you love him, but the thing about old magic is that there's more than one spell to do the same thing. Don't talk to Tamara if she tries to contact you. You're just a beginner, but she might try." There was a bite behind the old woman's words. Grandma rarely pushed when she spoke, but this time she did.

My lips sealed shut, and I bit the inside of my mouth. There were so many things I ached to say. So many questions. Maybe my grandmother sensed the rising anxiety I struggled to suppress. She tried to take my hand, but I slid out of the way and placed the sleeping baby back in the crib. Keeping my feelings inside wasn't going too well.

"Don't be disappointed," she said. "Tamara has chased too many problems. She is *beda*. The kind of trouble you don't need right now."

"What can you do, Grandma? What can I do?"

"Pray to God. I've contacted friends I trust. They are doing what they can."

"I appreciate that." I kissed her cheek and then Aunt Olga's. It was time to go. I had some thinking to do.

We said our goodbyes, and I headed home. On the way back to the small house I shared with Thorn, I noticed a dark-haired man waiting by the door. He had to be here for Thorn, since I rarely had visitors. When he turned around, my hackles rose and my fists clenched.

It was Rex, a man I wouldn't even call an acquaintance.

This day was getting better and better.

As he strolled in my direction, my memory replayed every single moment with him from the past that I tried so hard to suppress: disappointment, shame, and — even worse — betrayal.

"You seen Thorn around?" he asked, looking me directly in the eyes. As the pack's second-in-command, he should have looked at the ground in my presence. This wasn't the first time he'd challenged me.

"Not since this morning." I stared right back at his smug face.

"That's a shame." Rex used his right foot to kick around a small stone on the sidewalk. "He hasn't been easy to find the last couple of weeks."

"Your point?"

Rex gave me the very same expression he used on the day my parents tried to match me up with him after Thorn disappeared five years ago. It was the look a predator gave his prey. "An alpha should be accessible to his pack. He'd only hide if he was *weak*."

"He does have a cellphone. Why don't cha try that?"

The second-in-command smirked. "I already tried his phone, Natalya. Your mate's days are looking rather numbered if he keeps acting like this."

"Is that a threat?" An icy edge lined my words.

"What do you think it is?" He took a step toward me and smiled. Most of the women in town would've melted from his smooth smile and lean build, but I knew he had that asshole disease spreading around the East Coast. "Have you ever regretted walking away from me that summer? Or should I say getting *carried* away after your little panic attack? Have you ever wished you hadn't broken down in front of the whole pack so you could be by my side?"

I laughed at him. Hard. "Not really."

His sneer raised the fine hairs on the back of my neck. "Maybe after Thorn dies, you'll have a chance to prove you're an alpha female."

For seconds, I didn't breathe, move, or break eye contact with him. If his crazy ass was trying to scare me, he was doing a damn good job, but I refused to give him the satisfaction of showing how deep his words cut.

"That's not going to happen," I said slowly. "Not if I'm still breathing and have the will to find a way to help him."

"Don't get in my way, bitch." The word *bitch* came out as a long exhale. His curled lip revealed an elongated incisor, and he closed in, close enough for me to smell the pastrami sandwich he had for lunch. Extra onions. "I'm not going to have to lift a finger in a few months to get what I want, but it would be a shame for me to make sure both the alpha male *and* female make a quick exit."

Forty-eight hours passed since my encounter with Rex, and I was still shaken. I had too many questions and not enough answers. Saturdays were supposed to be a day where I worked at The Bends or I took the day off. For once, I actually took the day off, but I had things to do. I had answers to find, and there was only one person who could give them to me. It was so long since I touched base with one of my best friends. He was there for me during some tough times. When I had my worst days, he was at his best.

Every so often, I thought about Nick Fenton, the white wizard I met during my supernatural therapy group. I couldn't help but smile as I left the subway in the Park Slope neighborhood of Brooklyn. I came to this neighborhood many times with Nick. All the familiar smells from the restaurants we visited or the shops that we passed by were comforting. It was nice to have someone who understood what it was like to live inside my head and to see everything around me that bothered me to no end. But he saw me as so much more, and though I didn't reciprocate his romantic feelings, he never turned me away. He was a forever friend.

The street outside of the next brownstone was busy this morning. A family was moving out across the street. Burly men lugged boxes into a moving truck. Cars barely had enough room to squeeze by. Thank goodness, I decided to drive to the closest train station in Jersey and then commute into the city. Throughout my ride, at every stop, I'd had an urgency, an itch I couldn't scratch in my hide.

Nick had to know what was going on with the spellcasters. Maybe he'd even heard some news of what Tamara was talking about with the tainted weapons and such. My walk up the stairs quickened along with my heartbeat as I approached his door. Soon I'd see his smiling face and he'd reassure me that my hopes weren't in vain.

Yet when I knocked, no one answered. I pressed my ear against the warm wooden door and closed my eyes. Not a single sound. No faint hum from a fridge or even from any other electronics. Catching Nick's scent would be difficult. Based on my experiences with him, he usually hid his scent from me.

"Can I help you?" The door down the hall opened, and an elderly man with a balding head and wire-rimmed glasses peered out.

"Excuse me?" The faint scent of a spellcaster came to my nose.

"Are you looking for someone?" The man stared at me.

My mouth opened and closed. There was something familiar about his features as if I'd seen him before. When he blinked a few times, I remembered Mr. Blackowski. This man tried to hook Nick up countless times with his daughter, much to Nick's chagrin.

"I'm looking for Nick, Mr. Blackowski," I said.

"He's not here right now."

"I see. Can I leave him a message?"

Mr. Blackowski opened his door all the way and tugged keys out of his pocket. "I don't think you understand." He strolled over to Nick's door and placed a brass key into the lock. The door opened with a loud yawn. The emptiness in the room kicked me hard in the gut.

A conversation with Nick from months ago flooded my mind. *"You've given me a lot to think about — especially in terms of healing others... I've made the decision to enter medical school under Dr. Frank's direction."*

I'd thought I had more time. I'd thought that, like regular medical school for humans, Nick would have to take the MCAT exam and wait for acceptance into medical school. Things in the magical world were apparently beyond my understanding.

My footsteps on the hardwood floor echoed through the small room. Seeing his tiny kitchen brought to mind the day I came here and he cooked me dinner. Or I should say he "bought" dinner and shyly admitted it wasn't his food. A smile touched my face.

I slipped my hand into my pocket and rubbed my fingertips against my cellphone. Any attempts to call him resulted in a disconnected number. He'd severed his ties with the human world, or so it seemed to me. A part of me hoped he wasn't trying to run away from me because I'd chosen Thorn over him.

"Thanks so much for showing me he's gone," I said to Mr. Blackowski.

"Not a problem. He's a good man. I hope he finds what he's looking for out there."

"I do, too," I whispered. "I do, too."

Chapter 3

With Nick gone, I didn't have many options. So my next destination was Dr. Frank, who treated me for my OCD. The old wizard scratched my hide the wrong way on most days, especially since he didn't let me slide into my incessant need to shop. I did make a small pit stop in Manhattan on the way to his office, but compared to last year, when I made three or four shopping trips per therapy session, I considered a browse through — umm, brief purchase — at Nordstrom's to be a huge step toward improving my self-control. Only three things purchased, mind you, and that didn't even count, since they were gifts for Sveta.

When I reached the receptionist desk on the upper floor, I stopped in the middle of the hallway. The woman at the desk was new, a human this time. She smiled as I approached.

"Can I help you?" she asked.

"Is Dr. Frank available?"

"Dr. Frank was called away on personal business for a few months. Dr. Chainey is taking care of his patients until then."

Panic brushed against my stomach. "As one of his patients, why wasn't I notified?"

"It was an emergency leave," her smile was apologetic. "We just sent out notices about his departure a few days ago. Yours probably hasn't arrived yet. I'm so sorry."

So this was a recent development. Suspicion touched my senses. Not a good feeling to have. My imagination wanted everything to be like it had been before. With a quick glance at the meeting room doors, I imagined hearing my friends behind them. Heidi the mermaid's laugh bubbled up. Shy Abby the Muse replied to someone in her soft-spoken voice. Lilith, the soul-sucking succubus, would be complaining about her last date, or lack-thereof. The others would be there, too. But now Dr. Frank was gone, only to be replaced by a human, or so I assumed. Maybe he was another wizard for all I knew, but Dr. Frank had been my therapist since I was a kid. Telling all my secrets to someone new didn't sit right with me.

"Thanks for your help. I'll look for that letter." I tried to sound polite, but my voice came out stiff. It wasn't her fault that Dr. Frank had disappeared.

So where did that leave me?

As I left the building, I weighed my options for tracking down what could be happening with the spellcaster community and decided to make a few more phone calls. Heidi's phone went straight to voicemail so I left a message. I wasn't sure when she'd answer. Abby didn't really carry a cellphone, a rather useless device when only other supernaturals could see or hear her.

The third number I dialed finally worked, and a man with a low timbre voice answered the phone. "Hey, Nat!"

"Tyler! I'm so glad someone from therapy group is alive."

"What do you mean alive?" The sounds of traffic bled through his phone. A man near him swore at a biker who got too close to his cab.

"I tried to find Nick and he's gone. Moved out of his apartment. He didn't answer his phone either," I blurted. "Heidi also didn't answer, and Dr. Frank is gone."

"Yeah, I recently tried to call Dr. Frank's private line and was sent to voicemail. I never heard back. Are you doing okay?" He always had a kind voice, even if he didn't have too much confidence.

"Not really. I need some answers, and my spellcasting friends have exited stage right."

The sounds of his footsteps stopped. "Are you in New York right now?"

"Yeah, I'm in Upper West Side near Dr. Frank's office."

"Stay where you are. I just finished a go-see with a designer, so I'm free. Let's grab a coffee."

"You're the best, Ty."

Not long after our phone conversation, we met in a coffee shop off 73rd. The place wasn't the cleanest, but Tyler didn't stop me as I wiped off the small table. The tall dwarf even moved the napkin holder so I could scrub underneath it. A few ladies passed us and looked over Tyler's perfect blond hair, lean waist, and long legs. But he didn't return their gaze, so they moved on.

My poor friend made it damn clear he wasn't a ladies' man.

The dwarf scooted down in his seat with shoulders pushed forward, chin pressed near his chest. His bright blue eyes, almost the color of the ocean, reflected insecurity. Hopefully, he didn't act this way during his modeling gigs.

"You haven't heard about it, have you?" he asked.

"About what?"

"There's a war going on between the warlocks and the wizards, a pretty big one from what I've heard through dwarf circles."

"A shape-shifter said something about a war, but he didn't go into details. This had to explain why Dr. Frank is gone, and I've barely seen any spellcasters at The Bends."

"Folks are hunkering down for the fighting. I've heard they mask the fighting, but there's no telling what races will get pulled into this, including the dwarves."

"You might have to fight?"

He shrugged. "I don't know, to be honest. The wizards will expect us to choose a side sooner or later. Either way, I'm prepared to die as a free dwarf and not one of their damn minions."

Someone passed our table and gave Tyler a weird look. That "I'm prepared to die as a free dwarf" line was a little too *Lord of the Rings.*

I chewed on my thoughts before I spoke. "I need to go to Russia."

His eyebrow rose. "I know this website where you can get great deals —"

"That's not what I mean." I dished on what my grandma told me about Tamara and the wizards. About how they were looking for a way to remove death curses from objects. "As much as I'd like to sit around and wait for help to come to me, I can't. My husband's life depends on this."

He chuckled. "I know that from experience."

"I'm prepared to go alone if I must. I need answers." As my voice rose, the urge to bite my tongue hit. I'd let my eagerness get the best of me. "I can't stand waiting on the sidelines anymore to have what I fought so hard for taken away. I'm not exactly the richest person, so I thought maybe Nick or Dr. Frank could help me figure out the jump points spellcasters use so I could get to Russia somehow."

"Nat...I don't know if doing this is a good idea. Do you even know where you're going or what you'll do when you get there?"

He had a point. Still, I didn't care.

I rolled my eyes. "I've had plenty of time—a bit too much—to think about what to do. Through some digging, I've found where Tamara lives outside of St. Petersburg." I'd checked my parents' caller ID and found Tamara's phone number. I had enough amateur detective skills to help me track down her address.

"Did your grandma tell you to go?"

I gave him a death-glare.

"She wouldn't want you to get hurt," he whispered.

"I've had my leg broken with a crowbar, my forehead smashed into a dashboard, and I've had the shit beaten out of me. Being afraid is kinda out the door right about now."

Alpha female for the win.

Tyler sighed. "I shouldn't be doing this, but I can help you in a few days. Raj once got me to a photo shoot in Thailand. He didn't use a wizard jump point but something similar."

"Thank you." I couldn't resist grinning like a fool.

"I'll need a favor in return," he quickly added.

"Anything—well almost." I did have personal limits.

He paused for a moment and played with his coffee cup. What the heck did he need from me? It wasn't like I could hook him up with one of my cousins. He wasn't into werewolves.

"I need you to go to a dwarf matchmaking dinner

with me."

Chapter 4

"So you're saying you want to take another *woman* to this matchmaking dinner?" I asked Tyler again a few days later. "A dinner where you're supposed to hook up with someone?"

Maybe I'd heard him wrong or something.

"Yes." Tyler didn't look me in the eyes. He simply kept walking down the quiet East Village street. Evenings in NYC should always be pleasant like this. "Look, Nat, I wouldn't be too worried about it. Not to hurt your feelings, but you're not that pretty compared to dwarf girls and you're going to stand out."

Oh, yeah. No shit. "So I'm ugly, huh?" I tried to sound hurt but failed. Was I a bad girl for giving him a hard time?

"No, you're not that...unattractive. You're just too tall. And you need more...curves."

He glanced at my chest. I'd yet to hear any complaints from Thorn, so I just chuckled. To each his own.

I adjusted the gifts I carried. Even if I didn't think this was the smartest idea Tyler came up with, I decided to go and be at my best. I'd had enough home training from a sharp Russian mother to know I should wear a nice dress to a dinner and bring a gift of some kind.

The fairy at the bakery in South Toms River suggested thick loaves of bread and wine, so I bought a couple loaves from her and a cheap bottle of wine at the local convenience store. It didn't seem like the smartest move, especially with Tyler's harebrained idea of bringing me to his date.

"I'm so nervous," he whispered as we walked up to a brick apartment building.

"So this is where her family lives?" I asked.

"Only dwarves live here." He hesitated at the entrance.

I nodded and patted his shoulder. "C'mon. Where's the guy I remembered who battled werewolves like nobody's business?" Tyler, along with the rest of my therapy group, had come to the South Toms River Pack's rescue when an invading pack tried to take over. I'd always be grateful for his bravery.

"That was different. I wasn't trying to get married. I feel different on the battlefield."

"Fair enough."

Once inside, I expected us to climb the stairs to one of the top floors, but instead, we went down two levels. The stairwell was well lit, with sconces illuminating the whitewashed walls. My nose told me someone had diligently scrubbed these hallways with cleaning products. Tyler led the way to a door at the end of the hall. His fine leather shoes scuffed against the wooden floor.

Once we reached our destination, he froze.

"Do you want me to knock?" I asked.

He wiped a line of sweat off his brow with a handkerchief. His scent, heavy with agitation, filled my nose. "No need. Just give me a sec."

I hid my smile and tried to stifle the swell of nervous flutters in my stomach. Here was a man who'd make women tremble with his grin, and yet his nervousness seeped into me. His hand rose, then dropped again. By the third time, after a deep breath and wiping off his brow again, Tyler knocked on the door hard.

Poor guy.

"You got this," I whispered to his back.

His nod was barely perceptible as the door opened wide. Tyler blocked the doorway so I took a peek around him. From what little I could see, I spotted an older woman at waist-height.

"Right on time, Tyler son of Wendt," she said stiffly.

A sweet scent hit my nose and the wolf within me melted. Ham, baked with brown sugar and poked with lots of cloves. Just my kinda place.

"Greetings to Eosa, daughter of Kagte." He bowed at the waist then stepped inside.

This was my first visit to a dwarf home, so I followed Tyler inside and kept quiet.

The older woman didn't glance at me, only offering a disapproving glare in Tyler's direction. "Please understand the only reason we're granting this dinner is due to your esteemed lineage."

Tyler quaked at my side. The need to offer him a reassuring touch tugged at me, but I didn't budge.

"I'm honored you would invite me into your home." His heartbeat sped up, thundering in my ears like a trapped squirrel.

The older woman stared him down, crossing her arms while the sounds of a TV in the other room blared. Someone was watching a western. Just hearing the horses and gunshots brought back memories from another man who glared at me with discriminate thoughts. But that man wasn't the South Toms River Pack leader anymore, and just like him, the woman in front of me was probably more bark and less bite.

An instinct to save my friend from the awkward silence jumped in and I extended my hands with the bag of bread and wine toward Eosa. "Please accept my gift—"

Tyler's hand snaked out to snatch my wrist. "Don't speak yet. I must introduce you."

My mouth snapped shut.

"I've yet to have a wolf in my home; who is your guest?" Eosa asked.

He gestured to me. "This is Natalya, daughter of Fyodor."

At the sound of my name, I did a quick curtsy. As an alpha female werewolf, bowing my head to her would be a no-no.

Her eyebrow rose in amusement. "Greetings, Natalya, daughter of Fyodor."

"Greetings, Eosa, daughter of Kagte. Your home is beautiful—"

At that, Eosa nodded. "She has manners. That is good."

"Are you hungry?" she added.

"Yes, we're quite hungry," he replied.

My stomach growled at her words. I was quite hungry, but I didn't voice my thoughts, and I let him take the lead.

"Come to the dining room then." She strolled through her living room into an adjoining dining room. Since the apartment was underground, the windows were only for show, simply draped frames that probably went nowhere. The decorations were still nice, though, and the knickknacks here and there created a welcoming environment that made me feel right at home.

The dining room was larger than I'd expected for a New York apartment. It was a beautiful space with a long rectangular table and ornate china hutches on each end. Dwarf homes had a different setup though. Everything was lower than expected by at least three to four inches.

We were the last ones to the table. Six other dwarves waited for us.

"I can't wait to meet Giana," Tyler said with a shy smile.

"She's getting ready and will be down when I announce her," Eosa said.

"That sounds wonderful." He didn't hide his exuberance. "A proper introduction."

"Take your seats at the end." Eosa gestured to two empty place settings. As we sat, she continued to speak. "Let me introduce you to my family, who are here from overseas to assess her potential husbands. The woman on the end is Giana's aunt Hoyit. Next to her is Ntah, her husband. Then there are Rinrer, Kubde, and Berroh."

She pointed at the far end. "The handsome, virile man at the head of the table is my husband, Burt."

Burt? After all those exotic names, meeting a Burt was rather unexpected.

Tyler listened intently as if a quiz would be given at the end of the meal.

"What's going on?" I whispered.

"In dwarf tradition, during a match-making dinner —"

Eosa cut in, "The dwarf man may not look at his intended until after he is served his meal. After the first bite, he may look at her." Eosa smiled brightly now, revealing a shiny gold tooth. "That way, the suitor may find his intended as pleasing as the food."

I nodded as if that were a good thing. A man should appreciate a woman for who she was, but this wasn't my house or culture.

"Giana spent the whole day preparing the pig for tonight's dinner," her aunt Hoyit said with a bitter expression that darkened her small gray eyes. "We *hope* you enjoy it."

"I-I am grateful." Tyler stuttered a bit, but he tried to smile and offer a small bow. Like he always did, he crouched in the seat and kept his head low.

My stomach growled again. To keep myself occupied, I took my napkin and placed it in my lap. I glanced at his plate and he flashed me the "just wait a sec" look.

Soon enough I'd understand.

A question came from the other end of the table.

"How far back can you trace your lineage?" one dwarf man asked Tyler as one of his bushy eyebrows rose. If my memory served me right, he was either Rinrer or Ntah.

"Fourteen generations recorded, Ntah," Tyler replied, looking the man in the eye.

"I expect to hear you sing of them—" Ntah proposed.

"I don't wanna hear him sing!" Hoyit snapped. The next question came just as fast from Hoyit. "Do you have a proper underground dwelling for your new bride?"

"I've had trouble finding a place with all the requirements, but it's suitable," Tyler said.

"Suitable? A cave is suitable for a bear, but not a new bride from a respectable lineage." Hoyit frowned to Eosa, and she made the same expression.

"You're far too tall for a dwarf," Burt said, stroking his wispy blond beard.

Tyler crouched lower, and I almost bit the inside of

my mouth to keep my tongue in check. He took everything without fighting back.

Burt wasn't done yet. "Why should I let my beautiful daughter marry you when your children might be deformed?"

My hands clenched my napkin until they went numb. What the hell was up with the freaking Spanish Inquisition?

The words, 'Who do you think you are?' began to form on my trembling lips when an older round woman appeared with many metal cups on a serving tray. A silence descended on the table.

The silence continued as the older woman, who appeared to be about as old as Grandma Lasovskaya, served us each a drink. Her scent blended with the household. She had to be another relative. In my family, elders didn't serve. We served them. She moved so slowly with effort, her wrinkled hands unsteady as she placed each cup. Seeing the old woman, whom I would've taken care of, taking care of me bothered me to no end.

Eosa's family kept their eyes on Tyler as the older woman finished her task and hobbled into the kitchen. I tilted forward a bit to see a pale yellow fluid in the cup. Some kind of fermented drink, my nose whispered to me. The dwarves took a sip from their drinks, but Tyler didn't move, so I followed suit—until he nudged me with his foot. He jerked his head toward the beverage, miming with two hands as to how I should drink.

Here we go. The metal cup was cold against my palms. A bit damp with condensation. Like any curious wolf, I smelled it first, a brief sniff, then I took a small sip.

Ugh.

Good Lord, it was some awful stuff. About as

satisfying as drinking week-old beer left outside in a filthy wooden bucket. I still took another gulp and nodded with a weak smile. A foul-tasting beverage wouldn't diminish the Stravinsky honor.

Tyler downed his without taking a breath. He didn't wipe his mouth off either, letting it drip down his chin. "Good stuff."

Eosa nodded, at least she approved of that.

"So what is this?" I asked Tyler.

"It's fermented fairy sweat, mixed with lemons, buckwheat, and aged ale from the bottom of a barrel," Tyler said with pride. "The older the barrel the better."

So that was where that horrific wooden aftertaste came from.

A young woman stood in the open doorway to the kitchen holding a huge pot. Tyler's eyes brightened, but he kept his eyes on his plate. She walked in, standing at a height no taller than my waist, and managed to place the dish in front of Tyler. It was rather hard to see her at first, but by the time she backed away, I noticed she didn't look half bad. She blinked shyly his way with soft brown eyes. Her hair had been fashioned on top of her head in a fetching manner.

"Please enjoy," Giana declared.

I caught a whiff of roasted pig under the lid and fought off a wave of hunger. If it looked as good as it smelled...

It didn't.

Tyler lifted the lid with relish and placed it in Giana's small hands. With horror, I gazed, or, I should say, the pig's head gazed at us. The pig's mouth had been stretched open to fit the roasted rear end of a large chicken. Almost as if the pig had died while consuming its last meal. When I peered closer, I noticed the chicken's *head* poked out of the side of the pig's mouth.

The head was still attached.

Roasted, empty chicken eyes stared at us.

The words, 'Why did she?' came to mind, but, again, I kept my damn mouth shut.

Tyler nodded with approval, grabbed his knife, and then ate like he wasn't wearing nice clothes. He tore into the pig's head, flinging food about with gusto.

All the while, the older woman came out of the kitchen again to bring everyone else some food. She hobbled again, resting and grimacing as she worked. When she came to my side of the table to serve, I just couldn't take it anymore. I got up and tried to take the plate from her.

For an elderly dwarf, she had the grip of a Greek Titan.

"I just want to help," I whispered.

"What are you doing?" The old woman looked horrified.

"Grandmama, what is she doing?" Giana sputtered.

Everyone at the table stared me down as if I'd shifted into a werewolf and had taken Grandmama down like the big bad wolf in *Red Riding Hood.* Even Tyler stopped eating.

"Natalya, daughter of Fyodor," Eosa said crisply, "the family matriarch always serves at each matchmaking event."

Slowly, I backed to my seat under her scalding glare. "She looked like she was in pain—"

"Are you mocking my heritage?" Eosa sneered at me, and it reminded me of others looking at me that way in the past, relatives who enjoyed seeing me shamed this way. "You don't see me marching up to your weddings and spitting in the food, do you?"

Wow, what a bitch.

"Don't talk to my friend that way." Tyler's words were a low whisper only I could hear, even with his mouth full of pork.

I took my seat, head hung low.

Giana's grandmother continued to serve. When she reached me, she tossed the plate on the table. The pig's leg, still with the hoof attached, rolled off the plate and fell into my lap. The dark gravy stained my skirt before it finished falling with a wet plop on the hardwood floor.

"You should be mindful of the company you keep, Tyler, son of Wendt," Burt said with a growl.

At my side, Tyler's jaw tightened. Anger rose from him in waves. "The company I keep suits me just fine." He turned to me, his blue eyes darkening. "It's time to go, Nat."

He slammed his fork down, so I reached for his hand to calm him. He wrenched his hand free and then wiped his mouth off on the napkin.

"You don't have to do this," I said to him. "I made a mistake, okay."

I tried to switch gears, searching the faces of Giana's family around the table to look for a friendly face. "Tyler's a great dwarf. He's kind and thoughtful." I glanced at Giana, who looked away with disappointment. "He's gone out of his way to help my pack. He's a brave fighter, too."

"It's *time* to go, Natalya." Tyler stood with a straight back. He made his way out of the room, but paused briefly between the dining room and living room.

"Apologies, sweet lady," he said with a bow to Giana.

And then he left.

Using the napkin, I quickly wiped off my skirt, blurted out my thanks and goodbyes, and high-tailed it out of there.

I found poor Tyler in the hallway with his face in his hands, and my heart broke for him.

I reached for his back but didn't touch him. "It's all my fault."

"No, it isn't," he managed. "They just weren't a good match for me, that's all." He tried to sound upbeat, but pain stabbed each word he spoke.

Getting others to accept who you were still was an uphill battle, no matter the species.

"C'mon." He took my arm and tugged me to follow him out. "I need to wash that beer out of my mouth and make a phone call for you."

So the beer *had* tasted as awful as I thought.

Chapter 5

Listening to Tyler make arrangements with Raj from our therapy group was surreal.

Was I really ready to make the leap and go overseas?

I took a generous gulp of my martini. The bartender had added too much salt along the rim, but I didn't care.

Tyler tried to turn away, but that wouldn't do him any good. Even with the chatter of the evening crowd at this small pub, I could make out their conversations without difficulty.

"She needs help to reach St. Petersburg." He sighed. "Yeah, I know what we'll face, but I owe her one and well, you..."

Their conversation went on like that while I ordered another drink. By the time I emptied that last glass, Tyler turned to me with a one of his award-winning grins that charmed the co-eds behind us.

"Are you sure about this?" he asked.

I didn't hesitate. "Absolutely."

He nodded. "Then I have a ride for you. How

much time do you need to prepare for the trip?"

I wanted to say right now, but I did need time to go home and pack. I didn't like to just go on the spur of the moment anymore. It was too stressful for my anxiety. And, this time, I planned to just not tell people where I was going.

"I'll be ready at dawn tomorrow," I said with finality. If I waited any longer, I would question everything. I'd probably choose work over this trip. Or something else might come up and it would ruin everything. I had to take a stand now and not back out.

Tyler squeezed my shoulder with reassurance. "Then I'll see you at dawn tomorrow at Raj's house. I'll shoot you a text message so you know where you need to go."

I nodded and we parted ways.

That night, when I got home, I was a bundle of jitters. Thorn didn't notice, though. I found him in our bed, fast asleep. He didn't move or wake up as I slowly gathered what I needed in our bedroom. Indecision hit me a few times over the head. I'd need a jacket. But how many days would I be gone? Would everything fit in my backpack? Should I pick this? Would I need that?

I crept around, waiting for him to turn over and give me a questioning look. Fooling Thorn was damn near impossible. As the alpha, he had the kind of intuition I envied.

By the time I got into our bed, everything was ready. My backpack and coat waited for my great escape near the doorway. Even if Thorn got up in the night, he wouldn't question them. Every once in a while, I took my backpack to work instead of my purse, especially if I wanted to use it to hide my purchases...

He knew damn well what I used it for.

The night took forever to pass. I held Thorn close,

snuggling in his arms. I expected him to hold me back, but he didn't.

Worried filled me. He was practically exhausted from his work at the local mill during the day. As I ran my fingers through his hair, he continued to doze, oblivious to my worry.

I took his hand and rubbed it against my cheek. His scent was there, along with his strong heartbeat.

This was all for him, even if he'd feel hurt after I left. God, I hoped I was doing the right thing.

I managed to sleep for only an hour. A few hours before dawn, the vibrating ring of my cellphone receiving Tyler's text woke me up. I slipped out of bed and moved as if going to the bathroom. I made it without a problem.

Phase one of my master plan in action. With all the lights out, I crept downstairs and dressed in a T-shirt and jeans. Wearing my standard uniform of a blouse and pencil skirt on this trip wasn't gonna work. And I was mentally prepared to face that.

I checked twice and made sure my note for Thorn was where he'd find it. Thorn had his own morning routine, too. He didn't follow his as diligently as I did mine, but he'd find the letter. Hopefully, after I was out of town.

By the time I took the hour-long train from Jersey into New York, I looked over my shoulder less. From the note, Thorn would learn I was leaving town, but I didn't tell him *where*. The man was as good as my dad at tracking folks, so I had to be careful.

It wasn't hard to find Raj's house in Queens. I'd never been to my friend's house before. Matter of fact, I didn't know much about Raj other than what he told us during group therapy. As I stood outside of his bungalow with the dark red sun peeking over the horizon, I came to think of him as rather normal like everyone else instead of a minor Indian deity with a quiet nature about him. He had the picket fence, in a picture-perfect state, winter shrubbery cut at an amazingly level angle, and a stone walkway free from cracks. As I approached the house, I noticed everything was almost symmetrical.

"Hey, Nat." Tyler appeared at my side in a jacket with a backpack slung over his shoulder. He appeared disgustingly chipper like a catalogue model for a photo shoot. "You ready?"

"As much as I can be." I glanced at his backpack. "You don't have to come with me."

He snorted. "I've heard about your antics. Do you think I'd let you go alone after talking to Heidi and Abby?"

I rolled my eyes. The mermaid and the Muse could never keep their mouths shut. "The road trip to take care of the moon debt was a little one."

"You go ahead and call it little all you want." He motioned for me to follow him to the house. "Raj likes punctuality."

"That I *can* appreciate."

Tyler kept glancing at his wristwatch. Finally, he knocked on the door.

Raj immediately opened it. "Hey, Tyler. Right on time."

"We *just* got here."

I chuckled, realizing Tyler was catering to Raj's OCD, which pretty much extended into the house.

"Take your shoes off here please," Raj said. He smiled at us, revealing gleaming white teeth against his honeyed skin. He took a step back. "You can carry them inside."

A set of wooden shelves right next to the door had stacks of shoes. Many of them in gallon-sized plastic bags. Beyond the foyer, the dark wooden floor shined, almost as if a single shoe had never stepped on it.

After taking off our shoes, we followed Raj into his living room off the foyer. As I took in everything, the horribly organized part of me wanted to purr with happiness. The bright orange furniture had been lined up with care with easy chairs at exactly forty-five degrees to the sofa and the coffee table centered and at exactly two feet from the sofa. Not a single dust bunny lingered here. Every wooden surface was free from dirt, dust, or fingerprints. The smell of wood cleaner, bleach, and even vinegar was strong here, but I reveled in it, taking a moment to inhale, hold it in, and then exhale with a grin.

It was the little things that made a home.

All the knickknacks, like tiny wooden statues and lime-colored vases, had been lined up on the wall or end tables with the utmost care for balance and symmetry.

"Your home is *perfect*, Raj." I hoped I didn't sound turned on. I kinda was.

"I hope it is," he said, "with all the time I spend taking care of it."

"You'll have to let me know what you use on the floors."

"Oh, I have an extensive, preferred list. I used—"

"How about we talk about that later?" Tyler gave me a you-don't-want-to-go-there look. He shook his head pretty fast. "Don't we need to get Nat to Russia before it gets too late in the day in Derbent?" Tyler added.

"I've never heard of Derbent," I said.

"Derbent is in the southern part of Russia." Raj motioned for us to follow him toward the back of the house. The rich scent of incense reached my nose and wrapped around me. Sandalwood and cedar-scented incense had been recently burned. The odor came from a small room off the living room.

"Does anyone else live here?" I asked.

"My wife does, but she's at work," Raj said. "Would you like anything for breakfast before we go? Maybe some fruit?"

"No, thanks," I said. When we'd passed the kitchen, I didn't see any food on the counters. No fruits or bread. Every surface in the kitchen appeared barren without any knife holders, spice racks, or the like.

Compared to my home, it was a bit sterile for my liking.

We followed Raj into the room.

Raj gestured to the space. "This is our altar room."

We walked into the room slowly and my gaze swept over everything. Against the wall, there was a small table with fresh and used candles. As well as wooden incense holders along the edge. An empty silver bowl, where fruit had once been my nose told me, was in the middle. Other bowls, which appeared to be made from a metal like copper, were empty, but had traces of what had been in there before.

"Is this where you worship?" I asked out of curiosity.

"No," he replied. "This is how I receive praise from those who worship me."

Ohh. Now this was a new one for me. Raj hadn't said much about his place in mythology or his status as a deity. During therapy, he'd always said his time was divided in ways he didn't want it to be. He'd once said, "I need to stop wearing these gloves before I worry about how clean my altar is or where I have folks to come worship me."

During that session, my heart broke for him. He was one of the quieter therapy group members who only shared so much about his private life.

"So how do people worship you?" I asked. Not

your everyday question, but I might as well learn something new today.

"It's as simple as you'd think." He made a thoughtful face. "How do you worship? You believe in God, no?"

I'd been raised or, I should say, my grandmother had *tried* to raise me as a Christian, following the Russian Orthodox Church.

"Yeah, I guess I pray, and I take the time to talk to God," I replied.

"It's the same thing here," he explained as he took one of the smaller bowls in his hands to show it to us. A fresh peach was in it. "In the religion of my followers, they have an altar and they offer me food and other things. I listen to them from here. When they want to talk to me, I receive their offerings and they appear here."

I glanced to the altar and noticed there wasn't much. I was about to ask when something more would come, but that would be kind of rude. I didn't want to remind him he was just a minor deity and that few people wanted to make a paid call to his altar.

Raj's voice remained upbeat though. "My altars also have a special purpose, too. All of them are connected throughout the world."

"Really?" I couldn't hide my smile. Almost like jump points. So could Raj travel all over the world?

He slowly pulled off his white gloves. Something I'd never seen him do during therapy. "Take my hands."

"Are you sure?" I asked. I knew how I felt when holding others' potentially filthy hands. I used to be a lot more anxious about it, but I'd gotten better.

"We can't go without skin-to-skin contact." He extended his palm. "Don't worry about me. I'll be fine."

"Which hand do I take?" Tyler asked. "You got a few."

Raj's face scrunched up in confusion.

Tyler chuckled, a nice hearty laugh. "I've always wanted to ask you that."

He shook his head with a smile. "How about you pick the one your eyes can see."

Raj had multiple arms, but he had a glamour on himself that even I, with Bill's goblin magic clinging to me, couldn't get past. He was hiding some powerful stuff.

Raj's hands were baby-smooth and soothingly warm. His grip firm.

"Close your eyes," Raj advised.

"What for?" Tyler asked.

I was just as curious. What kind of magic did he have? Was it cool?

"Your funeral." Raj swung his arms forward, drawing us with him toward the altar. Then the world spun violently to the right in a swirl of bright colors. It was so intense I had to close my eyes, but even behind my eyelids, maroon light swirls dived into psychedelic orange-green dots. The strange visions flipped and rotated until they faded into black, leaving me a quivering puddle of mush on the floor.

My only tether to reality was the strong hand that continued to hold my limp one. I tried to open my eyes, but the world spun, so I kept them shut. My stomach continued to do somersaults in my gut. Not far from me, I heard retching and then the inevitable sounds of vomiting.

Poor Tyler hadn't listened either.

Raj just laughed.

We got what we deserved.

The disorientation left far quicker than it came as if a fog lifted from me.

"Does that help?" Raj asked.

"Was that you?" Tyler asked, his voice sounding numb.

"I can heal others when I'm standing on holy ground," he said as I looked at him and he went into focus.

The room where we landed was bathed in darkness. My keen eyes adjusted quickly and I scanned the rough corners of what appeared to be a cave. Only a narrow shaft of light from my right cast a glow on our legs.

Parts of the room were difficult to make out, but at least I could see a rotting table, about ankle height, with a handful of dull metal cups. A heavy layer of dust covered everything.

My stomach quivered and I closed my eyes for a moment to hold my anxiety at bay. Slowly, I got to my feet thanks to a friendly tug from Raj.

"I don't ever want to do that again," Tyler mumbled as he stood.

Raj snorted. "I even tried to hold back there — "

Then he stiffened at my side.

Something in the far corner of the cave moved, a small shadow that grew in size. The dark form quivered, taking a bold step toward us.

The hairs on the back of my neck rose and a low growl rumbled in my throat.

"What the hell is that?" Tyler whispered, putting down his backpack.

"There's another altar in the corner." Raj's hands formed fists. "That altar isn't for me."

The creature, still cloaked in darkness, hissed.

"Is that thing what's connected to the altar?" I asked as my wolf claws cut through my fingertips, ready to fight.

Raj nodded, never glancing at me.

Chapter 6

Raj was the first of us to advance forward.

He had no hesitation, practically walking scent-free. What came for us, though, smelled like an old carcass left out in the scorching summer heat. For over a week.

As my eyes adjusted to the darkness, what was clouded in mystery materialized into glistening skin with hints of serpentine scales. Lidless eyes, devoid of emotion, stared us down.

"Raj, what are you doing?" Tyler muttered.

"Defending what little I have left," Raj said.

Everything happened too fast.

Raj leapt on the creature, large fists swinging and punching. The sounds of hissing and hit flesh echoed through the walls.

My heartbeat thundered in my chest, but I was ready to help. I walked toward the fight, but Tyler stopped me.

"It's got big teeth. Hand-to-hand combat isn't wise." He dug into his coat pocket and pulled out a metallic box that was about the size of his outstretched palm. Using his other hand, he slid the top cover off, revealing a tiny axe inside.

Was he gonna pick its teeth with that?

My claws were a lot bigger than his axe.

He plucked out the axe with his fingertips. In one second, it was minuscule; in the next, it grew to the size of my torso.

Holy shit! That was awesome.

Armed with the axe, Tyler bounded in with a war cry.

Raj continued to wrestle with it. Indentations from Raj's invisible hands revealed where Raj grasped it. His control was slipping as the snake-like creature's tail wrapped around his leg and continued to head up Raj's body toward his neck. Before the thin tail reached its destination, Tyler came in swinging, delivering a sharp chop to the creature's backside.

A throaty hiss filled the room as blood splattered the walls.

"What else you got, you son of a bitch!" Tyler swung again at the thicker body closer to the head, which continued to thrash and writhe until it slipped from Raj's grasp.

Raj shouted. More blood dripped on the floor from somewhere, but I couldn't see where. With a roar, Raj clasped his hands together and brought them down fast across the top of the snake's head. The creature was flung onto the rocky floor with a hard thud. Not deterred, Raj pummeled the head until only a mushy heap was left.

Chest heaving, Tyler held his blood axe close by and watched.

Raj staggered from the head, not breathing as fast as Tyler. He clutched something and appeared to hold back a grimace.

"Are you all right?" I reached for him, but he

shrank away.

"It bit me." Raj added a grunt in an unfamiliar language and frowned in the beast's direction.

I tried to look closer, but all I could see was dark red blood running down something behind Raj.

"Did it bite one of your arms?" I asked.

"Yeah," he finally admitted.

"Is it poisonous?" Alarm rose in my voice.

"I'll be fine." He tried to give us a reassuring nod. "I'm tougher than I look."

"How about we clean it, at least. I have a medical kit, nothing too fancy, but since I like things sterile…"

Raj's right eyebrow rose. "You got alcohol?"

"And cute little band-aids with fluffy puppies on them."

He laughed, his chest shaking.

Tyler looked at me with an amused expression.

"If you feel uncomfortable about germs," I said as I opened my backpack, "you can always apply the first-aid on your own."

We setup shop near the entrance to the cave and got Raj squared away. He angled himself away from us as he worked, but he appeared satisfied once the job was done.

Once I packed up my bag, I couldn't resist asking Tyler about the axe.

"Oh, that's *A Battle Axe in a Box*," he said.

"I've never heard of those before."

"We can't exactly carry a full-size battle axe around in public. So the dwarves worked with the wizards and they helped us construct these boxes to carry a weapon for emergencies."

"How neat." I watched him wipe off the axe and place it back inside its carrying case. That thing took man-portable weaponry to a whole new level.

It was time to go. The light that extended into the

cave came from an opening to the outside. Raj helped
Tyler move the boulder wedged into place over the
opening. Sunlight flooded the room and I rushed
outside to get out of the stale air. The sun was low in
the sky. Over here in Russia, the day had already
passed and the evening would creep up on us soon.

Just a few steps onto the rocky ground and I knew
Derbent was the beginning of something wondrous. A
pleasant breeze brought scents of a beach not too far
from us. The wind whipped my hair into my face, but I
didn't care.

Tyler had already left my side. He'd abandoned his
shoes and was already barefoot in the water.

"By Tadth's left nut, this water is cold." The dwarf
scrambled from the shore back to us.

The breeze turned bitterly cold with the stench of
fish, but it was refreshing compared to the cave. It
reminded me of visiting the Atlantic Ocean.

"This is the Caspian Sea, right?" I asked.

Raj was in the middle of putting on a fresh pair of
gloves. "Yep, isn't it beautiful? It's been at least ten
years since I've walked on this beach." He glanced at
Tyler. "Get your shoes on. We don't have much time to
catch the last train to Mahachkala. It will be packed
with workers, so we need to hurry to buy a ticket."

From the shore, we headed inland past the brick
homes of fishermen, craftsmen, and peddlers. Many of
them weren't in the best shape with crumbling brick
and rusted tin roofs. The stench of dried fish was just
as strong here.

Now that we arrived, suddenly everything inside
me froze as I took in the land of my ancestors. The
open road into Derbent left a pleasant breeze on my
face, yet every step felt like I carried lead in my shoes.

"Keep going, Nat," Raj said at my side with
encouragement.

Nothing I imagined compared to this. Seeing the signs in Russian and Arabic. Smelling the citizens walking down the street. Everything was alarmingly familiar, yet so foreign at the same time.

Interestingly enough, not a single spellcaster was in sight. I scanned the streets ahead and spotted all sorts of fairies, a hobbling brownie in a bright purple coat, and a shape-shifter in broad daylight selling flowers in a basket. That would be unheard of in New York.

"So we're in the southern part of Russia?" Tyler asked. "It's been a while since I've brushed up on my geography."

"It's a part of the Republic of Dagestan. It's kind of like a country within a country. There are so many things I'd like to show you, like the fortress close to here. It was built long after my altar had been constructed around 900 A.D." Raj pointed inland where the land jutted up into hilly terrain. In the distance, I spotted a castle-like structure with old crumbling cream-colored bricks. In one blink, I could almost imagine the past, beyond a time even my grandmother had seen, when this place had been used as a stop on the Silk Road.

We weaved through the narrow streets until we came to the main road, by far, a lot more modern with enough space for cars and delivery trucks. Women and children passed us, scarves covering their heads. The children smiled and me, and I couldn't resist smiling back.

"So do you know who built your altar?" Tyler asked as we walked. He was rather chatty this afternoon.

Raj smiled. The memory must've been a pleasant one for him. "A trader, traveling along the silk road from Barygaza, in what you would now called Baruch, and he delivered goods in Derbent. While he was here, he found an alcove tucked along the rocks. He made a noble sacrifice of two goats and thanked me for his good fortune during his journey."

"That's pretty cool, Raj," I said.

Eventually, we reached the busy train station. A large crowd had gathered here, both in the lines and on the platform. These must've been the workers Raj spoke of. As we waited, I learned Raj could speak multiple languages, including Russian. His accent was barely perceptible. Tyler, on the other hand, only knew a handful of expressions — including how to ask for a taxi and where the nearest airport was, the standard vocabulary for traveling models.

I didn't expect us to make the train with so many people, but, by the time we made it on board, we entered a train filled to capacity.

"How about you two sit near the window and I'll take the aisle seat?" Tyler offered us a knowing grin.

We settled into the seats for a relatively short two-hour ride to Mahachkala. Compared to Derbent, Mahachkala was far larger with several train tracks instead of one.

It was the trip from Mahachkala to Moscow that was exhausting. As much as we wanted to see Mahachkala, another city off the Caspian Sea, we had another trip to take into Moscow. When we bought the three tickets to Moscow, my stomach dropped out of my gut and rolled away from the ticket booths.

"The trip is 38 hours long?" I gasped. "Isn't there some kind of magical portal or carpet or phone booth we can jump into and materialize in St. Petersburg?"

Tyler shrugged, not caring. "Apparently not. We get to travel *human* style." He wagged his eyebrows as he said "human style."

"The price for a *kupe* is more, but it's the best

option for us," Raj said, offering money to the cashier to pay. I tried to slip some money into his pocket, but he pushed my hand away.

"What's a *kupe*?" I asked.

"You'll see." Raj led us toward the train platform. "It's a much better option than the *platzkart* for you and me. Just trust me." He sighed as if the next thing he had to tell me pained him. "You should also go to the bathroom before we get on. Freshen up. Maybe even bring your own toilet paper products."

My mouth formed an "oh." So there would be very public bathrooms ahead of me for a while.

After we got on the train and passed through a few cars, I got drop-kicked even harder into reality. The *platzkart* was nothing more than an open dormitory-style room with bunk beds. As we walked down the aisle in the dormitory, we passed the assorted men and women talking, sleeping, and eating. Many folks held hearty conversations in a haze of cigarette smoke not far from a few babies that screamed/cried/babbled while their older siblings fought over God knows what. My loud Russian family gatherings quickly came to mind.

Several languages reached my ears, not only Russian but Arabic and a few I didn't recognize. One thing became apparent, though. There wasn't any privacy. None. A goblin, hidden under his glamour, scratched a balding spot on his wart-covered head, while an older man slept on the bench across from him. None of the humans disturbed a brownie, who perched on a high bed and gazed at everyone who passed with malcontent. Normally, brownies stood no taller than most dwarves, but they could be malicious when they wanted to be.

A grumpy, grizzled conductor showed us where we needed to go after checking our tickets. By the time we reached a door with the number on our ticket, I was quite convinced. Our room was a much better option for supernatural creatures who needed a door with a lock. I didn't want to wake up in the middle of the night in the *platzkart* section with some dude trying something. He'd get the fright of his life after I bit him in the ass.

The *kupe* wasn't the biggest space, but it was private with a locked door. From the door to the window, there were four bunks facing the aisle: two on the bottom, which doubled as seats, and two on the top. Against the window, there was a tiny table.

After grabbing some Russian tea, we settled into the bunks. Tyler offered to take one of the bottom ones so Raj and I could sleep on top.

"The bottom ones are used as couches too, so I'm sure you'll be more comfortable with those," he said with a grin.

Tyler even helped Raj and I wipe the place down with disinfectant. There was nothing we could do about the bedding though. One whiff told me they had been washed, but not to the degree I would clean them. Raj merely took his place on a bare bench, lay on his back, and closed his eyes. What puzzled me, as I watched him fall asleep, was when he crossed his arms over his chest. *So where did the other arms go?*

Night came quickly as the train rocked us into slumber. Tyler left one of the smaller lights on and he read for a bit of time. I, on the other hand, couldn't find sleep. What was Thorn doing right now? Were my parents freaking out? Would I come home to Aggie lining up to kick my ass?

I turned on my phone, but turned it back off just as quickly. I had no reception to check for messages.

Up in my bunk, with only my coat as my blanket, I drifted off, only to wake up again and again.

When the sounds of someone stirring underneath me made me twitch, I brushed it off and turned over on my side toward the aisle, only to notice that Raj was on the top bunk and Tyler was fast asleep with his book over his face below him.

So who the hell is under me?

The sounds of the intruder snoring floated up to me. Should I wake Raj and Tyler? Would the intruder hear me and attack us? I glanced at the door. It was locked as we had left it.

Slowly, as to not make too much noise, I angled myself over the edge and peeked. It was now or never, if it were truly a threat, it would have eaten us already. Something slept all right on the bottom bunk.

Our new roommate was sprawled on the bunk with one of the blankets provided on the train. His hairy limbs were too long for the blue blanket. His dark red hair partially obscured his face, but revealed a single eye where there should have been two. How the hell did a cyclops get in here after we'd locked the door?

I checked again. A cyclops in his underwear and nothing else.

Since I was checking him out, of course, the guy had to scratch his junk and then snort in his sleep.

I about tossed my cookies in my bunk.

I reached into my pocket and found an old receipt from the coffee I'd bought before I got to Raj's house. I slowly balled it up and threw it at Raj. The piece of paper bounced off his head. He looked over at me, irritated, until he noticed I was pointing downward.

The look on his face switched from perturbed to horrified. Raj took the balled up receipt and threw it at Tyler.

The dwarf didn't move at all. Raj reached into his pocket and pulled out something I couldn't make out.

But when he dropped it on Tyler's stomach, that got him moving. He rose to shout at Raj, but stopped cold when he spotted our new roommate.

He mouthed to me, "You know him?"

I shook my head. Raj shrugged his shoulders.

Tyler looked as though he was about to tap the cyclops's shoulder, but thought better of it and sat down on his bed. We were like that for a while until I dozed off. I wasn't sure if Raj or Tyler stayed awake the whole time. What I did notice when I woke up was that our poor dwarf friend fell asleep with his axe in his lap.

What was even more peculiar was that by the time we woke up, the cyclops was gone. The only evidence of his presence had been a musky scent and a folded up blanket. We shoved it under the couch.

After such a long trip, we finally reached Moskva Kazanskaia station. I was in Moscow. Just thinking that made me catch my breath. For years, I thought I would've made a trip like this with my parents and younger brother. You know, the family vacation where you seek out your roots and learn more about yourself? That kind of thing. What I didn't expect was for a train ride to remind me of how much I loved to be Russian. Each time the train stopped for about twenty minutes or so, we ended up in someplace new. There were old ladies waiting for passengers with hot, homemade food. The scent from piping hot *pirozkis* and fruit fresh from trees snatched me from the train every single time. This was the trip of a lifetime, but it also reminded me of one thing I still hated about myself: how much I hated to be filthy, to taste filth, to smell filth, and, if it were possible, to hear it, too.

I went nearly forty-eight hours *without* a shower.

The restless wolf in me could shake it off, but the human side picked at me at every opportunity.

In Moscow, no one voted down taking a shower before we got on the final leg of our trip, a ride on the famous Red Arrow Train to St. Petersburg. And after our surprise guest during the ride from Mahachkala, we bought four tickets instead of three to make sure we didn't have any uninvited guests.

The ride was uneventful, maybe due to the fact that Tyler slept against the door, axe in hand. He had three cups of tea and snored like the best of them.

We had come so far, yet my journey wasn't even close to completion.

Chapter 7

We made it.

St. Petersburg, a Tsar's modern city, lay before us. A massive city that beckoned me to spend a real vacation here. We took the *Frunzensko-Primorskaya* subway line from the train station into the northern part of the city. In the distance, I spotted the *Bolshaya Neva* River. There was a great deal of new growth and construction in the *Primorskiy rayon*, one of the districts in the city, but the touches of old St. Petersburg were still here in the grand, gray stone architecture. In many ways, this place felt like New York City, where you could stand at one corner and see a Japanese sushi bar on one side of the street and a modern Russian grocery store on the other side.

The whole city waited for us, yet my friends were already planning their escape.

"I'm definitely flying back home," Raj declared. "And I hate to breathe the air in airplanes."

"I'm flying back, too." Tyler sighed. "We need to get you some altars in England, Spain, and Greece. That should cast a nice and wide net."

"If you accomplish that, I'll take you anywhere you want, friend," Raj said.

"Where do we go now?" Tyler asked me.

That was the million dollar question. Was I ready to meet my family?

At least, I'd made it to St. Petersburg. Thorn was gonna kill me for this one. Tracking me, though, would be next to impossible. The man was legendary for tracking me down. In the past, I'd gone out on my own to set things right, and he'd spot me in the brush like a leopard wearing a bright orange cap with flashing lights. There was no way he'd find me by scent after going through Raj's altar.

So I hoped.

"I have family in town who can take care of me until I reach Tamara's. They live in the apartment block across the way." I tried to smile at them. "I don't know why you guys are still following me. Don't worry. Go to the airport and book a flight home."

Raj flashed a look to Tyler, one I recognized, since Aggie gave it to me all the damn time. *Yeah, right.*

"Okay, how about this compromise?" I offered as we began to walk toward the buildings where my cousin Yuri lived. "We go to my cousin's apartment, and from there, you can return home."

Raj frowned. "And how do you plan to reach Tamara's home from there?"

I grinned. "I'll figure it out. It shouldn't be that far if I find a ride or something through family. With some research, I learned Tamara is staying on a farm not far from a town north of here called Vyborg."

"How far?"

Boy, these two were nosy, but they meant well. And I couldn't deny their friendship.

"A good distance," I admitted, "but the Lasovskayas take care of their own. Once I make contact with them, I'll figure out a way to barter with them so they can give me a ride."

From the corner, we walked a few blocks down a wide three-lane road until we came to a concrete village of stone and brick. Tall apartment buildings extended into the sky, but it was home for many. Little kids circled us, pointing to Tyler and calling him Brad Pitt.

"What are they saying?" Tyler asked.

"They're asking if you're Brad Pitt." I laughed.

"Can I say yes?"

"Let's not." He shook his head, but I could tell he appreciated the attention.

We had yet to see a dwarf around here and I doubt we would. This area wasn't popular with the dwarves with such a high werewolf population. We tended to be territorial, and fighting between werewolves and dwarves were rare but happened once in a while. My uncle Boris always used to say, "Them dwarves couldn't dig their way out of a losing card game. If you can't scratch my hide while you're busy digging for gold, you're not worth much to me while hunting for women."

Go get 'em, Uncle Boris. Their women aren't exactly hunting for you either, pal.

The signs for the building weren't familiar. They used strange signs and you had to walk around the buildings until you found the right one. No rhyme or reason existed. Or even a complex map. Good 'ole apartment living.

The apartment where my cousin Yuri used to live wasn't too bad on the inside. Yuri didn't live here anymore, by the way. It was a long story but, basically, my cousin managed to weasel his way into hooking up with a succubus from my therapy group. Weird as hell, but you find love in the most unexpected places.

The rickety elevator took us up twelve floors before we reached a hallway leading to my cousin's apartment at the far end. The whole place stunk of werewolves. Not that my people smelled or anything, but when we lived in clusters close together like this, something happened that's rather hard to describe to humans. Have you ever smelled a house with a large dog population? Yeah, that smell where underneath all the cleaning chemicals and fine perfumes, lingered the scent of animal. In this case, enough werewolves had marked their territory here to create a billboard a mile high. Not that anyone took a real piss, but it was close enough.

It was overwhelming enough to kick me in the knees and tug me down a peg or two. This territory wasn't my own. A door opened as we walked down and an older woman peered out. Once she spotted me, she averted her eyes and closed the door again. As we passed more doors, more curious eyes took me in. I was an alpha female with an unfamiliar scent. Before we reached my family's door, another door opened, and the man who opened it stepped into the hallway, blocking our path.

"Who the hell are you?" he snapped in Russian. "Did Albert send you?"

"Who is Albert?" My words didn't have the kind of bite I'd like, but it was good enough to keep my back straight.

"You don't smell local." His gaze rolled from my forehead, lingered on my breasts and then stopped at my knees. "You're mated."

He crossed his arms and continued to block our path.

"What's going on, Nat?" Raj asked. He understood everything the guy said, like I had, but both of us were confused.

"He thinks we're here from a rival pack." I glanced at the man. "I'm here to see the Lasovskayas down the hall."

The man snorted. "Oh, those deadbeats."

"Eh-excuse me?" I might've been a hoarding loser back home, but one thing you didn't do was say bad things about my family.

"They never pay their rent on time and their rank has fallen for the past couple of years. I suggest you visit, but don't stay long if you know what I mean."

Channeling Aggie at that very moment came unexpectedly. "Look, I don't know when you caught that asshole disease that's been going around, but no matter how much your shit stinks less than everybody else's, you don't bad mouth my family. Got it?" The growl in the back of my throat came out of nowhere, too.

The man's jaw twitched. He shuffled a bit forward and my heartbeat quickened. There were certain things you just didn't do to werewolves. Had my bold attitude gotten me into trouble?

"Natalya? Is that you?" The door at the end of the hall opened and a full-figured, dark-headed woman peered out. The voice was familiar from long-distance phone conversations. "What are you doing here?" she asked in Russian.

"Cousin Inna. It's me." All the while, I kept my gaze locked on the werewolf with a bad attitude. Our staring match continued until my cousin stormed down the hall and smacked the guy on the back of the head.

"You buffoon," she snapped in Russian. She added a bunch of other words, far too crass for even my vocabulary. "This is my kin from overseas and you greet her like a nipping puppy that can't piss on a tree right."

Tyler cringed as my cousin slapped the man in the head again.

"Move!" She used her wide hips to shove him out of the way.

He complied and sulked away as if this had happened before. If there was a pack hierarchy on this floor, it was a weird one.

She herded us to the apartment and we ambled inside. I smiled as I took in her neat, narrow hallway leading to her living room. My second cousin had an eye for cleanliness that I appreciated. That smile died when I saw who sat in the living room.

"Hey, Lilith," Raj said. "What are you doing here?"

A familiar couple sat on the couch. There was Yuri and the woman sitting on his left smiled brightly, her garish red lipstick-covered lips parting to reveal teeth smeared with makeup. She crossed her bony legs, causing her kneecaps to poke out of her floral shift. You couldn't miss the unfortunate succubus from my therapy group.

Lilith's stomach extended as far as Yuri's beer belly. Why yes, she was knocked up. Yuri rubbed a balding spot on his head. The four brown hairs stubbornly pointed right.

"This my daughter-in-law," Inna exclaimed with pride in broken English.

"I see...," Raj murmured.

Lilith had a history of being the worst soul-sucking succubus I'd ever seen. And I'd seen some pretty broken-down supernaturals in the Northeast. I was surprised Lilith wasn't starving to death. Let me put it that way.

"Have seat, please. This visit unexpected, but wonderful nonetheless. I love to practice English with my daughter-in-law." Inna was all grins. The only free spot was a loveseat and the floor. The living room was cozy, but not that spacious.

Raj eyed the room and briefly adjusted the gloves on his hands. He glanced at the tattered rug on the floor, probably seeing and thinking what I thought when I first came in: *When was the last time they washed that thing? Had they ever?* Tyler tapped Raj's shoulder. "I'll grab a spot on the floor. You and Nat sit on the other couch."

Once we sat, I spoke first since everyone looked at me. "Thanks for inviting us inside," I said in Russian. "My friends were kind enough to help me travel here to visit family."

"Is something wrong with my aunt?" Inna interjected.

"Oh, no." I searched for the words to keep my business my own. The last thing I needed was a phone call to America.

"I'm here for personal reasons. A surprise for Grandma and the others," I quickly added.

"Oh, how fun!" she leaned forward and laughed.

I hid my relief and tried to keep my heart and breathing in check. My little speech worked all the time for my family back home. Surprises got most people to keep quiet. There were a few holdouts—Aunt Vera being one of them—but since she was in New Jersey, my journey here should work out.

A strange silence settled over everyone. The only noise came from a variety show on TV.

Raj's gaze slowly darted to Yuri, who was in the midst of picking his nose.

"Stop that!" Lilith slapped his hand. *Oh, God! She touched the hand he picked with.* "Go wash your nasty paws."

Inna glanced to each of us as if to change the mood, while Yuri went to the adjoining kitchen to clean up. "Can I get you drink, food?" she asked in English.

"No, thank you," Raj said with a smile. I translated that to *hell, no*.

"I'm good. Thanks." Tyler offered his brightest grin.

"I've been full for hours," I added in Russian.

An audible stomach growl came from the spot where Tyler sat.

Inna blinked and a wave of embarrassment came over me. I should've made sure Tyler got something to eat before we came. He didn't complain much about basic needs. Maybe it was a modeling thing.

Once Yuri returned to his seat, his wife spoke to him. "Go down to the corner mart and get our guests some sandwiches from the stand."

Yuri reached forward and kissed her stomach. "Anything you want."

That was the extent of their conversation.

I rubbed my eyes. This had to be an illusion. A trickery of light and I'd fallen on the floor unconscious. This wasn't the same lazy man who called my parents' home asking to "talk" to Grandma for money. In the background, I often heard my cousin's TV or the music from a video game. The guy had "deadbeat son who lived at home" written all over him.

Lilith waited for him to leave, all the while blowing on the fingernails she'd *attempted* to paint. She'd gotten a few streaks of red on her wrists, but the proud pregnant mother held up her hands with pride.

"When are you due?" I asked to make light conversation.

"I'm still early in my pregnancy. This place has been nice. New York wasn't a good place for me to be in my condition."

"How is that?" It wasn't like she had the tools to hunt for souls in the U.S. either.

"Yuri and his family take care of me. Every *single* need."

I shuddered, not bothering to ask *where* her food supply came from.

"What plan you have?" Inna asked. "You need stay here?"

My mouth opened to say no, but Tyler spoke first. "She needs to travel north to find a small town called Vyborg. Do you know the best way to get there?"

"Of course, my Yuri will take you tomorrow morning with his band," Lilith said.

We all turned at the same time to focus on Lilith.

"His band?" I asked.

"When we got here, I wasn't gonna have him sitting around on his lazy butt, so I made him work until he could afford to take his *balalaika* out of pawn. After that, I made him join a band." Her smile was coy, definitely the smile of a woman who wore the maternity pants in the house. "Can you guess when his next tour begins?"

Chapter 8

For the first time ever, I thanked the succubus. In group therapy, she drove us bat-shit crazy with her complaints about not being able to find a man or her lack of opportunities to find one. Heidi had once told me of Lilith's antics while the mermaid had taken her out to get a man. The succubus had sucked her date dry, but now that I saw her pregnant with Yuri falling in line with a couple of words, I couldn't help but smile like a proud mother hen. Well, I did little in getting her back on track, but she had to open herself up to a new relationship like everybody else.

The day wound down after Yuri brought back food for us to eat. The sandwiches had been wrapped with care, and with a sniff or two, I gave the thumbs up to Raj, who didn't look like he trusted his veggie wrap.

"So where you stay?" my cousin asked.

"I'll be fine until tomorrow morning," I replied.

"She'll be fine. We'll take care of her," Tyler said.

Inna chuckled, looking Tyler over like he was sizzling pork chops on a grill. "You are nice boy. Not werewolf, but handsome. You married?"

Tyler blinked. Was this his first werewolf proposition?

"I'm flattered, but I'm trying to get matched to a dwarf wife." He stumbled a bit while his face blossomed bright red.

"Dwarf wife." Inna's smile widened and then she laughed again. "Interesting. Never before I have dwarf in my home. You smell different."

Tyler frowned and sniffed his forearm. The guy was cleaner than most. I always smelled some kind of soap on him. I assumed he had to keep up appearances to find a wife.

After a round of goodbyes, I agreed to meet the band tomorrow morning at Alexander Park near the Leningrad Zoo.

The next things I needed to do was find a place to stay — which meant it was time for another round of goodbyes.

Once outside the building, I smiled at Tyler and Raj.

"You two have been amazing," I said. "*Again.*"

"Yeah, this has been fun," Raj said. "A nice adventure before I get back to the grind at home."

"You got work to do this week?" I asked.

"I always have work." Raj explained during the long train trip that he worked for a game development company as the lead over the writing team. The guy had a knack for coming up with really cool storylines for fantasy games. Go figure. I found it hilarious every time I thought about it.

"How about you, Tyler?" I asked him. "What do you have going on this week?"

"I have traveling to do. It will be hard, but I like challenges," he replied.

"Then you two should get going. I'm gonna try to find a clean hostel and get settled for the evening." I waved at my friends because Raj wasn't a hugger, and then turned to leave.

Then I noticed I had an extra shadow as I walked. "Tyler, what are you doing?"

"I'm traveling."

I faced him with my hands on my hips.

"I have business to handle north of here. With a friend." He shrugged.

"Don't you have to go back to New York? Maybe have another matchmaking dinner?"

"I think we both saw how that worked out. I need some time to get my shit together." Tyler rarely swore. He stared out to the street past us with a wistful expression.

"Not everything I see and experience will be vacation-like," I admitted.

"That's never the case with you, Natalya, but I'll be fine." He finally smiled. I couldn't resist returning it. He had that charismatic vibe about him that could make a ship sail backwards. "You have a way of bringing out the best in me. I need to spend more time with friends like that."

We began to walk again.

"Why can't I seem to bring out the best in myself, then?" I asked.

"I guess it doesn't work that way. If it did, we wouldn't be in therapy."

"You got that right. I wouldn't still be hoarding."

We slowed down a bit but kept going.

"It takes time, you know," he said. "I'm still not married and have panic attacks every time I want to meet a pretty girl."

"We're all a work in progress, huh?"

"I wanna be done."

I couldn't resist rolling with laughter. "You and me both, Tyler."

After asking the locals some questions and a short bus ride, we found a hostel to stay for the night in the neighborhood. The area wasn't too bad, rather like Brooklyn in a way. Men and women spent the evening heading out for groceries for dinner and the scents from their cooking drifted to my nose.

The sounds of conversation from the next building bled through the walls and reached my ears. I longed for home already.

Tyler was in the bed next to mine. The large room had several occupants already sleeping.

This was my first hostel and the second time tolerating a bed that wasn't my own. Tyler saw the look on my face when we came in and immediately turned around to find a shopping mart to buy me suitable bedding. The place smelled clean, but no matter how I tried to shake the bounds of my illness, I couldn't unsee things. Mind over matter was some useless bullshit in my opinion. I could sit on the bed and pretend I didn't smell the cat that had wandered around the place and lay on my bed. I could sit on the bed and pretend I didn't notice the tears in the sheet (seven of them.) And finally, I could pretend I was an alpha female and this was trivial. Humans had so many things that didn't concern them. Their lack of senses gave them blinders I wished I had.

I laughed a bit, and Tyler opened one eye to glance at me.

"Don't worry, I haven't cracked yet," I said with a bit of a smile.

"Yet," he mumbled.

I closed my eyes and focused on the TV show blaring through the wall from the home next door. I focused, allowing my ears to give me all the input I needed. I didn't need to worry about the room, the bed, or the occupants.

As I drifted off to sleep, listening to the laughter from the wife whose husband complained that his food was too cold and the kids arguing about some video game they heard about at school, a smile settled on my face. I thought about my brother Alex and my parents and a similar scene from decades ago when we were kids. Those were good times.

I held onto those memories and slept.

We were supposed to be at Alexander Park at nine a.m. But if you know me, I am a stickler for time. Matter of fact, I dragged Tyler out of bed to show up at eight forty-five sharp. In my opinion, the early werewolf could catch and munch on the bird that caught the worm. That sort of thing.

But not a single person was waiting at the designated spot.

"They are musicians," Tyler said with a shrug. "There's no reason for them to be on time. They might've had a late night gig or something."

Forty-five minutes later, the first person showed up. A tall man, wearing a wrinkled, bright red suit that stank of booze and smoke, ambled up to us holding a violin case. Using a small comb, he ran it through messy brown curls that refused to stay put.

"Are you waiting for the tour bus?" I asked him in Russian.

"Yes. Do I know you?"

"I'm Yuri's cousin, Natalya. He told us we could hitch a ride."

"Oh, yes, he told us about you last night at dinner. I'm Dmitri!" He glanced at my friend as if he wanted introductions. "Who is your friend?"

I introduced him to Tyler.

Tyler stumbled over saying hello in Russian, but he

managed to introduce himself with flair.

"Might as well prepare for any photo shoots in Russia someday," he said with a grin afterwards.

"Where is everyone?" I asked Dmitri.

"They all got sloppy drunk last night. The bandmaster even ended up passed out under the table."

I couldn't resist snorting. It sounded like my uncles after a few rounds of hard liquor.

"They'll be here soon. We need to get going, since we have a party in Vyborg tonight. We have to make it." Dmitri gave a half-hearted shrug.

A few minutes later, a few more players showed up. Most of them lumbered about with stubble on their faces and bleary eyes. A bunch of hungover werewolves made the worst travel companions. I tried to smile and introduced myself.

We stood in a wide circle. The smallest man, who had a tuba about half his size, seemed to be the only cheerful person in the band. He had merry cheeks and the most pleasant demeanor. He probably drank the least last night. Yuri arrived last with Lilith waddling ahead of him. She kissed his cheek, waved in my direction, and then headed back home.

"Where is the driver with that damn bus?" Dmitri spat.

"He probably fell asleep inside it," one man said.

"That slime bag is probably still between a woman's legs." He glanced at me. "No offense." He introduced himself to me as Andelov.

"You bark like a pup compared to my aunts," I reassured him.

He laughed. "A good woman knows how to handle a man," he said with a wink. He looked to be around my father's age, at least a century old.

An even older man shuffled up to us with a tiny

duffle bag in his hand, and Dmitri introduced him as *Stary Papa*. Old Papa. Wrinkles filled his face and he nodded to us with expansive gray eyes.

"He plays the cymbals for us," Dmitri said.

While we waited, Dmitri opened his case to reveal a beautiful fiddle. The fine instrument smelled of old wood and varnish. He'd cared for the fiddle a lot more than his appearance. With a flourish, he picked up his instrument, began plucking at the strings, and sang the opening line to *Korobushka*:

Hey, my carrier box is brimful, there's calico, print, and brocade.

Have mercy, my dear, with my juvenile shoulders!

It had been a few years since I'd heard the Peddler's Box song.

The others laughed and clapped, a few opening their respective cases. The atmosphere was hard to resist. I began to sing with them. How long had it been since I'd heard a live band playing Russian folk music? A crowd of bystanders strolling through the park stopped to watch the band. The short tuba player belted out the lively tune. Andelov played the accordion, while Yuri strummed the *balalaika*, a Russian guitar with a triangular body. Dmitri continued to play his fiddle.

Ever the showman, he even flipped it backwards in the middle of playing and kept going. The bow danced in his hands, and the growing crowd roared.

Tyler stomped his foot at my side, his head bobbing to the tune.

Naturally, right as they began playing the song for a second time, much to the bystanders' dismay, a grumbling tour bus pulled up to the street nearby.

Yuri continued to strum the *balalaika* and Dmitri played while dancing a jig, even as the others stopped and gathered their belongings.

Was there some kind of band member rivalry going on? While the others loaded up the bus, Tyler and I gaped at the two until Old Papa gestured for us to get on. "Those two idiots will play until we start to leave," he said in accented English.

"Why?" Tyler asked.

"I don't know." Old Papa shook his head. "They once played until Dmitri hurt his hands. Stupid idiots."

Tyler and I found empty seats in the middle of the bus.

As expected, the bus was loaded, still spewing black exhaust, and began to pull away as Dmitri and Yuri gave up their battle. They grabbed their instruments and cases, racing each other to reach the bus first.

"Wow, you weren't kidding," I said to Old Papa.

The elderly werewolf gave a short laugh. "I once told the driver to leave them and let them hitchhike. I was ignored, and you see what happens? Little boys who need their asses beaten."

The two found seats. Dmitri in front and Yuri in the back. They were breathless and glared at each other.

The ride north was a cramped one on lumpy seats with the stuffing poking out in places, but the mood was jovial. I expected sleeping and snoring werewolves, but the band had apparently shaken off the effects of their drunken night. Dmitri broke out another song at the front of the bus.

As much as I wanted forever,
my sweetheart ran away for another.
Would she come to me next full moon?
I beg you sweet princess.
She wouldn't come to me, for she'd found another.
"Ho ho ho, Anna!" another sang.
She had the fairest coat. As bright as sunshine, he

continued.

Old Papa handed me the cymbals and I tapped them with the tune.

They continued on with the verse again.

I beg you sweet princess.

She wouldn't come to me, for she'd found another.

"Ho ho ho, Natalya!"

I laughed when I heard my name.

The band kept playing like that until apparently they ran out of women's names. Maybe past girlfriends.

Two hours passed like that with the band playing and joking. All the while, the city-like scenery changed. City streets became the countryside with fields and roads surrounded by forest. Traveling by bus was much more pleasant compared to the train trip with Tyler and Raj. Speaking of Tyler, my friend slept in the seat in front of mine, his head leaning on the dirty window.

I stared out the window again. I wondered what Grandma would think of seeing Russia like this. I wished I could've taken her with me. She never mentioned why she wouldn't return to her homeland. Once she said something light-hearted like it cost her everything she had to come to America; why would she go back? But, this was her birthplace, the land where she'd buried Grandpa. Even some of our relatives still lived here. Was there something she had left behind that I didn't know about? Grandma was full of secrets. Many of them hadn't been revealed until she'd used old magic to save me.

Now that I was taking my own destiny into my hands, fear gripped me. Suppressing it had been easy every once in a while, but now, as I watched the miles between me and my destination decrease, apprehension tried to sneak in.

A wrinkled hand reached out and took mine. "You'll be fine, *devuska*," he said softly. "You're a good girl."

"Thank you, Old Papa." I returned the grip. His hand was warm and soft like Grandma's. I wondered if my grandpa Pyotr had been like him. Had he looked like my mom or my aunts? Grandma didn't have any pictures of him, which, in many ways, was a disappointment. Like a piece of my past had been denied to me. Of course, that didn't stop Grandma from saying he was a handsome man. "He had the most beautiful blue eyes, Natalya. Most of the females tried to get a piece of him, even after we were married. I had to slap around a few girls who got too close."

When she said that, Grandma had that flicker of mischief in her brown eyes she always had.

As I drifted in my memories, the bus came to a shaky stop.

"About time we got here," Dmitri said with a groan. "I need to piss for a day."

"You need to stop drinking then," Andelov said after him.

"Like you can stop talking!" Dmitri retorted.

I shook Tyler's shoulder. "We reached Vyborg."

He stretched his long arms. "How much farther until we reach the farm?"

I made a face while I pondered that question. "If we found a ride, we might reach Tamara's before nightfall."

"Do you want to wait and watch their gig?"

I snorted. "I've heard enough music to last me a few years."

He nodded. "Let's get something to eat and then see what kind of ride we can get."

We got off the bus. The city wasn't as big and sprawling as St. Petersburg, but Vyborg felt as big as

South Toms River. But there were so many differences compared to back home. The pine trees along the roads felt like home, but everything else was so different. All stone, gray buildings were everywhere. A touch of the old world. The cars and the architecture made the place completely new and different.

"Are you coming with us to eat?" Dmitri called out.

"Of course." Tyler followed Dmitri into the stone building with double doors while I tried to wear a brave face. My past history with unknown restaurants had never been a good one. America was a totally different place in terms of rules of cleanliness and serving. Not that I was saying my Russian kin would serve me food in a slovenly place with dirt lining the seats, but what I considered clean was at a different level compared to everyone else. And damn it all to hell. I'd made a conscious decision to leave my baby wipes at home.

The minute I walked through the doors, wonderful smells hit me. Fresh baked bread and grilled meat. I could practically predict the menu before it was even placed in front of us. Chicken *tabaka*, seasoned to perfection. Home cooked Russian dishes for a hungry appetite. A nearby customer, a werewolf, had fresh cabbage stuffed with ground beef. Tasty *golubtzy*. Matter of fact, there were a lot of us in here, which was probably why the band chose this place.

A hostess sat all of us at a few tables shoved together. The boisterous group filled the entire dining room. What few customers they had greeted us with smiles and inquiries about where the band would be playing tonight.

Glancing at Yuri, I had no idea my cousin had such potential.

The food was divine. Tyler practically wiped his

plate clean with his bread as I ate my fill. All the while, my friend joked with the one man who knew enough English to carry on a conversation, Old Papa.

"How will you two reach your destination?" Old Papa asked him.

"We'll find someone to give us a ride," he replied. "Who knows? In a town like this, maybe there are some workers or truckers who can offer a hand."

Old Papa nodded. "You should be careful, though. I noticed someone was following you."

Tyler froze in the middle of wiping his mouth. "Following us, what do you mean?"

"We've made two stops on the way here. Both times, I caught a strange scent. It was something I'd never encountered before. But I did smell it again when we stopped for gas. It was strange."

"Like what?" I leaned forward, my heartbeat up a bit. Had I been found?

"Could it be Raj?" Tyler asked me.

"Why would he follow us? Didn't he have to return home?" I said.

"Pretty much." He turned to Old Papa. "Do you think it was a werewolf?"

"No. I'm not that old, boy. I can sniff out my own kind easy enough. Whatever this was, it was something even I haven't smelled before."

I shrugged. "Maybe one of the other band members has a fan or something."

The old man shrugged. "I doubt it."

I stole a glance at Tyler. My first thought had been werewolf, too. Maybe Thorn or one of my relatives. But a nonwerewolf led me to believe otherwise. Something was going down and I couldn't run away from it.

Chapter 9

We managed to get a ride with a farmer who had
hauled his goods to Vyborg and was now returning
home. He had a cheerful demeanor, albeit a stuttering
potty mouth was included.

"T-that damn son of mine better have done his
chores," he grumbled. His remarks about his offspring
continued for most of the trip. I managed to learn the
boy wanted to be a good-for-nothing pop singer and he
couldn't hold a tune even if he played a mime, a rather
bitter insult.

Tyler covered his ears the entire way. We rode in
the back of the man's truck, huddling close to avoid the
chilly breeze from the bay as we rode up A124 road.
Soon enough, the forest blocked most of the wind, but
not enough for us to feel the frosty sensation deep in
our bones.

Tyler turned to me. "What will you say to
Tamara?"

"You mean what will I say other than please help
me learn how to remove Thorn's curse?"

He rolled his eyes. "I'm being serious. You traveled

all this way. Do you have a plan for when you meet her? The last time you met wasn't a pleasant memory, I'm sure."

The last time we'd met had been when I was fulfilling my father's moon debt to a werewolf named Roscoe. The guy was an asshole, a dead one mostly likely after the fairy child he trapped got a hold of him, thanks to me. I was forced to haul that fairy in a truck up to Maine. Once there, I met the pack leader and Tamara. There was a fight at the time between the fairies and werewolves. Tamara had cast some pretty dark magic that day, showing that she had my grandmother's powers of transformation.

"I guess I could say, 'Hi! I'd like to help you figure things out," I managed.

"You didn't think this through did you?" He sighed.

"I got it covered. Really."

I didn't have shit covered. This whole trip should've been better planned. I was the queen, the overlord, you name it, of planning to reduce my anxiety. But when it came to saving Thorn, I was willing to toss most of that planning aside. Damn! Love made folks do stupid stuff.

But it was worth it, I guess.

"Look, if you're not sure what to say, I got an idea or two," Tyler said.

"Like what?"

"Just let the professional do his thing."

"Tyler, you're a model. Do what thing?"

We reached a fork in the road and the farmer came to a stop. He pointed down the road with a smile. "Go that way about two miles, and you'll find what you're looking for at the top of a small hill."

I thanked him. Now it was time to get things over with. The walk didn't take that long. The road was still pretty wide, even though many of the dirt paths had gaping potholes. Tyler jumped over a few.

"This place is so quiet," he remarked.

"Do you want to raise a family in the city or in the country like this?"

He shrugged. "It doesn't matter to me. I just want to find someone who will make me want to live anywhere."

"That's what I like to hear."

Just like the man said, the house at the end of the road sat at the top of a small hill and couldn't be missed. Forests hugged an open meadow on all sides. The chilly wind whistled through the trees and whipped a clothesline of underwear through the air. Women's underwear. The two-story house had been kept up with dark grey shingles and a bright red door. A haphazard fence was the only thing in disrepair about the place. The dark wood was rotted in many places. A single power line extended from the road and raced up to the house. The only line for communication and power.

"Are you ready?" he asked.

"Stop asking and let's do it."

We walked up to the house. I was glad the wind was to my back. That way, I wasn't sneaking up, and whoever was inside could smell and see me coming. Werewolves didn't like folks sneaking up on them.

The door opened a crack as Tyler and I approached. From downwind, I couldn't smell who opened the door, but I hoped it was a werewolf and not some witch popping out who liked to eat little boys and girls. As much as I wanted to learn a spell or two from a werewolf, learning something from a spellcaster who was actually a witch wasn't welcomed.

The door opened and two sets of eyes peeked out. I grabbed Tyler's arm by the time we reached the circular courtyard in front of the house.

"Wait. Let them check us out," I whispered.

The wind shifted behind us and the hairs on the back of my neck rose. "Who are you?" A voice hissed to our backs.

The muscles in Tyler's arm stiffened. My grip on him tightened. Now wasn't the time to whip out his *Axe in a Box*. Not yet, anyway.

The scent behind us was wolf though.

"I'm Natalya Stravinsky," I said in Russian. "I'm here to see Tamara."

"Only people in America know me by that name." The voice circled us until a familiar face stepped in front of us. Tamara hadn't changed since the last time I saw her. She was a short, full-figured woman with thick brown hair, but it was the birthmark on her face that assured me I had the right person. The rose-colored birthmark filled most of her left cheek. "I've seen you before."

"You have," I said in English. I might as well keep the rest of the conversation out in the open.

She shifted and glanced at Tyler. "And the dwarf?" she asked in English.

"My friend," I replied. "He wanted to make sure I got here safely."

"You always seem to have friends...around you." She glanced toward the woods nearby. "Is the wizard here, too?"

She meant Nick.

"No, he didn't come with me. Only Tyler."

She kissed her fingertips, mumbled a few words I couldn't hear, and raised the fingers to the wind and waited. "You speak the truth. Now the next question. Why would you do something so foolish as to come here and see me?"

I took a deep breath. I refused to take my hand off

Tyler's arm. The guy was itching to speak, but for now, I needed to settle things. "I've heard some rumors from my grandmother, Svetlana Lasovskaya. You remember her, right?"

Tamara's eyebrow rose. "You are her granddaughter. Most interesting."

Hopefully interesting in a good way and not a bad way.

"You told my grandmother about a spell to remove curses. I am here about that."

At the mention of curses, Tamara's steady heartbeat rose.

"I wanted to—" I began.

"No more talking outside. We'll discuss your visit over tea." She glanced at Tyler. "He does drink tea, doesn't he?"

I released his arm.

"I most certainly do," Tyler said, giving me a stern eye.

We followed Tamara up the single step into the house. I expected to run into the double pairs of eyes, but the tiny living room was empty. Other than the bit of Russian culture here and there, it appeared like any other farmhouse with mismatched wooden furniture and little things here and there to make it a home. A wooden radio in the corner played classical music. The volume was turned down so low I barely heard it. Werewolves definitely lived here.

"Zoya, bring some tea," she said as she took a seat. "We have guests. Luda, bring some cookies. I know you baked some behind my back."

The two pairs of eyes appeared at the head of the stairs as we sat down. They belonged to a pair of fraternal black-haired twins. A shorter, full-figured one was dressed in a floral print dress, while a thinner, taller one wore a white T-shirt and jeans. They peered

84

at us with curiosity.

"Are they staying for dinner?" the one in the jeans asked. She pushed her chin-length hair behind her ears before she fetched a plate of cookies. That must be Luda, then.

"I don't know yet." Tamara leaned back in the seat. She gestured to the other places for us. "It depends on what they have to say. Whether I like it or not."

As much as I came here bearing goodwill and all, I wasn't a fool either. Tamara was a werewolf with spellcasting abilities. The only thing I could do was pretty useless in a battle against someone like her.

"I'm not here to threaten anyone. The reason I came was because —"

"You want to save the South Toms River Pack alpha."

I swallowed and tried to keep a straight face. "You know who I am."

She offered a slow smile. "Let's drop the pretenses then, Dearie. We met under fascinating circumstances, didn't we? I need fairy magic, you needed to save your father from his moon debt. I didn't approve Roscoe's method to bring me the fairy, but I needed the magic for my work. Everything was going so smoothly. Until you came and tricked all of us with the decoy in the truck." She laughed as Zoya poured a tea service and handed each of us a drink.

Tyler didn't touch his until Zoya sat and took a sip. He didn't trust them any more than I did at this point. I didn't blame him.

"You were quite clever," Tamara said. "Although, that wasn't too smart of you to let that wizard use you."

"What is she talking about?" Tyler asked.

I wanted to smack Tamara and I'd just gotten into her home. "Nothing you need to worry about." I didn't dignify her words with a response. "You shouldn't have taken that child from her parents. Your pack got what they deserved."

Tamara chuckled. "They weren't my pack—not formally, anyway. Just a means to an end. But, yes, you reap what you sow, right?"

She took one of Luda's cookies and continued. "Are you ready to entangle yourself in my web? Are you ready to harvest from my tainted fields of knowledge?"

My gaze never left hers. "Some prices are worth paying."

"Great advice from your grandmother. She told me that once, too. Not that I paid attention, though."

I got to the point; I didn't feel like waiting. "So have you found a way to remove curses?"

"Not yet, but I'm close, and that's why I have to be careful. I wanted to find others who practiced old magic. Other werewolves like your grandmother who had the skillset to help me, but most of them don't want to touch dark magic and try to change it into something else." She shrugged. "Touching darkness is a scary thing. Like jumping into a pit and hoping the world is waiting there to break your fall." She touched the birthmark on her face, making me wonder if she'd truly been born with it.

"I can help you," I said softly, "especially if you taught me once you figured it out."

Tamara made a face I was getting tired of during this trip: *Yeah right.* She crossed her arms and a sinking feeling soured my stomach.

She was gonna ask me to leave.

"I might be a beginner," I said quickly, "but what I do have is an undying will. I can remember things, and I'm willing to do whatever is necessary to save my husband."

"I don't think the term *beginner* is close to what you are. Can you command fire? Can you transform? What can you do?"

"I can't do any of those things," I admitted. "But I'm willing to learn."

She shook her head with disbelief and I could feel my only chance slipping through my fingers. "How will your *learning* help me?"

"That's the thing about solving problems. I can take what's scattered and bring it together. I see organization, or what you'd call patterns, in chaos." Like the shitty way The Bends was before I got that place together.

Tyler, who sat at my side, placed his hand on my knee. When I briefly peeked at his face, his expression told me to let it go. Like hell, I would. If I had to get on my knees and soil my family honor to beg, I'd damn well do it.

"That's your argument?" Tamara said.

"Don't you want to learn how to remove curses?" I replied.

Tamara sighed. "More than you know."

I glanced at Luda, Zoya, and then Tamara. Zoya took a deep breath and briefly closed her eyes. Luda reached for her twin's hand and offered a reassuring squeeze, but it was the pained expression on their faces as they glanced at their grandmother that hit me hard. What happened to them? Secrets seeped out of the cracks in the wall and hovered over us like a suffocating cowl. Was someone in this house cursed, too?

"I'll let you stay for a few days," Tamara said to end the silence. She didn't look my way, simply looking at the black and white landscape photos on the wall. "If you don't show me you're worth my time, I'll either send you back home or — "

"Or what?"

Her smile widened and made my throat go dry. "I guess you don't want to know what happens when I curse someone, do you?"

Chapter 10

Afternoon tea with Tamara turned into dinner. I expected Tyler to bolt and make a run for it, but the dwarf merely smiled and followed me around like a good friend. The twins, in turn, followed us. As to whether Luda or Zoya liked him remained to be seen. The taller twin hid her smile often behind her hand, grinning whenever Tyler said something. The shorter one was far darker, casting a smirk in my direction whenever I spoke.

"You smell. How long have you been on the road?" Zoya asked.

She didn't need to remind me. My nose worked just fine, thank you. "Not too long. We stayed in a hostel last night and, after that, we traveled up north with my cousin's folk music band."

Zoya nodded. "That's still not an excuse for filth."

Kill her with kindness, my *babushka* would say. "No, it's not." I glanced at the coffee table and couldn't resist running my finger along the edge. I drew a line in the dust, collecting it into a pile of dust bunnies.

Her smile faded. *Touché.*

"How about we let you two get settled then before the evening. During dinner, we can discuss our 'arrangements' for the week," Tamara said.

"That sounds good," I said.

As much as I wanted to get to know Zoya and her sunshine-like sister Luda, I really wanted to remove all the filth from our trip. Luda darted up first, gesturing for us to follow her up the stairs.

The wood creaked with each step. "How long since the stairs have been checked?" Tyler remarked.

"This is my parents' home," Luda said in heavily-accented English. "They've been dead now for the past ten years, so it has been a long time since Papa had fixed them."

"If you have tools, I'd be glad to look them over." He offered the kind of smile that would make any woman melt between the cracks in the floor, but Luda simply chuckled.

I poked him in the back and gave him the I-know-what-you're-doing look. He shrugged back. For a guy who only preferred dwarf girls, he didn't mind flirting with a stranger.

The top of the stairs opened to a hexagon-shaped room about the size of my bedroom. The farmhouse had been well-constructed — many years ago, though. A few cracks and water stains in the wallpapered walls showed the age of the home. A single light bulb hanging from the ceiling added needed light due to the narrow window along one of the walls. Dark red curtains with a pattern resembling gumbo in a bubbling pot clashed against violet pattern wallpaper.

The whole place needed someone handy for upkeep. The outside was in far better shape compared to the inside.

Five doors from where we stood led to other areas. Luda pointed to the closest one. "That room is for Zoya and me. We won't be sharing forever..." She stumbled on her words. "But for now that's where we stay. Across the hall is my gram's room. And next to our room is the bathroom. It's the only one in the house I'm afraid."

We nodded the whole time while she explained things. Tyler and I each got our own room. They were small, but as Luda promised, they were tidy. Not to my standards in terms of cleanliness, but after a few days of living here, every dust bunny would end up on the endangered list. I nuked those suckers on a daily basis back home. Here they'd get the same treatment.

No one disturbed us when we were in our rooms. Based on the steady breathing from his room, Tyler must've taken a nap. I took a long, hot shower.

While I was in the ancient bathroom drying off, I couldn't help thinking about my cellphone. Except for the brief time I'd checked for messages on the train, I'd kept the phone off. The temptation to turn it on nagged me. Had something happened back home? I rarely turned it off. With so many things going on with my pack over the last year — the attack from the Long Island Pack, my brother's kidnapping, my father's moon debt — the idea of cutting myself off from the others seemed unforgivable.

An alpha female never abandoned her pack.

I chose Thorn over them.

My heart clenched as if someone punched me in the chest. The pain circled around my ribs and sucked away the breath in my lungs.

All I could do was face myself in the murky mirror and accept what I'd done.

Because if I had to do it again. I would.

Some prices are worth paying.

When I got back into my room, I turned on the phone briefly. I had reception this time. There were thirteen messages, all of them from Thorn. He'd called the phone twenty times.

Oh, shit! I should've expected this. I quickly turned off the phone. I was so gonna hear it from him when I saw him again.

Not long after I freshened up, the sky opened to rain. I opened the window a bit and let in the fresh air. The crack didn't let in too much rain, but the breeze removed the stagnation in the air.

Dinner time came with a call from downstairs. No knock was necessary. In a werewolf household, if you couldn't smell the food cooking or hear someone whisper "chow time" from the basement, you didn't value your stomach all that much.

Tyler's earthy scent wasn't in the hallway so I knocked hard to get the dwarf up. He came out looking pretty rough—clothes-wise anyway. The guy could be in rags and he'd probably make them look good enough to be photographed. But he did smell like somebody who had slept into their sweaty clothes.

"You might want to change clothes after you eat," I whispered.

"Oh, I smell bad?" His face scrunched up.

"Kinda of."

To a werewolf, he stank. Most humans would consider him sweaty from a hard day's work.

He darted into the bathroom. "Tell them I'm on my way."

I stifled my laugh.

Dinner that night was garden potatoes, asparagus, and generous portions of pork sausages. Everything was fresh from the farms around us. They tasted so good. Tyler kept eating what Zoya scooped and placed on his plate. Even Luda and Zoya grunted with each bite, scooping large portions on their own plates.

As good as the food tasted, I couldn't help but feel

a set of eyes on me. Whenever I glanced at the head of the table, I spotted Tamara staring back at me, her brown eyes pensive. For every five bites Tyler took, she ate one. She chewed slowly, too. Pretty weird for a werewolf. Half of her plate still had food by the time everyone else finished. I offered to help with the dishes, but Tamara shooed the girls away with Tyler to help.

"You should go to bed now," Tamara said. The way she said it made me pause.

"It's not even nine."

"We're on a farm. There's work to be done in the morning." She jerked her chin to the stairs to indicate that I should go.

"I understand."

"Oh, and Natalya."

"Yes?"

"If you want to stay here, I suggest you keep your phone turned off."

Asking how she knew would be pretty fruitless. The damn thing beeped as it booted up. But as to why she wanted me to keep it off was another matter entirely. Whether sinister or not, I'd find out soon enough.

The morning didn't come with a knock. It came with a violent push off my bed.

I flopped onto the cold, hardwood floor with a hard thump. My noggin hit the floor last, but whether that happened or not didn't make a damn bit of difference. Tamara stood in the doorway. My door usually squeaked, yet she'd entered without a sound.

"Move your ass, girl," she said. "We got work to do."

As she turned to leave, she threw behind her back, "Meet me in the middle of the field."

Waking up on time was something I always strived to do. In anticipation of what was to come, I had set the ancient alarm clock by the bed to five a.m., a great time to wake up. This woman shook me out of bed at four. I blinked at the ticking alarm clock, finally raising my wobbly arm to turn it off. It was pretty useless now.

My morning routine made the day start right. After the stay in the hostel and now waking up at Tamara's, I damn wished I'd taken my happy pills. My stomach churned with discomfort as I quickly washed my face in the bathroom and threw on my shirt and jeans. With a sigh, I touched the jean's fabric, wishing for my skirt. Another day, another opportunity to adjust.

I could do this. *Big girl panties, right?*

Tamara waited in the middle of the field behind the house.

The sky had opened to a downpour that had turned into a soft rain. But the damage had already been done. Between the house and Tamara was a field awash in mud, wet grass, and who knows what else.

Was this some kind of test? I took the two steps down from the house and hesitated before hitting the ground. This was supposed to be the easy part, yet during my time in Russia, it hadn't rained. My sad jacket would be soaked after some time out here.

Instead of taking a step back toward the house, I marched right out into that damn field. I even stomped in a puddle to gather my confidence.

I ignored the wetness seeping into my shoes. I ignored the mud covering my shoes. And I even avoided a panic attack by constantly reminding myself why I was here. My purpose.

Damn. My purpose really needed to work better when I was cranky in the mornings. Just the thought of scraping gunk off my shoes just about made me go back.

Tamara gave me the evil eye, so I decided to stand there with a straight back.

"You're not very fast," she said.

"You're not very good at keeping time. You said in the morning."

"It is morning."

"I mean like dawnish morning."

Tamara didn't show amusement. "The last time I saw you, you didn't defend yourself with magic. Was there a reason for that?"

"I only know so much."

Tamara chuckled. "You mean you know nothing?"

I shrugged. "Kind of."

Tamara sighed. "You're not much use to me like this."

"Give me one week. I might surprise you."

Tamara's eyebrow rose. A trail of rainwater formed on her hair and streaked down her cheek. Her clothes were soaked, but she didn't care. She merely blinked when the water got into her eyes. She sighed deeply. Her cheeks caved in as if she were chewing on it. She smacked her lips and glanced at me from head to toe.

Time stretched out, and I hoped she would say something. My jacket was soaked by this point, but somehow, through sheer willpower, I remained where I stood. My Aggie would be proud.

"Lesson one," she finally said, "know your power." She held up her hand and presented the palm. "The amazing thing about power is that it's in everything around us. Power swims in this whole hand. It's all over me. Do you understand this?"

Nick had taught me a lot about this. Once he'd showed me how he saw me through his eyes. That power pulsed bright white under my skin like a fire. As to how I could use this inner strength was the important question.

"Yes."

"The fundamental exchange is the driving power behind the spellcasters. They have the ability to draw power from a source and manipulate it to do what they want."

Fundamental exchange. This was a new term. I nodded.

"Think of them as master clay molders. In the range of things, we are a source of power. Our power to shift comes from within. Without our power we cannot change from one to another."

That I knew, too.

"For us, drawing from our power isn't the same as shape-shifters. As a conduit, the path to using the power isn't the same. They have to work less than we do. They're better at it too, since they are playing in the pool you could say."

"But..." I tried to find a way to ask without bringing Nick into it. "A spellcaster once told me he draws from himself sometimes."

She chuckled. "They can, but compared to us, their inner strength is a pebble next to a mountain. Most of them could never change their flesh like us without an imbued weapon."

I shifted and my feet squished in the mud. "You said most of them."

"The world is a massive place, Natalya. You should never assume the shadows don't hold new dangers." She glanced to the woods in the distance. Her eyebrows lowered as her nostrils flared.

"Is something wrong?" I asked.

She took a deep breath, and then shook her head. Nothing you need to worry about. "Now I will most likely have to undo the garbage you've learned before. I bet all somebody taught you to do was light a campfire or something."

I couldn't light a cigarette, even if I wanted a smoke. Lighting a fire right now didn't exactly seem like a genius thing to do anyway.

"Just go ahead and teach me."

"Let's start with water, then. All around you is matter to be manipulated. Either you move it, freeze it, or vaporize it. You can play with it like clay. Are you following me so far?"

"Yep."

"Manipulating matter requires two things: tapping into the inner source, and the words to do the push for us to make the connection."

I didn't interrupt her. It was nice to learn something my grandma was so eager to hold back about. This was something I needed to learn.

"The memorization is the easy part. Finding your way to unleash your power is another thing entirely." She went through a series of phrases for the manipulation. And it wasn't something simple like move water around. Each way you could alter water had a three-word phrase. And Tamara was perfectly able to info dump them all.

Instead of mumbling like a damn fool, I chewed on each phrase and swallowed it into my head.

Pretend like she's Bill, I told myself.

Every morning Bill went though his work list, his order list, and a bunch of other bullshit he remembered at the moment but would forget by the time he grabbed his morning coffee.

For a goblin who loved money more than his relatives, he sure didn't work hard toward learning more of it.

"What are you doing?" she asked out of the blue.

I opened my eyes to see her staring me down.

"This is what I do to remember stuff."

"So how do you freeze water then?"

I read the phrase in my head.

"Vaporize water."

I read the next one underneath that.

Three-word phrases weren't so bad compared to the one spell Grandma had me learn. Now that took some time.

"Let's go through the rest of the elements then. After that, I'll give you a demonstration."

Something my grandma said came to mind. "Wait a moment. What about the consequences? Doesn't the fundamental exchange have rules? Energy is never used up. It's merely transformed. If there is a consequence to changing matter, what is it?"

A slow smile formed on Tamara's face. "You're a smart girl. What happens to an object if you slowly grab bits and pieces of it?" She took a step toward the house. "What if you took this hand and removed a sliver of the cells on a finger? Not much. There are massive amounts of power there. But the sad thing is that, as spellcasters pulling from ourselves, we have little say in where we pull from. You could be pulling from your fingertip. You could be pulling from your stomach. The worse spots are your internal organs." She laughed as dread rose through me. "Or even worse you can pull from your heart. How about a bleeder from there? The ones who truly lack self-control pull from up here," she tapped her head. "And then it's all over."

Grandma had been unconscious for *five* days due to one spell to save my life. What the hell was I getting myself into this time?

"You ready for a demonstration then?"

The word *no* came to mind, but I nodded instead.

Tamara mumbled under her breath, the words weren't discernible to me. First, there was nothing but the sounds of the rain and the feel of the drips on my coat. The chill in the air flowed from my forehead down to my toes. She was strangely calm, serene. I never had such a feeling. The only person I'd ever seen with such a calm spirit was Grandma.

Then I saw the drops of rain that fell go back up again almost as if gravity had flipped. The very sight made my jaw drop as I watched even more rain that normally would fall to the ground being sent up towards the sky. The best way to describe it would be as if time went backwards.

"Amazing," I whispered. "How do you do it so easily?"

She opened her eyes and gave me a knowing smile. "Ten years to discover what the werewolves had lost. Another twenty years looking for a master to teach me werewolf magic. Another ten years to find the spellcasters who would teach me." Her voice rose as her determination shone in her brown eyes. "Time was on my side to master what I needed to know. But there are still secrets to be found, and I want to find them all."

Her head jerked to the left. The upside-down rain changed direction, coming back down as it did before. She shoved me in the back toward the house. "Demonstration is over. Back to the house. Now."

"What's going on?"

A strange smell drifted toward us from downwind. To the east, something a few miles away advanced quickly. The rustle in the trees increased. The crack of a branch reached my ears. "What's out there?" I whispered. The need to freeze touched me, but Tamara kept pushing me toward the house.

We rushed up the two steps and past the red door. She slammed it shut behind her, and, shortly afterward, leaned against it to whisper something to the thick wood.

Luda thundered down the stairs in a nightgown with a robe. Tyler wasn't far behind her.

"Is it here again?" Luda asked.

"What is *it*? What's going on?" In a few minutes, I'd be turning into a damn parrot with these people.

Tamara pressed her palms against the door and spread her fingers wide. She continued to mumble, ignoring me as I paced the space in the living room.

She stopped to turn and look at me. "Shut up! Luda, send them back to their rooms. I need to concentrate."

Luda took my arm and tugged me toward the steps. Outside the windows, the sky had darkened instead of lighting up with the sunrise. Rain continued to belt the glass, removing any opportunity to listen for what lurked outside.

"Why can't you tell us?" I hissed at her.

"We're under attack!" Luda said.

"No shit. From what?"

As we approached my room I tried to slow her down, but she was stronger than she looked.

She shrugged and I smelled the truth in her confusion. "I don't know. I've never seen it and Grandma said I wouldn't want to know."

"Well, I do."

"We could help her fight it," Tyler said.

A laugh came from downstairs. "You go ahead and come try," Tamara said.

"Did you see anything?" Tyler asked.

"Not really," I replied. "I just caught a scent. One I've never smelled before. It was really weird."

Luda leaned in to whisper to us. "I've never seen it, but I know it did walk up to the front door once. When it first started attacking us, she said it couldn't cross the field. Then she said the wards in the house walls should hold it back. That the beings trapped inside — "

The front door creaked as if the wood shuddered from something hard leaning against it. Then the wood rattled and shook.

Screw standing around. I raced into my room. My backpack should've been on one of the chairs by my bed, but it had fallen over onto the floor. One of the objects I'd brought with me gleamed on the floor: the goblin blade. It had come in handy during my road trip to save my father, so I took it with me. The goblin blade had transformed again, leaving something long poking out of the zippered opening.

The door downstairs shook again. Zoya screamed while Tyler tried to calm her. All the while, I stared at what the blade had become. Each time it changed like this, I dreaded what had to be nearby. What evil force did the blade try to prepare me to face.

The knife's hilt had elongated to baton length. The sharp blade was now an opaque crystal. My breath caught as the crystal pulsed with a strange dark blue light. The stench of burnt hair made me blink. Before my fingers touched the weapon, the house went silent. For seconds, I hovered, waiting for the next sound.

But nothing came. Nobody moved.

The dark sky brightened as the rain retreated.

When I glanced back at the goblin blade, it was back to its original form.

Chapter 11

It was time for answers. Now, as to who was willing to give them to us was another thing entirely. When Tyler, Luda, Zoya, and I came downstairs, Tamara was gone. Her scent trailed out the door and disappeared a few feet from the house.

"Where did she go?" I asked Zoya.

"I don't know. She does this sometimes. She'll be back, though." Doubt circled her words. She laughed to add levity as she urged us to come inside. "We're safe now. Let's have some breakfast."

I didn't want food. I wanted to know what threat I faced. When the Long Island werewolves came to South Toms River to take over, the pack had an idea of what was coming. They could form a defensive plan and place pack members at the best position. Such a luxury vanished when the threat was unknown.

After an early breakfast, a trip to the bathroom for a shower sounded so wonderful. The trio remained downstairs while I finished up.

On the way from the bathroom to my room, I spotted someone inside. A short figure hovered over my bags: Tamara had returned without coming through the doors. I froze to keep the floorboards from creaking. The need to rush in and shout, "Hey, those are my things," was the first reaction, but I stopped when I saw her tilt my backpack to force the contents to spill onto the floor. The goblin blade was at the top of the pile.

"Now this is unexpected," she said with a grin. "You're far too powerful of a toy for a little wolf to play with." She leaned toward the floor, her hand stretched out to pick it up. I expected the blade to form the weapon used on me, a silver knife, but something else happened entirely.

For each inch she advanced on the knife, it scraped along the floor away from her. When she was finally within reaching distance, it shimmered and vanished. Tamara chuckled. "Fair enough. You've made your choice, but sooner or later she'll have to learn your secrets." She turned to leave but paused. "You're too much for her to handle."

As she turned to leave the room, I sprinted back into the bathroom like a deer escaping an oncoming truck. I hid in the bathroom until my heartbeat and breathing slowed. By the time I poked my head out, Tamara was gone again.

When footsteps echoed across my floor the next morning, I was ready. My eyes snapped open and I turned into a roll off the bed, somehow landing softly on the hardwood floor.

"Damn, I really wanted to raise the bed off the floor like in *The Exorcist*." Tamara tsked, pulled a granola bar from her pocket, and ate it. There wasn't a wrapper on it either.

With my palms, I rubbed my bleary eyes. Such a gesture hopefully helped me avoid the fact she pulled the unwrapped snack from her *pocket*. "You do know that's kinda messed up."

"It's a dark world, honey, and magic is a gumbo with the darkest ingredients of them all."

Memories of my grandma flashed in my mind. "Something tells me magic is only as dark as you let it be." I put on my shoes.

"You enthusiasm is disgustingly sweet." She finished the food, wiped her hands on her skirt and headed outside.

Wow, Aggie had competition in terms of eating habits. At least my best friend cleaned up after herself.

Instead of heading out to the field, our next lesson took place in the kitchen. Day two would begin with a bang.

"Time for fire," Tamara said.

"Are you sure about this?" I asked.

Zoya was in the middle of frying up eggs and Luda had a bunch of stuff out to make what appeared to be cakes and pastries. Luda had a bucket of water while Zoya had enough grease to contribute to a huge ass grease fire.

"The house has only caught fire two or three times." Tamara patted the wall. "She's a pretty tough broad."

"Tough broads burn just as easily," I replied.

"Let's get started. Recite everything you learned yesterday."

Zoya added eggs to a plate and with a wary eye watched me recite all the words to manipulate water. As I finished blurting everything out, she frowned. "You said you didn't know anything."

"I didn't," I said, keeping my voice calm. "I learned this yesterday."

"Some people actually have talent, Zoya," Tamara said. "Finish cooking breakfast. Just because you couldn't remember your own name even if it was taped to your forehead doesn't mean somebody else couldn't figure it out."

Zoya's black eyes seemed to darken. "I can remember just fine."

She opened her mouth as if she had more to say, but turned away to concentrate on her cooking.

"Just as I thought. Don't write a check you can't cash. I have work to do, and I need folks who can keep up."

"You don't have to talk to her that way," I whispered.

"Whose house are you staying in?" She placed her hands on her hips.

"Yours, but that doesn't mean you should belittle her either."

Tamara walked right up to me until our noses almost touched.

"She's been trying to learn old magic from me for the past few months, ever since I moved back here. Every day, she recited each spell, but none of them ever stuck. Not every one has the skill." She tapped her forehead. "Memory is a tricky game, and when it comes to knowing things that can potentially save your life, you either know it or you don't."

My mouth formed a straight line and I stared right back at her.

She laughed a bit. "If you feel the need to play Mother Teresa and get her up to speed, that's up to you."

"If she wants my help, I'll offer it," I said.

Tamara snorted. "Good luck with that. Zoya's more stubborn than the foxes in the field. Enough discussion. I speak. You repeat."

She stood over the double sink and began to go over fire spells. The words to manipulate fire were similar to water except the verbs were different. Not hard to figure out. I listened intently, closing my eyes again as if I had an order to fill.

"Got it?" she asked as she soon as she finished.

"Yes."

"Hop to it, then."

"Huh?" The last thing I expected her to do was ask me to perform.

"I'm not showing you all this for fun. Learning the words is the easy part for you. Executing the spells appears to be your flaw." She gestured to the sink. "Set that old piece of food on fire."

My lips went dry. How long had it taken me to master my first spell? I usually could do it when I really needed it. Not when I didn't want to do it.

I glanced at a piece of crust from toast. How the hell was I supposed to do this? Nick's words came to me at that moment.

"Magic comes from within or another source. If it's from another source, they must be touched by magic as well — like the transformation magic that shape-shifters have..."

That part I understood, but there was more I wanted to grasp.

"Even if you do have that ability, you must understand that to harness it, you have to put in what you expect to get out of it. An equal exchange..."

How simple it sounded. Take your inner strength and use it for another purpose. Whenever I cast my calm spell, I was in the height of anxiety. There was only one purpose: freedom from the pain, from falling into an abyss from which I couldn't escape.

"Magic isn't a simple formula," he'd said. *"It isn't like a chemistry set you can put together and expect results every time you put together the ingredients. It comes from your heart. When you have the right tool, the right words, and you believe without a doubt, magic can happen."*

My hands gripped the counter as my heartbeat escalated. My breath quickened. From the corner of my eye, I spotted Luda watching with curiosity. I was on the spot to perform, the court fool asked to do a song and dance. This was my chance to impress Tamara, and I was falling into a panic attack. It had been weeks since my last bad one. My right hand let go of the wood to reach between my breasts for something. The spot was empty. A seashell necklace had been there a few months ago, a gift from Heidi the mermaid that I'd willingly given back to her. I'd have to do this on my own.

Sweat formed on my brow. The crust stared back at me, mocking me as if to say, *Your sorry ass can't set me on fire.*

Ha, still not burnt.

Closing your eyes isn't gonna help.

Holding your breath isn't gonna help either.

A voice entered my din. "Are you all right, Nat?" It was Luda.

"Just a sec." My voice came out as a wheeze.

Somehow, I had to find that tool Nick spoke of, and I had to believe. Disbelief was my worse enemy. That was the source of the panic attack: fear that everything was out of control and I couldn't control it. I spoke the calm spell, reaching and straining for a place that would give me peace. Grandma told me I could have it if I really wanted it. Warmth spread over my chest and spread to my head and limbs. In the next breath, I spoke the fire manipulation spell.

The crust of bread exploded into soggy pieces and rained down as multiple fiery masses all over the kitchen.

"Holy shit!" Luda grabbed the bowl with pastry dough and flipped out as one gooey mess landed on her shoulder.

Tamara hardly moved, merely blocking an incoming fireball with a flick of her wrist. The hint of amusement on her face made me want to run from the room. Tyler stormed down the steps and rushed in to offer a hand.

With a frown, I used a wet dust rag to pat out the tiny fires.

"I think it's safe to say you have little control over your abilities," Tamara said.

I threw a dirty look in her direction.

"I'd check the towel over there." She pointed to the other side of the room to where Luda tried to clean off the table. She managed to take care of one fire. On the other hand, a quilt on the other side of the table had a nice growing flame. Black smoke filled the room. My victory had turned into a burning mass of madness.

"When does she plan to work on the next element? Can she do wind outside? Away from the house?" Luda laughed and offered me a wink.

I shook my head. Dorothy from the *Wizard of Oz* came to mind. If I blew the house away, could it land on Tamara?

Tyler offered me a hand to stomp out the burning quilt. He tried to help with the other fires while I took care of my mess. When I picked up the poor blanket, I noticed something weird about the wood underneath. Instead of a minor scorch mark, the dark wood had lightened, almost turning into a reddish hue. I stooped down to touch it. When my fingers pressed against the spot, I heard a piercing scream in my ears. But no one else reacted, so only I must have heard it.

"What the hell?" I whispered.

I looked for Tamara to ask what happened, but she was long gone. My gaze flicked to the reddish spot again. Had I imagined what I heard? Why would a house scream out in pain? Something Luda had said

108

during the attack pecked at my memory—something weird about the house—but I couldn't remember. I reached for it again, but Tyler touched my shoulder.

"You okay, Nat?" he asked.

The need to say something tugged at me, but I kept my questions to myself. I must've been standing here for a while. Tyler looked as if he had worked hard to pitch in. His clean shirt was now covered in soot. He even had smudges of black grease on his face.

"I've had better days. I'm so sorry about your clothes."

He shrugged. "I planned to work on the fence today. I'll get started on that and then shower outside. I don't want to mess up the bathroom anyway."

While Tyler headed outside, with Luda not far behind after she finished her cake, I cleaned up the kitchen and tried to forget about the burn mark. I settled into the familiar rhythm of cleaning. Of taking away what was tarnished and making it fresh and new. This was the most relaxing activity to be honest. I didn't know where everything went. But that didn't matter. I organized all the cabinets, wiped the sink until it shined and I scrubbed the floor until it was clean enough to eat on—if you were into that kind of thing.

By the time I wanted to go outside for fresh air and to check on Tyler, the day had passed by. After the rough morning, the cleaning had done my soul good. Yeah, only someone like me with OCD would fall into old habits, but doing what I did back home was like therapy. This place was far too new.

The outside had experienced an upgrade, too. The yards of rickety fence along the street in the distance had been replaced. My friend, though, wasn't still working. But his scent was still here—he'd definitely spent the day working up grime and nastiness. My nose directed me toward the barn. The building didn't have any animals inside, but their presence lingered here. Cows and horses had lived here once before. The chicken coop next to the barn still had the sounds of clucking and such. That was the source of fresh eggs every morning.

As I rounded one side of the structure, I spotted Luda trying to keep her sister Zoya from leaning around a corner.

"What are you two doing?" I asked.

Zoya shushed me and gestured for me to get back.

"We should go back inside," Luda said.

Were we under attack again?

I peeked around them and blurted out the first thing that came to mind: "Ohhh, my."

Right there in bright daylight, Tyler's ass was in full bloom. The tan line from a bikini brief had left part of his buns pasty white, but the view was quite nice by werewolf standards. Water from the outdoors shower dripped down his back. His muscles rippled in his shoulders as he scrubbed his back. I glanced at the twins. The Peeping Tom Twins.

"I'd rub gravy all over that and lick him clean," Zoya whispered.

Eww. What a waste of gravy.

"Zoya, you're so bad," Luda said. "We should give him privacy."

"Forget gravy," Zoya purred. "I'd rub olive oil all over him. Rub him down to get rid of that grime. Get 'em nice and clean."

Uh, no to that, too. I opened my mouth. "Tyl—" A hand slapped down over my mouth.

"Don't you dare ruin the show." Zoya twisted me in the opposite direction and pushed me toward the house. "Go learn a spell or something. Quit messing with grown folks' business."

I contained my laughter and headed back to the house. By the time I rounded the corner and the house came into view, my insides locked. A lone man blocked the path to the red door.

You may not see me, but I'm always around.

Thorn Grantham had found me.

Like he always did.

Chapter 12

Thorn Grantham had the kind of feral beauty most men would envy. When he met others, they came to like and respect him. His facial features, with a strong jawline and piercing hazel eyes, were my favorite.

I still remember the day he walked back into my life half a year ago. It was almost impossible to forget when sunshine cleared out a storm.

But the man who stormed in my direction wasn't the same though. His stride wasn't as strong. He took the footsteps of a man with aches and pains in his joints. With each step he took toward me, reality pressed against my heart. Once blond hair now had speckles of white and grey. Crow's feet touched the edges of his eyes.

That beauty had faded.

He frowned at me. That part of him hadn't changed a damn bit.

"Look, I can explain," I began. "I know you're mad —"

Strong hands grasped my shoulders and pulled me into his arms. He pressed me close, his breath fanning my forehead. "Don't *ever* leave me like that again."

My heart tugged painfully. "I have a plan. I really do."

Thorn merely snorted. "I've heard that before."

A perfect calm spread over me from my head to my feet. How had one man given me the same kind of feeling only a magical spell could do? He had that kind of power over me.

He kissed my forehead first, lingering just long enough to take a deep breath. I did the same. When his lips found mine we settled into a set of motions that never got old. Our heads tilted. His hands found my hips. His heartbeat quickened like mine.

When we finally parted I kinda forgot he tracked me down. For a second there anyway.

"How did you find me?" I asked quietly.

"A little detective work. A visit to see your grandmother. Then a visit to Nick's place. A talk with a rather nice older gentleman who lived there. I followed your trail to a coffee shop where I smelled a dwarf. Then I took another trip to your dwarf friend's apartment. Tyler's landlord told me his tenant would be gone for a few months since he had a photo shoot in *Russia* of all places."

I rolled my eyes.

"From there, I dialed in a favor to a friend, who got me overseas. From there, I found the Lasovskayas and I visited with a most peculiar succubus in St. Petersburg who directed me north to Vyborg. Your trail was faint, but fresh enough to follow you here."

Damn he was *good*.

"So what now?" I mumbled.

"Your parents are worried about you." He tilted my chin up. "They deserve a phone call."

"You know what they'll say."

"That they are disappointed? That you leap

without looking?"

"You sure know how to make a gal feel shitty."

"I'm telling the truth. I know what you're trying to do, but this isn't the way to do it."

I sighed, enjoying the warmth of his arms. "But I have a feeling this is the place. Tamara has to have a reason to solve the problem as much as I do—"

"I don't like this place. We should leave." Thorn glanced over my shoulder toward the barn. I turned to see Luda, Zoya, and a now clothed Tyler.

"Is everything all right, Nat?" Tyler asked.

"Yeah." I pointed to my husband. "Guys, this is Thorn, my mate."

I introduced Thorn to everyone.

"Nat, you've been holding out on us," Zoya said. "He's beautiful."

Thorn gave me a side glance.

"They don't get out much," I said. "Tamara really needs to find them husbands."

After everyone met Thorn, we went inside for tea. I was tempted to ask Tyler if he knew about the peep show he gave the twins, but doing that in front of my mate wasn't the smartest idea. He didn't appear all that pleased and even passed me his cellphone with an expression that said, "Do I make the call or you?"

With a grimace, I dialed home. Dad picked up on the second ring.

"Have you found her yet on that farm?"

"It's me, Dad." I waited for it, even cringing for the blow.

A long sigh. "Natalya, of all the foolish things to do!"

I caught the sounds of footsteps on the line, of others surrounding Dad.

This wasn't gonna be good. At all.

"Where is she?" one person snapped. Maybe Aunt

Olga. "I can hear her breathing on the line," she said.

"How could she do this to her grandmother? Her grandma is worrying and practically near the grave. What an ungrateful girl." That had to be Aunt Vera. Grandma always had some ailment of some kind when one of her relatives didn't do something the family expected. I waited patiently to hear that grandma was blind and deaf and perhaps slowly heading for her deathbed.

Then the crackled overseas phone conversation turned to swearing in both English and Russian. My cousin Inna had nothing on Aunt Vera when she was livid.

"You can't be serious! She is really there?" Aunt Vera spat. "That little troublemaker better not come home anytime soon."

The sharp sounds of someone snatching the phone made me pull the phone away from my ear. That kinda hurt. "Where are you?" Mom's voice was pretty easy to make out. Normally it was honeyed, but now I was getting the full brunt of her anger.

"I'm in Russia," I admitted. "I'm *harasho*."

"*Harasho?*" She stretched out the word as much as possible, her voice rising into a shriek. "The pack alpha had to come after you and move heaven and earth to get there, and you call that *fine?*"

This was going nowhere fast. Explaining myself wouldn't help Thorn. Listening to them berate me would only make it harder for me to save Thorn. And if my father got on the phone again and commanded me to come home, I'd feel compelled to comply. He was my sire and still had a measure of control over my behavior. But I felt more compelled to stay and discover the secret to save Thorn's life.

Time to end this conversation.

"Oh, no, the reception is going bad." I made

hissing noises into the phone. "Sorry, I gotta go. I'll try to call later."

I hung up on them, hoping they wouldn't have a fresh grave waiting for me in South Toms River.

After hanging up on my family, and then ignoring every call and text message that came afterwards, the next three weeks passed quickly with Thorn at my side. He didn't do much, merely watching over me while Tamara trained me. I noticed she had become far more polite with him present.

This particular morning he didn't get up, deciding to lay in bed and rest.

"I'll be fine," he reassured me. "I've never had a vacation like this. I'm gonna enjoy it while I can."

I hope he was just saying that for my benefit and not because he wasn't feeling well.

The farm had been quiet all night into the day. Whatever had attacked us the day after I'd arrived hadn't showed itself again. I took that as a good sign. There'd be less for me to worry about.

"What attacked you?" Thorn asked me that night before bed.

"I don't know. I was in the middle of the field with Tamara when something spooked her. We were just standing there and then I heard something in the woods. It seemed pretty big, like a large animal. We were upwind, but there wasn't any scent I recognized."

Thorn's face appeared thoughtful.

"You need to be careful around here." He made me look him in the eye when I tried to look away. "There's something out there. I've gone out a few times to try to track it, but I never get a good trail. Almost like it leaves for a period of time then doubles back when we stop paying attention."

I nodded. "I'll watch out. Anyway, she told me

we'd work on the earth today. We can do that inside the house."

"Be careful," he advised.

An hour or two later, Tamara had me in the house in the sitting room.

"Do you know why I've chosen this element to be the last one for you to learn?" She stood not far from me.

Not really, but I wanted to sound like I'd been listening, so I tried to say something intelligent. "The others hadn't been too complex. But I suspect when it comes to changing matter itself, like ourselves and the earth, that's a tall order."

She pursed her lips. "You could say that."

She opened her palm to reveal dirt.

"What do you want me to do with that?" I asked. Hopefully, she wanted me to toss it outside where it belonged.

"I want you to feel it."

I had a feeling this was coming. I took the offered soil and pretended it was glitter. Shiny glitter didn't feel this grimy, though.

"I want you to close your eyes and just listen. Not with your ears per se, but with everything. Listening is the hardest part for us, since, as werewolves, we don't know how to listen to what the spellcasters can hear already. You've been touched by magic of some kind. I can sense it on you. So, you'll have to listen carefully."

Did she mean the goblin magic caused by Bill or something else?

She began to recite the words and I followed along like I always did during a lesson.

After some time, my palm warmed and an array of other sensations ran along my fingertips. From wet to warm to scalding. It was amazing.

"What is this?" I finally asked. I told her what I

117

felt.

She scooped the dirt from my palm and placed it back into a flowerpot near the window.

"That is dirt from a very special place far south of here where there are tropical forests and volcanoes. What you're feeling is the residual magic in it. Everything in the earth has some kind of negligent pull, but if you touch the *right* things, there's a lot more." She offered her hand.

"Go on," she must've seen the confused look on my face. "Take my hand."

Her grip was strong when I grabbed her hand, but I quickly caught on to what she meant. An electric hum pulsed from her fingers into mine, growing stronger each second. My breath caught as my knees buckled and I collapsed on the floor. My vision blurred. A fire boiled inside Tamara, so hot, I let go of her.

"What was that?" For some reason, I felt weakened after touching her.

"That was me drawing from you. The sensations you felt was the same thing I felt when I touched you. It was our untapped potential."

I blinked, trying to take it all in. But why had she hurt me? "But why did you take away my power?"

"As a lesson." Tamara crossed her arms. "A valuable one. You can take from yourself as a source, but others can steal what you have, too." She approached me as I crouched on the floor.

"I don't like that."

"Are you willing to take from others to save your husband? Playing with the magic from others requires a little finesse, though. I don't think you're ready to do that."

"I'm not willing to do it, either," I finished for her. I had enough of a bad taste in my mouth after what Nick did to me.

"Your husband barely made it outside today," she said softly. "Do you want the tools necessary to survive long enough to figure out how to remove curses? You'll need strength to do that, Natalya. More strength than your weak body can imagine."

She said the word "weak" like a swear word. My fists clenched and I wanted to smack the smug look off her face.

She extended her hand. "Take back what I stole from you." She poked me, and I couldn't suppress the growl stirring in my chest. "Do it!" she snapped.

I snatched her hand and waited for the pull. The tug didn't take too long. I spoke the words again to manipulate matter.

And I took more from that bitch than she took from me.

As strength returned to my limbs a bitter taste raked the back of my mouth and dizziness smacked me hard. But I didn't let go of her.

"You learn fast," Tamara said with a chuckle. "A stubborn bitch, though."

"Takes a bitch to know one," I remarked, not bothering to hold in my rising anger.

As the day wore on, the lingering effects from the spell made it hard to touch anything or anyone. In particular, the house itself. The whole place and its inhabitants were weird. I still couldn't forget that scream from the other day or how the house shuddered when that creature attacked us. Luda had said something important. Something about beings trapped inside the house. As to what she meant, I didn't know. Questioning Tamara came to mind, but if I pried too much, would she force me to leave?

Tamara had too many secrets, but I had no choice but to stay unless another opportunity came up. Also, even though I had grown to dislike her, I had to admit one thing: I knew more now than I did when I first came here. I just wished I knew how to manipulate the darkness inside of Thorn. I wished I knew how to pull out what ate away at him and protect him.

But even Tamara didn't know how to do that.

With a slight sense of accomplishment, I settled into bed that night and wrapped my arms around Thorn.

Chapter 13

Instead of daylight tugging me awake, it was a hand over my mouth that yanked me out of slumber. Thorn leaned in close to me and whispered, "Don't move."

He kept his hand over my mouth. In the darkness, I watched his eyes shift toward the window. I froze, slowing my breathing as much as I could.

What the hell had spooked Thorn?

Then the moonlight filling the room vanished as something covered the window. After a few seconds, it reached the roof and the moon's glow bathed the room again.

Something big as hell had come for us.

Thorn uncovered my mouth.

"I wish that had been a squirrel," I whispered.

More creaking echoed along the rooftop. A form passed over the window, that of a man. With a deep inhale, I caught a whiff of cinnamon.

Spellcasters. And maybe their monster minions. And they were all over the freaking house. They'd made it past whatever barriers Tamara had erected.

My breath hitched painfully and heartbeat sped up, but Thorn pressed his hand on my stomach for reassurance.

"Not now," he said softly.

I closed my eyes to hold back my anxiety. I wasn't weakened anymore.

A creak outside our door drew our attention. Had they come inside already? Thorn shifted to rise without sound, but failed. He wasn't as stealthy as he used to be.

The door opened without a sound, and I was prepared to pounce on the goblin blade, but the face we saw was unexpected. It was Tamara.

"We're surrounded," she whispered. Her words were simple, matter-of-fact. "You need to leave the house. I can draw them away, but you won't have long to run."

"Who is here?" Thorn asked. He pushed me to put on my clothes.

"The warlocks don't trust their minions anymore to do their dirty work. They've come here personally to take me out." She sighed, her eyes appearing tired for a moment. "I'm rather disappointed they sent weak ones."

My mouth dropped. *Holy shit.* Actual warlocks had come here to attack us. I reached for the goblin blade. The weapon had already transformed into a metallic, golden box that could fit in the palm of my hand. Was this the same box I used when I was in Atlantic City fighting Roscoe's warlock? I didn't know how it had worked last time, but the goblin blade had disarmed a warlock. A rather handy trick.

"What about the twins and Tyler?" I asked.

"I've already spoken to them. Tyler will follow them to the south. You're going north."

A thud against a wall to the east of us shook the

house.

"They're persistent." She coughed and brought up a handkerchief to her mouth. When she pulled it away, there was blood on the cloth.

"What's wrong with you?" I asked.

"Does she always ask questions at times like this?" Tamara rushed to hand me my backpack.

"There isn't enough time to tell you how often." Thorn finished dressing. "How much time do we have during your diversion?"

"Not long, unfortunately. Two inexperienced spellcasters is a lot for even me to handle. Once they breach the spells protecting this house, all bets are off. It will be just me and them."

I reached out and touched her hand. "Are we meeting up somewhere?"

Thorn tugged my hand to leave the room with Tamara behind.

"Just worry about now, girl. We got bigger problems than figuring out what will happen tomorrow." She shoved us toward the stairs. "Go to the cellar. Down there will be a door. Hold your breath as you go through and you'll find a path to safety on the other side. Lock the door behind you, though, and don't look back."

Thorn nodded. "Safe journey."

"To you as well. If you travel along the closest main road north toward *Bol'shoye Tsvetochnoye* lake, you'll enter Finland and find the *Yhdeksän Männyt* Pack in a small town called Nuijamaa near the border. Their alpha is an old friend of mine, and he'll protect you."

The trip down the stairs was hard going with Thorn's weakness, but we made it. Offering to carry him wasn't even a question. I'd never belittle him like that.

By the time we reached the staircase for the cellar,

we noticed the dwarf had taken this path, too. This must have been how he escaped with the twins. Upstairs, the house shuddered as if the roof would come down any minute. The lights flickered and the air was saturated with the sticky sweet scent of cinnamon.

At the far end of the dank cellar was a door I'd never seen before. Where I'd once seen rows of preserved food in jars was now a dark wooden door made from large planks. The knob was made from tarnished brass with deep scratch marks in the metal. I helped Thorn across the room and soon we reached the door.

"Are you ready?" I whispered to him.

And that's when the upstairs exploded.

The explosion drove us to the ground. Thorn didn't move when I tried to revive him, so I hoisted him onto my shoulders. I held my breath and opened the door. No turning back now. My ears popped and something stung my eyes like onions. There was no smell or sound, just a dark path ahead. Heat fanned my back from the fire above. I entered the doorway and closed the door. I remembered to lock the door behind me and I carried Thorn down the dark path, all the while holding my breath.

With each step I took, my body begged me to breathe. To help get through the tunnel, I reminded myself that at any moment we could be attacked. I couldn't hear my footsteps, but something told me I walked a dirt path. Eventually, I emerged through a hole in the ground to the outside. Fresh air fanned my face, so I took a deep cleansing breath. How wonderful the air was. The golden box in my pocket hummed. When I retrieved it after putting Thorn down, I noticed it had transformed back into its original form. We were safe from our threat. For now.

Miles away, I saw an orange glow and a line of

smoke extending into the air. That had to be Tamara's home. With a sigh, I said a prayer for her and wished her well. She made a sacrifice for us I wouldn't forget. After all the dark things I learned about her, this one moment of light was one I wouldn't forget. She could've gone through those doors and left us behind. Yet she hadn't. Her final words echoed in my head as I picked up Thorn and headed north.

I still have cards to play, Natalya. You haven't seen the last of me yet.

Thorn had carried my knocked-out butt a few times. I had yet to return the debt and there was a good reason. The guy was heavy as hell.

A few human guys I've met could stand to get a good meal or two on their bones, and the white wizard I'd carried home once in the past required nothing more than a fireman's lift. So I'm guessing I needed a challenge to keep me frosty and fresh, like a werewolf with solid muscle mass. While lugging him up a hill, I groaned, "Good Lord, did you eat Little Red Riding Hood on the way to Russia?"

The night stretched out as I carried my charge. The goblin blade, my usual alarm to trouble, remained inert at my side in a knife scabbard.

The countryside was so beautiful this late at night. I had no choice but to enjoy it. Maybe it was because I had Thorn with me. I leaned my head against his side. He didn't stir, still sleeping. He always had a way to make me feel like I could face the world. The very idea that I might have to live for centuries without him tightened my throat and faltered my step.

Even five years was a damn long time to be without the love of your life. It almost seemed like a lifetime since Thorn had left me behind five years ago to go to San Diego. It was a long story I tried not to dwell on, but he'd tried to keep his father from killing me, so he left. In the end, he nearly died at the hands of a warlock who trapped him for five years. In order to escape, Thorn had cursed the warlock, an act that blackened Thorn's soul and left him dying.

Both of us had been through so much. Would all our efforts be in vain?

A few hours later, the sun rose to my right. Its warmth was welcomed. From Tamara's house, I ventured to the nearest country road and continued north. Earlier, I used my phone to figure out our position and determine how far we had to go to Finland. If we had to do it all on foot, the distance was insane. I needed to find us a ride sooner or later. I couldn't carry Thorn that far while we were both so vulnerable.

Suddenly Thorn chuckled. "You can put me down now." His hand tapped my back.

"Good morning." I tried to sound cheerful.

Thorn staggered a bit, but he was steady on his feet once he found a set of bushes to relieve himself.

While I gave him his privacy, I checked the phone to determine our location.

The phone pretty much read "middle of nowhere" in Northern Russia.

Not a single car had come down the rough country road. We had at least twenty miles until we reached the Finnish border.

"How are you feeling?" I asked him.

"Pretty rough. What the hell happened back there?" He rubbed his hair, which now stuck up in the cutest manner.

"I don't know to be honest. While we were on the way to the door, the house exploded."

Thorn frowned. "It was going to happen sooner or later. She was playing with shit she didn't care about."

"What do you mean?" Did Thorn know something I didn't?

"I left out a lot of things while we were there." He tugged me to stand so we could keep walking. I offered him water from a bottle and he drank it.

"Like what?"

"Tamara had wards all over that property. I could sense them the minute I stepped past the fence."

"*Sense* them?"

He grinned at me. "I'm not the same man I used to be, sweetheart. Old magic has changed me in ways I still don't understand." Thorn revealed he knew old magic when the Long Island Pack leader had cornered me to kill me. That warlock who had imprisoned him taught him a thing or two.

"What else have you held back from me?" I asked.

"Tamara has weaved everything there in dark magic. Hardly anything on that property is defensive light magic, the house in particular. Didn't you say something attacked the place the day after you arrived?"

I nodded.

"Whatever was trying to get in had to be crazy powerful 'cause the house was built like a tank."

As he shook his head, everything weird about that house flashed before my eyes: the scream I heard on the burned floor, the walls that reacted as if alive when the attack occurred, and Luda mentioning the trapped beings.

"It wasn't a house, Nat. It was made from the...bodies of other creatures. Every time I walked in or left, I could feel them crying out in pain."

I slowed down. "What are you saying?"

"She took shape-shifters, like us, and used their bodies to create the house to protect her and the twins."

"No way!" So that was what Luda meant.

"Why didn't you tell me?" I snapped.

"Tamara had her fingers in everything. The whole property was her dark magic playground. From the grounds to barn to the house walls. Every single conversation was heard. Every sound," he said.

"So why did we stay?"

He shrugged. "Maybe I had hope," he admitted. "Foolish hope, anyway."

I took his hand. We were both fools, hoping for the best even under these circumstances.

A ride finally came by after an hour. A woman and her family appeared all too kind and offered us a ride to the nearest town where they lived. The ride was pleasant, even with the suitcases and such in the back.

"You feeling all right?" Thorn asked. "I'm sorry I couldn't tell you sooner. I wasn't in any shape to face Tamara."

The back of the truck wasn't the cleanest, but I was too shocked and numb to notice. All that time I'd stood in that kitchen. I lit a fire and burned the walls with my lack of control. I'd caused those…shifters pain. I hadn't even known they were trapped. Just the thought of it made my stomach churn.

When we reached the nearest town, we stopped and got a bite to eat. A local werewolf offered us a hand and took us to his alpha. From there, we were given a ride to the border.

"You two are smart to leave this area," the older man who gave us a ride said in broken English.

"Why?" Thorn asked.

"The war between the warlocks and wizards is starting to spread out. We thought they'd keep to themselves and stay out in the north where there aren't as many people, but their conflict is carrying over into the human world." The man sighed. "Those wizards have the nerve to ask us for reinforcements. Like I want to bring my pack into their mess."

"Are you serious?" I asked.

The man huffed. "We have no reason to trust any of them. It's crazy shit, if you ask me. I wouldn't help them if they offered to help me on my death bed."

The ride was quiet after that. On the way to the border, we stopped at a gas station. Our driver pulled over to pump the gas while I got out to stretch my legs. Thorn was fast asleep in the passenger seat. The temperature was a bit cooler here, but it was pleasant nonetheless. I walked a distance to the side of the road. What I spotted made me stop.

Across the road from me were sets of white tents. Like a campground of sorts. But none of the humans who pumped their gas or pulled out of the station glanced in the direction where I looked. I rubbed my eyes in case I was seeing things.

Nope. The camp was still there. A man emerged from one of the tents. When he noticed that I was looking directly at him, I quickly glanced away.

Oh, shit, shit!

Act normal.

Along the edges of my peripheral vision, bits of the campground appeared muddy, as if I were looking through a dirty window. I wasn't meant to see him or the camp. All of this was probably thanks to Bill's goblin magic that helped me see past most glamours.

I turned around and hauled my butt back to the truck. Our werewolf driver was still pumping gas and whistling along with the radio. I settled into the backseat so my twitchiness wouldn't wake up Thorn. I placed my hands in my lap and tried to act natural. Maybe staring at fingernails would work.

The Russian werewolf did a little folk music dance at the pump oblivious to my behavior.

Also, he didn't see the man who stood in front of my window.

Oh, fudge.

The guy had no smell and didn't make a sound. There wasn't the telltale odor of cinnamon or any other indicator he was there. Was he a wizard? It was impossible for me to tell. Even worse, had I stumbled upon a warlock encampment? They could be walking around all over the place.

If so, we were dead werewolf chow. I rested my hand against the goblin blade hilt as my heartbeat rose to blinding levels. I even closed my eyes for good measure.

Go away. Go away.

Don't force me to fight you.

Did I even have it in me to use the old magic Tamara taught me? When I heard a car door open and the Russian driver got inside, the man who had approached my door was long gone.

I finally exhaled.

"You okay?" Thorn asked. He'd awakened and promptly joined me in the backseat.

"Fine." I tried to sound like everything was okay and probably failed. "I've been awake too long. A little fried."

If he only knew.

"Get some sleep." He tilted my head to his shoulder. "I'll stay awake."

Sure, sleep with spellcasters roaming around. I turned my head to glance at where the encampment lay.

"You see something?" Thorn asked. So he didn't see it, which meant there were things my eyes could see that his couldn't. I had to remember that for the future to keep us safe.

"Nothing you need to worry about," I replied.

The ride toward the border left me wary. Would we be followed?

Not far from Finland, our driver dropped us off. We'd have to cross through the forest. "Good luck, you two," he said with a wave.

We thanked him and set out.

As we hiked through the dense forest toward Finland, I wondered how this would work out. Would we encounter a fence or some other structure? Was the border guarded? As we made our way deeper into the woods, we came to a small clearing. There were men waiting for us there.

My stomach dropped when I spotted the man I saw from the encampment. They looked like a bunch of humans going out on a camping trip with their jackets and such.

I grabbed Thorn's arm. He had tensed up, too.

"We can't go this way," I hissed.

He pushed me behind him and took a step back. "Do you know them?"

"Not really. I saw that man at the gas station."

"And you thought to keep that to yourself?" he grumbled.

He picked a shitty time for a squabble. "I didn't know who he was. He showed up, disappeared, reappeared. I wasn't gonna roll down the window and say, 'Hey, whassup?'"

Thorn turned in the opposite direction and ran into a full sprint. This was the man I remembered. As to how long he'd be able to keep it up was uncertain. We ran as far as we could until Thorn slowed down first. His grip on my hand loosened, but I refused to let go of him.

One minute we were running through the forest, the next we had five men blink into existence in our path. There was no way we could outrun them if they could teleport like that.

"This land isn't safe for you, wolf." The man from the gas station stepped forward. He was the shortest among them with dark eyes and hair. He had that twinkle in one of his eyes that I noticed on Nick once in a while.

At my side, Thorn's body vibrated with hints of the change.

"Let us pass," he growled.

"We're not those war-hungry bastards," the man said.

So they were wizards, a rather scruffy looking band of them.

"Then why are you following us?" I asked.

"Where did you get marked by a darkling?" His words sank in slowly.

A darkling?

"I don't understand what you mean?" I took a step around Thorn.

"He has to be referring to those things that went after Tamara," Thorn said.

Out of curiosity, I glanced at myself. Nothing appeared out of sorts.

"Which one of us is marked?" I asked.

The wizard in the front with the longest hair spoke. "The female was marked first, but hints linger on the male. Only one of you has been near it."

Realization hit and I tried to process all of it. "First of all, what is a darkling and once you find out where we got marked, how will you use that information?"

"A good question," a voice behind us said.

We turned to see a white-bearded, older gentleman strolling toward us—Dr. Frank. Now that was a face I hadn't expected to see. At all.

"Dr. Frank, w-what are you doing here?" I stammered.

It was rather strange to see my therapist out in the middle of the woods like this. His gray eyes shined with amusement. "A scout from this party told me they were questioning a woman fitting your description. I was…surprised to confirm it was you."

"There have been some developments since my last appointment," I admitted.

"For both of us," he said.

He nodded and an understanding passed between us. He knew based on past therapy sessions that I was here for Thorn, and I suspected he was on the frontlines to assist in the war.

"Now as to your original question before I interrupted your conversation. We've been hunting a warlock named Cato Fillian who has unleashed his minions to the countryside. His superiors apparently want him to keep others from learning how to remove the curses. And that includes werewolves who use old magic. I have a feeling you're included in that group, yes?"

I nodded.

"These creatures are difficult to track," he said. "We lost a trail in Finland and only happen to come back across the border and find you here. I wonder how deeply you're involved in all of this."

Thorn grabbed my hand. When my mouth opened, his grip tightened. His apparent signal to keep my mouth shut.

"What happens to us once we tell you what you want to know?" Thorn asked.

"I've taken care of Natalya for a long time, Thorn," Dr. Frank said to reassure him. "I've known her far longer than even you have."

With Dr. Frank here, I couldn't resist confessing everything. "I have been working with another werewolf to learn old magic to find a cure for Thorn.

We just happened to become a target when these darkling things attacked us, too."

"They are probably just as clueless as we are as to where the darklings are located," the short wizard said.

"I agree, Wilhelm. We're chasing troublesome shadows, and the threat from the warlocks is growing worse day by day as they take our weapons away."

The stricken look on their faces filled me with dread. How badly had things gotten over the past three weeks?

"So no one has come up with a way to remove curses?" I asked. "I mean, c'mon, you guys can do amazing things. Why not something so simple?"

"Nothing is simple in the world of magic," Dr. Frank said with a sad smile. "But yes, we do have something. We're holding out hope that our brothers on Stolobny Island can escape and teach us what they've learned."

I approached Dr. Frank, hope renewed. Wilhelm materialized next to us. "Please tell me you're not joking. The wizards know a spell to remove a death curse."

Dr. Frank nodded. "But there's no way to reach them, Natalya. The warlocks have surrounded them and any wizard who approaches the island is left weaponless. Those who get too close are slaughtered."

My mouth opened to speak, but I didn't know what to say. What could I do to help them? I searched my mind for anything, but couldn't think straight.

"Don't worry, sweetheart." Thorn touched my face. He must have sensed my unease. "You can only do so much."

"No," I said firmly. "I can do anything." I faced Dr. Frank. "What if I found someone — something that could punch a hole in the defenses? If I helped them, would you help me?"

Dr. Frank's face reflected pity, and I hated it. "I can't help you, Natalya, but there's a chance the elders would grant you an audience if you can bring help from the local werewolves to the frontlines."

There was no way the werewolves would come. I wasn't dominant enough to gather rival packs together. Thorn wasn't in any shape to do that either. Just knowing my goal was insurmountable made me want to throw up, but I breathed through the moment and spoke the first thing that came to mind.

"I will find a way," I promised Dr. Frank. "I don't know how, but the one thing I have on my side is stubborn determination."

"You're a good person, Natalya. You should stay away from Cato and his darklings. You can't miss him. He's a tall man with red hair and eyes. It would be even better if you returned home as soon as possible." Dr. Frank turned to Wilhelm. "Offer them assistance to go wherever they wish." He patted me on the shoulder and vanished before I could say goodbye.

Wilhelm looked us over before he spoke again. "You two are quite the pair."

"We've been through a lot. It's hard to explain," I said.

Wilhelm chuckled. "I'll say. One of you is like a black hole getting sucked away into nothingness, while the other one glows bright enough to blind me. I'd like to ask why, but I have a feeling you're not going to tell me." The man glanced at me.

Thorn grunted. "No, she's not going to say a damn thing."

I had a past record of running my mouth. Thorn had learned his lesson long ago.

One of the other wizards stepped forward. "I can heal either of you," he offered.

What ailed Thorn was beyond any of them, but I'd

let him try. Before Thorn could refuse, I said, "Could you give him a bit of strength? He's weak from a long journey."

My husband's pride rose to the top of the trees around here, but he couldn't refuse me when I gave him *the face*. If you're married, or have someone you love, you know exactly what I'm talking about. It's the I-care-about-you-and-will-make-you-feel-guilty-to-no-end-if-I-don't-get-my-way face.

The wizard who wanted to help materialized in front of Thorn. He touched his shoulder, and then pulled back. "What happened to you?"

"It's a long story," Thorn whispered.

"I suspect." He grasped Thorn's arm. "I can't reverse the effects, but I can give you the strength to reach your final destination tonight."

While one of Wilhelm's cohorts healed Thorn, another wizard stepped up to me to offer the same. It felt weird getting healed by someone other than Nick or Dr. Frank. The feeling was just as good though — hands down, I wouldn't be surprised if there were junkies who enjoyed getting healed by wizards.

By the time the man let me go, I felt ready to take on the world. "You didn't need much," the man said. "You're quite strong."

"I wish I was," I replied

He gave me an expression I didn't understand, but I smiled politely.

"Where are you headed?" he asked.

"To a village across the border called Nuijamaa. The *Yhdeksän Männyt* Pack will hopefully give us sanctuary."

Wilhelm spoke to the others. "I'll make this quick. Report back to base."

The others vanished as Wilhelm took Thorn's hand and mine. "This will be a rough ride, since I normally don't do this spell with passengers."

Before I could even agree to the free ride, we were whisked away in a blur of white dancing lights.

And plopped back into another place in mid-air. We landed hard on a riverbank and missed falling into the water by a few feet.

I was the lucky one to land on my head. Based on past experiences, this was a spot I couldn't seem to avoid in terms of trouble.

I groaned. "I thought wizards couldn't teleport long distances."

"The town isn't that far away. About two miles from where my friends met you." He rubbed his side as if he'd fallen hard on it. With a scowl, he dusted off his pants. "I'm not sure where you'll find the alpha."

"We'll manage just fine from here," Thorn said.

My mate probably already had a scent. The whole place reeked of werewolves. As to which one was the alpha, would take me a bit of time.

The man lingered for a moment. "I'm sorry there's nothing we can do to help you." A range of emotions crossed his face. One of them was regret. "We'll do our best to save the trapped wizards to the south, and we hope you'll do the same."

Chapter 14

After nearly a month at Tamara's farm near Vyborg, my path to finding help for Thorn seemed muddied and unclear. Thorn and I walked into Nuijamaa, glancing furtively around us. Not a single sign made sense since we were in Finland.

"Do you know Finnish?" I asked quietly.

Thorn took my hand and rubbed the palm. "We'll be fine. I can already smell the pack that lives here."

That was obvious, but as to how we'd find them was another story.

"This place is so beautiful," Thorn said.

On that, I had to agree. This far up north, there was more forest than man-made structures. With a single inhale, I caught evergreen and spruce trees. It smelled almost like New Jersey when you went deep into Double Trouble State Park near South Toms River. I used to run there with the pack before I was kicked out that summer, an event that Rex loved to bring up all the time.

"I've heard that many Scandinavians know English. We should be fine once we reach a business."

I nodded, checking my phone. The cell was long dead. All the time I'd spent checking the GPS had drained the battery.

"Are you hungry?" I asked him when I heard his stomach growl.

"I'll be fine. How are you holding up?" He gave me a reassuring smile.

"Other than the fact I had a helluva night?"

"We're alive. That's a blessing."

And we were together, I thought to myself.

Nuijamaa couldn't even be called a small town. Our hometown was a metropolis compared to this place.

On the paved road we followed, we came to a set of red ranch-style buildings right off the street. My nose told me there had to be a restaurant nearby, maybe a home or two.

"Could this qualify as a honeymoon?" Thorn asked out of the blue.

I couldn't contain my laughter. "This is the most jacked up honeymoon ever. You owe me the Virgin Islands after I save your hairy butt."

"The Virgin Islands? I'll have to remember that."

We didn't go anywhere after we were mated. It was for the best. I needed to recover from the fight of my life, and Thorn had too many pack responsibilities to handle. The pack needed money and the only way to make that was to work toward getting pack members with income. And South Toms River wasn't exactly a billionaire mecca.

Speaking of money.

"Do you have any money?" I asked him as we walked up to place with a sign I couldn't read.

"I have some, but it's rather useless, since it's not the local currency."

I reached for the doorknob, but someone

approached us from around the corner. He walked with caution, looking over Thorn and me with curiosity.

When he was close enough, he waved and spoke English. Based on the man's scent, he wasn't the alpha, but he was dominant enough to qualify as someone with ranking. He introduced himself as Jorge and we told him our names.

Once we had a brief chat, he told us to follow him. After walking for hours, I welcomed some rest in Jorge's home. Also his mate knew a bit of English and kindly offered us clean clothes, food, and a place to sleep. Since she was expecting her first child, she let me pick whatever clothes I wanted. As much as the thought of wearing someone else's clothes bothered me, I wanted to burn what I had on—other than my jacket, which was still in pretty good shape. Anyway, our host's clothes smelled clean, and that was good enough for me.

My new attitude was a welcomed change compared to a year ago when I would've collapsed on the floor, twitching with stress. My reflection in the bathroom mirror appeared haggard, but I was a survivor. By the time I joined Thorn in bed that night, he was fast asleep. He'd washed his face and that was it. My poor guy was tuckered out.

I, on the other hand, was far from it. Too many troubles danced around my head: the warlocks, Tamara's secrets, and the trapped wizards who knew how to save Thorn but couldn't escape from their prison without help from an outside force.

It was as if circumstances were pulling me toward a burning bridge over a chasm with rocky rapids at the bottom. On the other side of the turbulent waters was my husband's salvation. All I had to do was gather enough nerve to cross.

Instead of lying with Thorn, I glanced out the tiny window to the forest outside. My fingertips twitched as my anxiety threatened to rise. A sink was close and with it came an old compulsion, the need to wash my hands. But I ignored it as purpose echoed through in my head: *I could go again. I could take another chance to see what I could do.* I heard my husband wheeze from the next room. He'd never made that sound before and just thinking about how much he weakened every day tore into me. The pain resurfaced again and tears threatened to fall, but I pushed them away.

But the truth was laid bare. My mate was dying and this trip to come after me had taken more of his life away.

Something inside told me I was so close to a solution. So close to helping him, I could taste it if I tried. I just needed that first step. I could rally my relatives and any friends they had. I could return to St. Petersburg and go door-to-door if necessary. I nodded as if such a gesture could make the decisions come easier.

Thorn stirred and coughed, but drifted back to sleep.

I took a step toward the window and opened it, letting the fresh air drift over my face. With the cool air came the promise of possibilities if I remained strong. Staying here and watching him die until it was time to go home wasn't an option.

My dad said it most eloquently when I saved him from his moon debt, "You too can be honorable for your family."

Thorn was my family I reminded myself as fear coursed through me. I would be all alone for this mission.

But, then again, I should be used to that. After five years of going to work everyday, this should be easy peasy.

Swallowing past the lump in my throat said otherwise.

When I finally lay in bed next to him, I expected him to sleep, but he pulled me into his arms like he always did. When he brushed his lips against mine, the man I loved touched me. As much as I wanted to make love, it wasn't right to do that in a stranger's home, so we held each other, touching the places that always pleased the other. Every hard line of his body belonged to me, a familiar territory for me to explore again and again. He knew the perfect way to hold my face while he kissed me, cupping my cheeks ever so gently while his lips brushed against mine. Even if our bodies never became one, we still felt as if we were that way.

Afterward, he tucked me in the crook of his arm with a smile. I couldn't resist returning the expression.

"I wish you'd smile more," he whispered.

"I try. When the moment warrants it."

He rubbed a cold spot on my arm. The chill in the air didn't bother me, but I appreciated the gesture. "You have so many good things in your life, Nat. I wish you could see things the way I do. Your life has turned around. You have your parents. You have your brother, too."

Hearing him say the word 'parents' made me sigh. Thorn lost his mom when we were kids.

"Do you miss her?" I searched his eyes when he looked away. We've never talked about his mom at length. Or the fact she died after a massive snowstorm swept over the northeast a long time ago. He usually clammed up when the topic came up. Maybe one of the reasons was that at the time he was too young to search for her — to use his tracking skills to find her like he found me.

"I think about her all the time," he replied. "Every

day."

"I've seen the picture you carry in your wallet of you and her. She's beautiful." Saying she was beautiful was an understatement. The photo had frayed edges and a water stain or two, but her eyes radiated life. She had a toddler on her lap and the sunset behind them cast a purplish-red glow on their shoulders.

Beside me Thorn only nodded, his jaw twitching. His stomach muscles clenched and I sensed the unease growing in him.

"We don't have to talk about her. I'm sorry," I whispered. I shouldn't have brought up his mom until he was ready.

"No. It's all right." He sighed. "It's just that the emptiness never goes away. I push it down so deep, but every couple of years when I believe I've gotten over her death I find out I'm not *even* close."

We sat in silence for a bit, my thoughts circling around the ceiling fan. All this time my mate had been suffering when I believed hardly anything got under his skin.

I snuggled closer to him, wrapping my leg around his. Why couldn't I take his suffering away like he did mine? For once I wished I knew how to use my *babushka's* calming spell on him. What I did have to offer in reality was just as good: The love of my family. "You have more than one mom now. A grandma, too. My mom isn't perfect," I chuckled. "She's loud and stubborn like her daughter, but she's willing to move heaven and earth to protect her own."

I sensed the grin on his face. "I appreciate the offer. They are rather loud, but I don't mind. Thank you, sweetheart."

Our sad moment ended with a long kiss that set my soul at ease.

Somehow, Thorn fell asleep not long after our

conversation.

I, on the other hand, didn't sleep the whole night. After such a long trip, I should've been exhausted, but I refused to lose the moment. I wanted every second and every sense locked in my memory: his smell, the warmth of his skin, the feel of the rise and fall of his chest against my arm.

My beloved would live forever in me if I *failed*.

At dawn, I got dressed. When I packed what I needed, I gently nudged his shoulder.

He smiled at me with sleepy eyes. "Why you up so early?"

Then he noticed my backpack and tears in my eyes. His mouth formed a hard line. "What are you doing?"

"What must be done. You're going to stay here until I get back—"

"Nat, damn it—"

I kissed his right hand. His left locked around my thigh. "I'm going to find a way to get those wizards out, Thorn."

"I told you not to do foolish things without me."

"Too late for that."

His grip on my leg tightened. "Don't go."

"You have to admit this is an improvement. I am saying goodbye this time. You have to give me credit for that."

"I don't want to say goodbye." Sadness touched his hard features.

I couldn't stop the tears from falling. What if I were making a mistake? What if I left, and he died here all alone?

Doubts tried to eat away at me, but I shoved them aside.

Screw doubt. Doubt could take a long jump off a short pier. I kissed his forehead and stood.

Damn this was so hard.

"You're the love of my life, Thorn Grantham." I'd said that once before with all my heart, and I meant it now just as much.

"You're perfect in all the right places," he said as his voice broke.

"I'll be back soon," I promised.

Every step out of that house killed me. A thousand reasons hit me stronger than any panic attack I'd ever had before. The walls of fear tried to close in on me, but I kept walking. The air outside tried to choke me with heat, but I kept walking. The backpack on my back turned into a ton of bricks, but I kept facing forward, not stopping once.

The wind was on my back, the first good thing to happen to me today.

Chapter 15

Touching old magic beyond a spell to calm my nerves was one thing, but really using werewolf magic to do the things wizards and warlocks were capable of was another.

Today seemed like a good day to try out my powers, no? I'd set fire to a kitchen, but that was a while ago when I didn't have Thorn weighing heavy on my mind like I did now.

There was no choice but to get it right the first time.

Next test: find the nearest jump point to take me to St. Petersburg. Months ago, I'd made my first jump with Nick from Jersey to Brooklyn. It had been quite the experience, pretty much comparable to getting teleported with Wilhelm. One minute, I was in a field with Nick, and in the next, I was in a basement in Brooklyn.

Even after several months, the jump from that large rock in the middle of that field was still vivid in my mind. We tapped or, I should say, Nick tapped into the strange sensations coming from the stone. Tamara had prepared me for this, and I didn't even know it until now. I chanted and pressed my hand to the ground and waited for the feeling Tamara told me would be there.

I got nothing.

Yep, that's dirt and it's as disgusting as I imagined.

Other than that initial feeling, I drop-kicked what I usually worried about into a steel trap and tried to focus on the task at hand.

Listen this time, Tamara would tell me. *Say the words and* believe *them 'cause you don't have a choice in the matter.*

I waited and waited. *It will come,* I reminded myself. I didn't dare move.

And that was the key.

Something tugged at my fingertips from the east. I wasn't sure about the mileage or whether I'd have to break into a building to get to the jump point, but I'd sure as hell do anything necessary.

The march east was long, taking me back into Russia. Walking all alone, with no cellphone for direction, felt strange, but I kept going, one foot in front of the other. By the time the sun began to set, the vibrations turned into a rough yank along my arm.

I was close. The forest at twilight cast too many unfamiliar shadows. The noises here weren't familiar.

Caw caw.

The chorus from a flock of crows joined the crickets.

A branch snapped behind me, but I didn't turn around. My hand touched the goblin blade on my hip for reassurance. A hum resonated from the blade's hilt and vibrated in my palm. With the wind blowing into my face, I didn't have the advantage of being downwind. I kept walking. Was my mate foolish enough to follow me or had I stirred up another kind of trouble?

My steps quickened as the rumble of broken brush kept following me. I reached for the nearest pine tree, its pungent scent growing stronger as I pressed my body against it.

The warning signal from my blade bounced off my side like a painful slap. The sensation was jarring to say the least. The sounds of water falling along rocks sounded louder. My stride turned into a full-out run. The wolf in me urged me to run faster. Footsteps came from the far right now, too.

I leapt over a rock formation and landed with a roll on the other side. The forest opened into a clearing, exposing a cloudless sky and a peppering of bright stars. Instead of taking in the beautiful sight, I made a run for it toward what called to me, a single pine tree in the middle of the field. The need to look behind me was strong, but I ignored it. Only a damn fool would check behind them to see what was about to tackle them and potentially eat them for lunch.

By the time I sprinted to the middle of the field, my pursuers had to be no more than ten feet or so behind me. My thoughts bounced around my head, but one in particular rang true: whatever you plan to do, you better make it fast.

As I approached the tree, it bounced up and down in my vision as I ran. I extended my hand reaching and hoping that by the time I collided with it, I would figure out whatever mystery Nick had known and I would teleport.

The vibrations increased with each step. I was almost there. The pine filled my nostrils. In one inhale, I hit the tree hard. But instead of bouncing backward, which the laws of physics dictate should happen to geniuses who run into trees, I continued forward, every limb twitching as something pulsed through me.

My tongue rattled around my mouth as something built quickly in my belly and spread outwards.

I was flung from one place to another and landed with a hard thud on the ground. Twilight became day and the sand on my hands — and in my mouth — told me I'd gone a lot farther than I intended.

The open sky as far as my sharp eyes could see was a vivid blue with flecks of white clouds. No more than ten feet or so from me, waves rolled onto a white-sand beach. Somehow, I jumped from a dense forest to a single palm tree sitting near the shore. In the distance, I spotted tropical vegetation waving with the breeze.

It was all so refreshingly beautiful.

I even laughed a bit. Hadn't I told Thorn I wanted to visit the beach? Maybe even the Virgin Islands? Not like this, though.

The wind whipped my hair about as I managed to stand. Sand clung to my clothes, but I reminded myself I was alive. I had teleported. I'd done something I'd only seen spellcasters do.

I turned and glanced at the tree where I'd come from. Not a single thing grew near the beautiful palm. Only the seashells kept the tree company. My watch said it was nine p.m. on the dot, yet it had to be at least midday. Quite a jump forward in time.

The sounds of movement pricked my senses along the tropical tree line. I darted to what little cover I had and pressed my back against the rough, still vibrating surface of the tree.

One voice whispered, then another responded.

"Is someone there?" one man asked. They spoke Russian, but the words were older in origin — like Old English. Once in a while, Grandma slid into speaking Old Church Slavic, her mother tongue and a precursor

149

to the modern Russian language. I knew enough bits and pieces to understand what they said.

"I can smell the female." The second voice came from farther down the beach.

My mouth opened and snapped shut. What could I even say? I peeked around the tree and didn't see anyone, but I could hear them. Branches rustled from one spot and then another.

The wind shifted and I sensed someone behind me. So they played the diversion game, eh? I palmed the goblin blade, which had been silent on my hip. Why hadn't it changed to a new form? By now, its Spiderman-like warning system had become rather handy.

I looked up to face my attacker — only to discover I should've looked down. An amber-haired, burly man, who, by far, wasn't as tall as my massive father, pointed a spear in my direction and stared me down.

His brown-eyed gaze flicked to my weapon. "That maiden's blade wouldn't even open one of these hairy fruits on the beach," he said in Old Russian.

The wind brought his scent to me and fed information without words: he was a werewolf, he was about my age, and his health was good.

His clothes screamed that he was either a historical period reenactor or I'd taken a very wrong turn during my jump. Something about the way his long-sleeved, white shirt reached his knees and the fitting of his red trousers made me pause.

"Good day to you," was all I managed.

He glanced at the tree, and then took in my jacket, jeans, and backpack. "What kind of old magic is this?"

"I-I was in one place and now I'm here," I stammered.

Three other werewolves cautiously approached us from down the beach.

"That's what happened to us, but how as a werewolf did you do it? My friends and I have been trapped here for over five thousand moons."

Holy shit. I did the rough mental math: around 400 years. Dread shot into my gut. Was I trapped here, too?

"Blazh, it wasn't an accident," the tallest one claimed. He marched right up to us and his violet eyes formed slits at the man he called Blazh. "You were trying to send us to Kyjev before we were ready."

Kyjev was an older name for Kiev, the capital of the Ukraine. That definitely dated them.

Blazh made a rude snort. "You and your brother always drag your feet—"

"Don't bring Radomir into this again," the tall man snapped. He pushed a man with similar features back. That must've been his brother Radomir.

"Oh, shut your mouth, Dragomir! We were this close to finding a new master, but you always hold us back!" Blazh said.

"Hold us back?" Dragomir growled and closed in on Blazh. "We've been *held* back for endless moons on this forsaken sand-covered oven thanks to you!"

They continued to argue, and I glanced to the fourth man, who gave a half-shrug as if to apologize. His narrow black eyes danced with amusement. While they went on, he bowed to me.

"Greetings, lady. I'm Chestibor. These are my arguing companions." He gave their names and pointed to them as Dragomir shoved Blazh to the ground. Fists flew as the two men swore. Radomir could do little to keep them apart.

Chestibor just stood there.

"Are you going to do anything?" I asked him.

"I used to. Now I let them release their anger that way." He led me away a bit. "Are you an old magic master? We've seen countless wizards and warlocks arrive, but they left soon after." He appeared so hopeful. Was I the first werewolf to come?

"A master? Not at all. I'm a *beginner*." I walked over to the tree and touched it. The vibrations I felt before weren't as strong. "Why can't you just leave like everyone else?"

"We've tried countless times. It's past the point in the day when the sun is in the middle of the sky. We even made a sundial, but it's not that accurate. We only see others show up at that time."

"Noon," I murmured. "So it only works then?"

He nodded.

The warm sun made me uncomfortable, so I shrugged off my jacket and pulled my hair into a ponytail.

"You're an acolyte like us." Disappointment pushed Chestibor's shoulders down, but he perked up when he spotted sweat gathering on my brow.

"Do you have discomfort?" he asked. "We have a meager shelter in the woods."

Should I go off alone with this guy? Technically, he was still a stranger, but as I watched the other acolytes continue to fight like a bunch of rambunctious high school boys, I suspected I didn't have many options.

Either way, I had a *maiden's* knife, and I was willing to gut any guys who got a little too friendly.

So we left the beach and ventured into the jungle.

What Chestibor had referred to as a "meager" hut was an expansive island hideaway with two stories, a covered patio, and even a creek as a fresh water source. I held back a laugh. They didn't have windows, per se, but with all the time on their hands, they'd built something grand.

"This is…amazing," I blurted as we walked into what appeared to be a common room with a central fire pit. It was like visiting the set of one of those castaways-on-a-deserted-island movies like the *Swiss Family Robinson*.

Everything set the scene, except for a far wall, filled with written words. They'd burned the words for spells into bark slabs and attached the pieces to the wall. Many phrases I recognized as the basics for manipulating the elements, but there were many longer spells I hadn't seen or heard before.

And they called themselves acolytes...

"It isn't much. I hope you like it." The look that flashed across his face reflected a little interest. It had probably been a while since he'd seen the opposite sex.

Time to make things crystal clear. "Whoa, there! I've got a mate, buddy."

"Who is buddy? My name is Chestibor."

"It's what you can call someone other than their given name." I sighed. "Don't worry if I'm not making any sense. What I'm trying to say is that I have a mate back where I came from."

"That's too bad." He nodded with understanding.

Chestibor offered me cool water, a coconut (the hairy fruit—ha), and some tasty fish jerky. They hit the spot after a long night—or should I say afternoon?

The other guys joined us a bit later, one with a black eye and the other with a ghastly split lip. As werewolves, they'd heal soon enough, though. They settled into a routine, doing chores around me, only glancing my way once in a while.

What else could I do until tomorrow at noon when the tree "activated?"

A question came to mind as I finished my food. "Why haven't you guys built a ship?"

Radomir stopped what he was doing first. He was in the middle of braiding his long, brown hair. They all looked at each other, and it was Chestibor who spoke first. "We're not too good at shipbuilding."

"The last three attempts never made it past the reef," Dragomir said quietly.

"Two shark attacks," his brother Radomir added.

Dragomir shook his right leg as if something dreadful had happened to it. "You mean three."

Radomir shuddered. "I'm trying to forget that attempt."

"Awww." Poor guys.

"Old magic can only do so much," Blazh remarked. "We've cast countless spells, but none of them have helped us escape this prison."

I tried not to let their words sink in, but the feeling was there. Would I regret leaving Thorn behind for the years to come on this deserted island?

The day stretched on into the late afternoon. Dragomir and his brother left with fishing poles while Chestibor had disappeared elsewhere. After Blazh finished gathering firewood, he settled next to the fire pit and mumbled to himself.

At first, I thought he was crazy and talking to his imaginary friends, but I caught a few words in the ancient tongue.

After some time, curiosity got the best of me, so I found a spot to sit nearby and asked, "What spell are you reciting?"

"A special one." He grinned. "For the longest of time we searched the land for a master, but we couldn't find one. Luck found us when a traveling merchant told us of a legendary band of old magic spellcasters. During Batu-Khan's invasion they had been called to Kyjev to offer reinforcements for the wizards stationed there."

"Fascinating." I'd never heard of these people before.

"They never made it, though, and Batu-Khan destroyed Kyjev. Legend says there was deception of some kind in their ranks, and, somehow, they were imprisoned."

"Where?"

"To the northwest of Kyjev. I don't know if the site is still there, since so much time has passed, but my friends and I wanted to set them free. We thought maybe they would be grateful and teach us what we've wanted to learn for so long."

A sliver of hope pulsed through me at that moment, but I tried to ignore it. Blazh's tale could be what he called it: a legend and nothing more. But what if they really existed? What if there were werewolf spellcasters who had the strength and bravery to face an army as formidable as Batu-Khan's?

Blazh continued. "In preparation to set them free, I've been reciting a spell to manipulate the earth to pull them from their prison."

"Amazing. Can you teach it to me?"

He nodded and began again, tapping his knees with each syllable.

"Ndinae kodo maeda maeda..."

The spell went on and on, and I had the impression there was no end to it, yet when that first word came up again, I recognized it since he always said it with flourish.

After some time I couldn't resist smiling. "You've had a lot of time to practice."

"We've practiced simple spells, but we banded together in the hope that we'd find a proper master."

"I've had the same problem," I admitted. I told him about my husband's curse and how my grandma and Tamara were the only old folks who knew anything.

He was surprised at how much the attitude toward old magic had changed due to the Code.

"So only women are interested in old magic now?"

Blazh sputtered, his short torso stretched considerably. He still didn't reach my chin, but his spirit towered over me.

"Pretty much. My mate learned a thing or two, but he's the only one I know."

We continued to chat and Blazh even tried to teach me a few more spells as the sun set. It was refreshing for once to have a kind teacher like Grandma.

Dragomir and Radomir soon returned with our dinner: fresh fish. The hot coals in the fire pit crackled as Dragomir placed the fish on heated rocks. The enticing aroma floated over to me and I sighed.

At noon tomorrow, I better get us out of here or I'd have many more dinners by the fireside.

Chapter 16

I was thrilled to leave. The acolytes not so much.
How many times had they approached the tree filled
with hope, only to walk away in defeat?

How the hell was I supposed to get us all out of
this? What did I know that they didn't?

Nick had told me there were all kinds of jump
points. To travel from place to place, magical folks like
fairies and other mystical beings, had punched a hole
in the fabric of magic and these places had been what
was left over.

While the guys took their time to get here, I sat
under the tree's shade. A few coconuts had fallen
overnight, but I stepped around them. Blazh was the
first to show up, but doubt touched his features. He
probably expected me to become the island's newest
resident. The others followed, not carrying much with
them except a weapon and a meager sack over their
shoulders.

I almost reached out and touched the rough bark,
but I stopped and laughed. Hadn't I gotten myself into
trouble when I didn't think things through last time? I

hadn't had a choice, but this time was different. If I remembered right, when Nick and I used a jump point that connected Jersey to New York, he hadn't just touched the rock. He'd taken a moment to really pause before he did the deed. Maybe he thought about his destination. Perhaps it was that simple—along with the timing factor.

Now all I needed to do was think about the nearest jump point to St. Petersburg so I could accomplish my next mission: contact the local packs and rally them to help me. I hesitated, thinking about what Blazh told me.

What about the legend? Could I take them there to fulfill what they wanted to do, and, in turn, the old magic spellcasters could help me? My fists clenched in frustration. I didn't want to make this choice right now. Thorn's life hung in the balance if I got this wrong.

"Damn it," I muttered.

"Natalya?" Blazh said.

"Everything is fine," I whispered. "If this tree does its job, we'll reach Kiev in no time."

So I had made my decision.

But what if there wasn't a jump point near Kiev?

Damn it! Don't think that way!

I'd have to take that chance.

"It's almost time, Natalya," Chestibor said. The sundial must read noon. I checked my wristwatch. The hour was wrong, but the timing to the minute was accurate. We didn't have long to wait.

"Everyone take each other's hands," I instructed. "Blazh, grab the bag on my back and hold on tight."

Once everyone had a good grip to form a chain, I placed my hand on the smooth sand near the base of the tree. The pull was there, growing stronger every second. The timing had to be damn near perfect. I looked at the watch again, staring intently. A gal like me made sure any timepiece I used was accurate to the second. Atomic clocks could be set with the damn thing.

As my hand hovered over the bark, waiting for the watch's minute hand to hit twelve, I thought of Kiev. Every landmark I remembered from books and my studies in Russian literature. The Pechersk Lavra, with its golden-tipped buildings built so many centuries ago. Then St. Sophia's Cathedral and Independence Square flashed through my mind. I just needed a place close enough for me to do what needed to be done.

When the minute hand struck twelve, I fell toward the tree and grabbed it. The full power from the jump point shot through me, rolling over me like hard ocean waves. There was no escape, no way to fight the overwhelming feeling of drowning—then all that disappeared as the day turned into night and the ocean breeze became another kind of wind altogether.

I'd placed us right on the edge of a tall downtown building.

Chestibor cursed, turning sharply to grab the thick, gray bricks on the wall. The brothers followed suit.

"Have we reached hell?" Dragomir whispered.

Not hell, but close to it—rush hour in downtown Kiev.

Wind from between the grand buildings whistled to us. I tried to scoot right far too quickly, and plummeted down.

I expected to see the ground racing toward me, but I fell onto a balcony instead.

Thud!

Blazh called my name from above. The stone structure held my weight just fine, but the concrete wasn't forgiving and my cheek slammed into it with a hard thunk.

Ouchie. Why did everything have to hit my face?

Balance was one of my fortes, but not like this. I rolled onto my back and cracked open one eye to see the guys climbing down after me.

"That didn't look good at all," Chestibor tried to whisper to Dragomir.

"I heard that," I muttered. Blazh helped me stand. As much as I was in pain, I couldn't help feeling exuberance. In the distance, I spied Independence Square and tried to grin. My face exploded in pain. Reaching up gingerly, I touched the skin. My cheekbone was broken and the puffiness meant I'd done other kinds of damage. An audible crunch along my jaw told me my body had begun the process of healing. *Lovely.*

But the good news first. I pumped my fist. I did it. I'd set them free!

Now the next question remained. How the hell would I get them down? I glanced through the balcony's glass doors into the dark room beyond. Breaking in was an option, but getting them through the building would be a problem with security. A sigh escaped me. I'd have to either break in or get down the old-fashioned way.

As I took in the busy street below I wondered if I dared to jump and see how well I manipulated the wind. Or maybe how fast I'd meet the ground to break more than my face.

After climbing off the balcony, our ragtag group descended slowly down the wall, taking it easy to remain in the shadows as much as possible. With my luck though, we were seen. The guys had medieval garb on and Dragomir had a pretty big sword sheathed at his hip.

When I reached the second floor, a small crowd had gathered, their phones out to record our progress to the ground. *Well done, keeping things undercover, Nat.*

"Are you doing a stunt for TV?" one man asked in Ukrainian. "Are we on TV right now?"

"Oh, yeah," I replied in what little Ukrainian I knew.

Folks glanced around and we beat a hasty exit before the cops showed up. As we ran down the street, the sounds of sirens increased behind us. Damn they were fast around here.

The food smells hit me next. Not that what the acolytes had served me had been bad or anything, but grilled fish wasn't the same as creamy fettuccine or even Dunkin' Donuts. *Yep, downtown Kiev has one.* All the stores I passed smelled so good. Even the street vendors I passed made the wolf in me pant with excitement.

Culture shock flashed across the guys' faces at every corner. From the women to the cars and bright street lights. The crowds here in the city center were thick and I tried to get us out of there as fast as I could.

According to Blazh, we had to head northwest toward the town of Kozelets off the Oster River. So northwest we went. The trip out of the city took forever, especially with a pit stop to a goblin's coffee shop to charge my phone for a spell. I had plenty of messages, but not much time to check them. The goblin was about as stingy as Bill, charging me by the minute.

"I don't know why you werewolves think you can push people around," the goblin said under the glamour of a balding young man. "I own the power here. If you want to chit-chat away on your little talking box you can pay me the money I deserve."

The acolytes remained quiet, taking the coffee I offered without sour comments to the irate shopkeeper. Maybe this new world was too much for them.

I didn't know the bus system, so we took the

subway to Kiev's outskirts. From there, we walked northwest.

According to the map on my phone, the place Blazh described had to be at least eighteen hours away by foot. That was way too much of a jaunt for anyone on a quest.

We kept going anyway. Another option would present itself sooner or later. As we walked, I couldn't help but think about my friends. *Oh, Tyler.* What had happened to him and the twins? I called him, but he didn't answer his phone. Had they escaped the house okay? I could only hope the twins took good care of him.

The city turned into the countryside. The guys cheered up a bit when the distractions from the city melted away.

It was amazing how within the last couple of weeks I'd gone from Russia to Finland and now the Ukraine. As much as I wished I could've had a real vacation here, I'd settle for this much.

With a group so large and so strange, we had trouble finding transportation to take us out of the city. I was the only one who had any money to speak of — in the wrong currency — but we found a truck driver who took the American dollars and was eager to earn his pay.

"It's not often I get a pretty girl in my truck. Are you married?" he asked.

"Very much so, but I'm flattered." I tried to be friendly, really I did.

He shrugged. "You can't blame a man for trying."

By twilight, we reached Kozelets. The historic town that was the final resting place of the band of werewolves who never made it to Kiev. Along the way to the town center, we passed beautiful white cathedrals with green rooftops. The place had a small-town feel to it.

"Any ideas where we'll find the site?" I asked Blazh.

"The merchant told me the original location was at least a mile to the east of the town center. The only important descriptors were that the house had a stone path with pine and spruce trees. A well was not far from the house, too."

"That could be anything…" I said.

Chestibor gave me stern eye. "Back in my time, we'd have no problem with this. Right now, not so much."

He had a point there.

Blazh found a patch of grass in front of a shop and rested his hand on the green blades. He mumbled a bit under his breath.

"Can any of you sense them?" I asked him.

"There's something to the east, but I'm not sure if it's them." Blazh sighed and ran his hand over his head.

We had no choice but to search.

So we went east, following the pull Blazh detected in the ground. After a long walk, we reached what was left of a house on an embankment. All that remained were the stones, covered in grass high as my knees and a nearly hidden well.

"There's power hiding here," Blazh said firmly. "We have found it, my friends."

Everyone nodded with smiles all around.

My smile ended when I looked beyond the stones to where the green grass died. The yellowed patch of earth was circular and extended wide enough for a group of people to stand within it.

Not a single living thing grew here.

We really had found it.

A dying place for trapped souls.

Chapter 17

No one followed me as I approached the dead patch. I didn't go all the way though, just lingering along the edge. A wise wolf didn't jump into danger. A stench, similar to rotting flesh, reached my nose and my face scrunched up.

"Death lives here," I whispered.

Radomir joined me and nodded. His older brother paced not far from us, his grip tight on the sword on his hip.

"So what do we do now, then?" Chestibor asked.

"Someone used dark magic to seal them inside," Blazh said softly.

"Any ideas as to what trapped them?" Dragomir asked. "Now that we're finally here after all this time, I thought the answer would be clear, but it's not. I wondered what would keep such powerful men and women in this spot."

"Something terrible indeed," Blazh said. "This type of magic was before our time. As to what trapped them I hope it isn't around here."

I glanced at Blazh. "So what do we do now?"

"We prepare." He appeared thoughtful. "For the next one hundred days."

Dragomir and Radomir gathered wood while Chestibor prepared a fire faster than most folks lit gas fireplaces.

"Whoa there!" I grabbed Blazh's arm. "I don't have one hundred days for us to *prepare* to set them free. Thorn might be…My time might run out before then. Is there a reason why we have to wait?"

Blazh rolled his eyes as if he wanted to humor me. "I've waited countless moons for this day. Everything must be perfect. We must feast to gather strength! We must rest! We must cleanse ourselves."

"I feel clean. Didn't we sleep last night?"

"That is not what I meant, Natalya." He left me behind to go through his bag.

I couldn't help but feel disappointment. Maybe after some rest I could think of a way to convince them.

Soon enough the other acolytes had set up camp. The two brothers had left to hunt up the evening meal.

I didn't have the heart to tell them their options were limited and we were better off finding a butcher shop.

I plopped down on the cold grass, not caring to look where I sat. All I felt was regret. I could've been in St. Petersburg right now. I might've had a longshot chance to convince the local packs to help the wizards, but I could've tried.

Time passed, long enough for me to doze off. A hard tap to my shoulder woke me up.

It was Blazh and his eyes were wild and harried. "We need to move!"

He pushed me toward the dead field.

"What's going on?" I blurted, trying to find my bearings.

"Something is following us." Blazh found a spot

near the edge of the field and sat.

Not again. *Had the warlocks found me again? If so, how the hell did Cato pull this one off?*

Blazh continued. "While the brothers were out hunting, they spotted something strange along the river. Dragomir led it away while Radomir returned to warn us. He said we won't have much time before the diversion falls through."

"Why don't we run away and come back later?" I took a spot next to him and the reality of the situation was like getting dunked in cold water.

"I'm not letting this opportunity go. Not after waiting for so long." The eager look in his eyes vanished, only to be replaced with hesitation. He'd been put on the spot to perform.

"Might as well get this done and over with, right?" He gave me a shaky smile. "It shouldn't take long to bring them out of the fold and reform them here. We'll be done before Dragomir comes back." He offered his hand and I reluctantly took it.

"The earth magic is like a piece of parchment here," he whispered to me. "Like someone has folded it multiple times into a shape that covered those who are imprisoned here."

My face scrunched up. "Like origami."

"I've never heard of such a thing."

"It's an art form where you take thinly flattened paper-like materials and fold them into shapes like birds or animals. It's quite beautiful."

"You'll have to show me sometime." He took a deep breath. "Are you ready to begin?"

"As ready as I can be," I murmured.

The night sky was clear as we began chanting. I stumbled over the words — it was far too a long a spell for me to memorize in such a short time. But he should be able to say it backwards at this point.

When he paused for breath, I remarked, "You're not much of an acolyte anymore."

His grin was brief and his brown eyes shined. "A student should learn humility before he becomes a master."

I nodded in agreement.

He began to chant again, encouraging me to follow. As I listened, I recognized many terms from what Tamara taught me. The best way to describe it would be like a chef putting together a recipe. Earth tugging against water, fire pulling at the wind.

As we continued to speak, in my peripheral vision I spotted Chestibor pacing and Radomir with his gaze fixed on the horizon.

Blazh tapped my leg and pointed toward the tainted land.

Focus, his eyes said. *Not much time.*

I closed my eyes and continued to chant. As time went on, something happened. A buzz formed in my toes and another strange sensation fluttered against my face. Almost like a hand holding my head in place.

In the back of my mind, Blazh continued to work. The stench of ozone grew stronger and made my nose run and eyes water.

The first sign of true werewolf magic.

Blazh's voice deepened when Radomir shouted something behind us. I wanted to tear away, to straighten and listen, but whatever I drew out of the field forced me to look straight ahead. Visions of light danced before my eyes. I spotted what looked like twelve men and women not far from us. Their eyes were trained on Blazh and me, their gaze blank and unwavering. I wanted to look away, to focus on where Radomir and Chestibor had gone. I couldn't smell them anymore.

"What's going on?" I finally whispered.

"Radomir..." My voice sounded far away to my ears.

A hand touched my leg, the grip firm. *"We're under attack, Natalya,"* Blazh said to me. Yet I didn't hear him with my ears. The message came from elsewhere.

"How are you speaking to me right now?" I asked in my head.

"The spell has bound us together until one of us breaks it apart. If either of us breaks it, we will never save these people."

Our bodies were vulnerable. Anything could be happening right now. *"But what about the others? What's going on?"*

"We can't look behind us anymore. Only ahead."

My heartbeat was loud to my ears in this place. I looked at the people in the field and watched as the discoloration over them passed from reds to greens. What once had been a scene frozen in front of me moved like a movie going from slow motion to full play. One man looked to me and pointed, his eyes growing wide in fear.

Shouts behind me increased. What the hell was going on beyond Blazh and me?

The fold around the spellcasters was shifting. Whatever boundary existed in front of us collapsed. Like fish caught on a line, they floated in our direction.

Blazh chanted faster and I stumbled over the words. The faces of the people in the field contorted into an angry sneer, and I tried to keep my focus.

One man in particular was taller than the rest. I couldn't make out his eye color, but he had the most piercing eyes. He stared at me, or maybe he stared right through me. Then the bubble containing them shrank down to a point of light.

At that moment, I had no idea what was going on. Did Blazh plan any of this?

A hand touched my shoulder in the haze, but I

ignored it. Someone was reaching out to me, someone other than Blazh. Their breath fanned my fears. They were shouting at me, but I couldn't hear them. What were they saying? Was it something important?

Were the acolytes in mortal danger?

"Nat?" The voice was faint. Somehow, I stopped chanting.

"Natalya, you have to wake up." Blazh's voice entered the din as my eyes slowly opened to see the real world.

Smoke now filled the countryside. My whole body ached. When I tried to turn my head, it throbbed.

"What's going on?" I mumbled.

Blazh touched my shoulder again, his movements sluggish. "We can't stay here anymore. We're under attack."

"From what?" I blurted.

"Dragomir couldn't lead them away anymore. Radomir said he saw some warlocks coming so he left to help his brother." Lights danced along the horizon. The breeze to the west brought the stench of burnt flesh, ozone, and thick smoke. I could barely see Dragomir and Radomir fighting in the distance. They were holding back whatever was coming for us.

"We need to help them," I managed to say.

"Neither of us is in any condition to assist." Blazh's eyes were still toward the field, toward the floating point of light.

"Blazh?" I whispered.

"I had them." His smile widened then faltered. "I did, but—"

"But what?"

"There's no time left to finish what must be done."

I tried to stand, but my legs had turned to jelly. Weakness clung to my limbs. I hadn't felt this way in a long time. The memory came to me and I sucked in a breath. I hadn't felt this way since Nick had drained me of power to save our lives from the pack in Maine when they'd attacked us.

Pain blossomed anew when I moved my head.

My voice was firm when I spoke though. "How much time do you need?"

"Too much. They're getting closer."

The cloud of fire and dust advanced. I couldn't make out our friends in the haze.

"But we can't give up! Are we close?" I asked.

"I don't know," he groaned, obviously in pain.

I couldn't just sit here and let them die. I ignored my discomfort and managed to stand.

"You will abandon the old magic spellcasters and leave us!" he thundered. His words had a sharp finality.

We had to be close. We'd freed them from the field. With a final push, we could take them from the light into physicality.

"I'm not letting them go," I snapped. "You've worked for years on this spell. We can do this." I had to believe Chesibor, Dragomir and his brother were fighting to offer us a chance at success.

"I'm going to give you the boost you need to send them back, Nat," he said. "If I save one person, all my efforts will mean something."

"Don't you dare!"

"I'm going to do this for everyone. You can't escape otherwise."

"Don't give me that chivalrous bullshit, Blazh."

The man scoffed and didn't listen to me.

When Blazh let go of the trapped werewolves and bent his chin down to his chest, I sensed the strain on me. The ton of bricks he dumped on my doorstep. But I held it, however tenuous. I had to hold it. I had to preserve. I had their lives and Thorn's life in my hands.

But what the hell could I do with this burden other than send it back to its original place in the field? I was too weak to set them free.

So what other option was there?

The burden grew heavier on my soul and the pain in my head grew monstrous. Blood seeped from my nose. I choked on my breath as fear pulsed through me. As the fear increased, I decided to make a rash choice. Looking out at the field a spark of an idea came to me. Could I be the same as the field? Like the soil that held them all this time? Could I take these people within me and protect them until I was strong enough to free them? Hadn't Nick told me I had more power than I could imagine?

Suddenly the burden lifted and my pain lessened enough for me to yell at Blazh.

"Don't make me come for you," I warned Blazh.

But there was no answer. I twisted my head to see he'd vanished. In one moment, he was there, and the next, he was gone.

What the hell had he done to himself?

But that didn't matter anymore. What had once existed in a field floated into me.

And like a fool, I swallowed them whole.

Chapter 18

The Ukrainian countryside continued to burn with unnatural lights behind me as I ran, or, I should say, stumbled from the field where the band of old magic werewolves had been trapped toward the unknown to the east.

The goblin's blade elongated into a sword and glowed at my hip, ready for me to face my enemies, but I was in far too shitty shape to do a damn thing.

So I ran with what strength I'd been given, Blazh's final gift. My chest burned as the pace grew long. I was never the best runner, even when Thorn tried to train me to reenter the pack. Most of his efforts had been most likely early morning attempts to see me.

What I wouldn't give for a car or even a horse. Shit, a spell to take me anywhere other than where I was right now was preferred.

Turn back, a part of me begged. *Face your enemies with honor. Help your friends like they helped you.* Like a heavy block of lead in my stomach, the vessel containing the old magic spellcasters slowed my progress, but I didn't stop.

My legs pumped faster and I urged the wolf within to work harder. I darted around clusters of trees. Leapt over fences. Burst through cleared farmland. Faster and faster.

A sign read Pylyatyn for the next small town, then Kozary. After that, everything was a blur until I collapsed in a thicket, my chest heavy and body soaked with sour sweat.

Every part of me was filthy, practically beyond anything I'd endured.

Instead of feeding my anxiety, I closed my eyes and curled on my side. I told myself I'd care tomorrow. Just tonight, I'd sleep and rock myself and try to ignore the words I whispered again and again.

"I'll be clean soon. I'll be clean soon. I'll be clean soon."

Somehow, someway, I had to reach Stolobny Island. A place over twelve hours away by car.

An elderly couple picked me up on the side of the road. They were on their way back to Russia to see their fifth grandchild who had recently been born. They couldn't take me all the way to my destination, but a town on the border was just as good.

"A girl like you shouldn't be walking alone," the older woman chastised as she pushed me into the front seat between the couple.

The need to speak was there, but I only nodded. When I peeked at my hands, they shook uncontrollably. To not frighten the couple, I kept them clenched in my lap.

After sleeping in the thicket overnight, my body had changed in unimaginable ways. Tamara's warning rang through my head, but I shoved it away. *The exchange requires a piece of you. In ways you can't control.*

What was the catastrophic price I was paying this

time? I didn't sleep for several days like Grandma. So what was changing inside my body and could I slow the process so I could make it? Another shudder passed through me.

The older woman clucked like a concerned mother hen. She pushed a soft piece of bread into my mouth, and then pressed a warm hand on my forehead. "We need to get blankets on this girl. She's freezing."

Werewolves usually had a high temperature. After what I'd experienced, I expected to carry a higher one due to the energy I expended to carry these people inside me.

I had yet to think about how I was keeping them there or how I'd get them out other than doing Blazh's chant again, but one step at a time.

The couple pulled over, the woman helped me into the backseat, and she laid a few blankets over me. They smelled like her vanilla perfume. I snuggled under the covers as a trail of blood ran from my nose. I quickly wiped it away. The couple kept driving, unaware of my rising panic.

We reached *Troyebortnoye,* a small town along the border in Russia, around mid-day. The rest had done me some good, but not much. All around me, the land was flat, like rolling plains. Trees peppered the landscape here and there, but there wasn't much.

"You need to be careful, Irina," her husband whispered. Even at the lowest whisper, he was loud and clear to me. "She might have a bad infection. You might pass it to the baby if you're not careful."

"I've been a nurse for twenty years," she clucked. "She has nothing more than a basic cold. I've been exposed to much worse." She laughed off his concern. "Maybe I should be more afraid of you after bringing home that disease from that woman."

The man scoffed. "Are you gonna bring that up

again? I've apologized for the past ten years."

"I itched for days after you lay with that bitch."

I hid my laugh. Maybe this guy was a distant human relative. In a way, he reminded me of my man-whore uncle Boris.

"Thank you for the ride," I told them. "I'm feeling much better." With a trembling hand, I managed to open the backseat door and angle myself out. The werewolves trapped inside me churned in my belly and pressed against my bladder. It was time to find a bush before I had an accident.

"We're already at my daughter, Alyona's home," she said with an annoyed tsk tsk sound. "God helps those who take care of their own. Freshen up and eat before you go." She got out of the car and was on me faster than I could move. I hid my smile. Even my aunt Vera didn't have the quick reflexes this human possessed.

"Get the bags out," the woman commanded to her husband. He nodded, apparently whipped into submission after he did the deed ten years ago. "Have Alyona prepare the bed above her garage for our guest."

I didn't protest as the woman's husband helped me into the house. From there, a kind human around my age took me under her wing. Her children huddled and followed her around, but like eager pups, they fed me and tucked me into a warm bed with crisp sheets. Pure heaven.

As the half moon rose and the night creatures prowled, the wolf inside me tugged me awake with a violent shake.

My head flicked to the double window above the one-room garage apartment. I held my breath. Shadows crossed the windows and the goblin blade twitched on my hip.

Time's up.

I sprang into action, grabbing my belongings and stuffing them into the backpack. My cellphone glowed bright. Nice and fully charged.

A single message flashed on the screen: *Nat, where r u?*

I had plenty of other ones, but the one from Tyler was at the top. As quickly as my fingers could move, I typed: *under attack. heading west from troyebortnoye. thorn safe in finland.*

Nothing moved outside my window. I crept out as fast as I could. Without a sound, I leapt off the second story and landed softly on the grass outside. Still good. On the other side of the house, I caught the faint sounds of heavy footsteps where the cars were parked. It wasn't bipedal like me. Death had found my little sanctuary.

I hightailed it west outta there.

My sprint took me a few miles into the middle of a small woods, my only cover. There was nothing else out here but flat plains, fields, and small towns.

And whatever circled the house had to have followed my trail. Was it the creature that attacked Tamara's house? Or something worse?

I hungered for a forest. A place where there was nothing but miles and miles of thick vegetation. In the trees, I could try to blend in and hide. Out here, I was exposed and vulnerable.

The need for sleep tugged at me as sleet soaked through my jacket and chilled my skin. With trembling hands, I chanted and pressed my palm to the wet grass. The earth was still. Nothing pulled at me.

I was so screwed.

There was no place for me to go. No jump point.

A little help wouldn't hurt so I recited the calming

spell Grandma Lasovskaya taught me. Warmth and calm immediately drenched me from my head down to my feet.

The blade stirred to life so I grabbed it.

The hilt elongated in my hands going from metal to a smooth wood finish. The blade hollowed and twisted upward to a beautiful, spindly spiral point.

My heart beat like a trapped animal. I glanced around, but nothing came at me. *Yet.*

C'mon, c'mon, finish transforming already.

The tip of the blade turned bright and crystallized. I gripped the middle tightly as the blue crystal at the end whistled. The rain drops that hit the metal strips circling around the crystal evaporated.

I had a freaking hot and cold fireplace poker in my hands.

Shit. Shit. Shit.

What was coming for me to need this kind of thing? It better have a trigger somewhere.

The short staff in my hands began to vibrate faster, but I held firm. The wolf within me urgently tugged at me to transform and run away. To chuck it all and flee.

But could I even transform into a werewolf while holding the spellcasters inside me? I'd gone all the way from Finland to the Ukraine yet my pursuers had found me. There was no more running. There was no more escaping. This was the point where I'd either die or make a final stand.

Slowly, I backed into a tree trunk. I listened and waited. At first, there was nothing but a strange silence as the tree branches stretched out their barren limbs like arms reaching for me. They didn't bring comfort.

The quietness meant one thing: I was being hunted and my pursuers didn't want me to hear them coming until it was too late.

Get ready, Nat. You got this.

The trees not far from me to the west shook. A powerful blanket of cinnamon filled the air, so strong I could taste it on the edge of my tongue. My heart beat against my ribs and I tried not to think of all the reasons why Tamara made us run away, why Tamara used her house for protection instead of facing it head on.

The pine trees directly in front of me fell over. Whatever was coming for me was closing in fast. The goblin blade shook so fast, my knuckles whitened from the grip. The army stirred in my stomach. An ominous form approached me in darkness with bright red pinpricks in the center — almost like the bioluminescence from deep sea fish. The crimson dots blinked as my attacker grew larger and larger. I'd hoped that whatever was coming for me would maybe be as big as a horse, but what came for me was almost as high as some of the trees. My sharp eyes made out what had to be its face — a mass of wriggling tentacles with eyes in the center. It had a squid-like face, but a lion's torso. Sharp claws snapped the fallen brush at its feet as it slowly came at me like a predator approaching its prey.

Cato Fillian's darkling.

A growl formed in the back of my throat. My incisors lengthening in my mouth. The wolf within was hungry for a fight.

"C'mon!" I snapped.

A thin line formed on the darkling's face and spread open to reveal dagger-like teeth that glowed like hot coals. From its back, longer tentacles squirmed. As its mouth twitched, opening and closing, a clicking noise bounced off the trees.

I turned the goblin blade so that the business end pointed at the darkling. Power pulsed from the glowing crystal and raced into my fingertips. Sparks jumped along the tip. The tiny hairs on my head rose. The burden I carried in my stomach rumbled and a strange aquamarine glow grew along my limbs.

The darkling trembled and like a fellow predator, I knew the next sequence of events. I waited for it, watching the muscles in the darkling's legs tense up. Any second now, it would strike and I'd be ready. The darkling leapt forward. I lunged and spun to the left, avoiding a swiping claw by inches. The darkling crashed into the trees behind me. As I turned around, I pointed the goblin blade at my target.

Where the hell was the trigger?

I didn't need one. As I thrust the goblin blade forward, a dual arc of cold and flame shot out of the crystal. In the path of where I fired, branches turned to cinder, and the ash immediately froze afterward.

Now that was bad ass.

The darkling dodged my attack and came at me hard with one of its tentacles. I jerked out of the way, but wasn't quick enough and the tip of one barbed tentacle snagged my shoulder, tearing the skin that blossomed with pain from the hit.

Keep moving, Nat. I thrust the weapon at it again, and, this time, a blast of wind rocketed through the thicket, sending the demon one hundred feet into the trees again. But it didn't stay down for long and scrambled after me.

My quickened breath came out as mist as I tried to dodge and outrun the darkling, but it was far faster. It swooped in again, its wide mouth biting deep into my leg. The pain didn't keep the wolf in me from fighting back. At the same time, I plunged the crystal tip into the darkling's shoulder. Blood and flesh sizzled. Our mutual screams filled the air. The darkling immediately released me and scooted backward with a limp.

I did the same as hot blood coursed down my leg. God, the pain was awful. I bit back the scream in the back of my throat as black dots danced around my vision. With my shaky left hand, I clutched my leg and with my right, I tried to hold on to the twitching goblin blade. A tree hit my side hard as I backed into it. All the while, I continued to face my enemy.

Stay in the present. Never look away.

The darkling hissed at me from a few feet away, crouching low again for the next attack.

The staff began to vibrate again, this time too much for one hand to steady. I used both hands this time, recognizing the power build-up again as white sparks snaked around the staff. My knees buckled as fatigue swept over me so I used the tree for support.

Time to play again for the last time.

Static electricity tickled my arms. The hairs on the nape of my neck rose as the goblin blade began to glow so bright I had to close my eyes and pray that a final strike was coming to end it all.

The goblin blade shuddered and a missile of white-hot heat from the crystalline tip rocketed into the ground. From there, it shot heavenward into the stirring clouds and then rained down onto the darkling.

The creature fell over as a burned and blackened husk. All that moved was its mouth and teeth. A second later, it moved no more.

Chapter 19

For good measure, I jabbed the beast a few times, burning a few more holes. When the goblin blade grew cold, I gave up. It might've been dead, but I'd seen too many movies to know the bad guys got up if you didn't do them in well enough.

The ground was so cold, but I welcomed the support as I collapsed. My leg throbbed as my body fought to heal itself. The pain was far worse compared to when Erica Holden had taken a crowbar and broken my leg. With a quick peek at the ground, I confirmed the worse. I was bleeding profusely.

My cellphone vibrated again in the bag. There was a new message from Tyler.

I'm close! hide if u can.

Kinda late for that, I thought with a chuckle.

Not far from me, the darkling's mass continued to stink up the place like burnt cinnamon toast. I shook my head at the sight.

"All this time you were nothing but a..." I chewed on the thought. "Squid-thingy, and I thought you were much bigger."

I sighed. "I'd hoped you would've been smaller."

Fatigue crept into my chest, forcing me to take shallow breaths. To staunch the bleeding, I took one of the shirts from my backpack and wrapped it tightly around my upper thigh. Pain sliced through the limb, but I grimaced and tried to ignore it. I fell back on the snow, unable to stop the strange bubble of laughter that came over me.

Maybe I'd finally lost it.

I would've never seen myself like this while I was training for the trials to reenter the pack. Never in a million years, while I was running laps on that stupid high school track, did I foresee that I'd be in my grandmother's homeland running away from conjured demons that looked like mish-mashed seafood.

Snowflakes, which were feather light and frosty, drifted to my nose, but I didn't wipe them away. They were such simple things — not really a nuisance.

A few months ago, I'd been stressed out. There had been no wars. Just my life within the pack on the line. The South Toms River Pack was one tiny dot in a world full of creatures.

I was such a damn fool for being so close-minded, letting my world with my ornaments and the werewolves in a small town keep me from growing and learning. I could've explored my grandmother's old magic a long time ago.

The urge to cry suddenly came over me. I fought the tears and took deep breaths. I wanted to be alive to return and take my place as alpha female.

Hell, I wanted to live to show those kids who was boss around that town. The trees above me grew dimmer and dimmer as the snow under me grew colder.

I tucked in as best as I could, leaving my leg stretched out. As I closed my eyes for a brief moment, I imagined Thorn was behind me, his warm lips resting against the nape of my neck, his arms offering comfort.

"How badly is it broken?" a man's voice asked within the haze of my sleep.

My eyelids were heavy. Far heavier than my numb limbs. The goblin blade, which I'd clutched in my right hand, was gone. A warm hand held it instead.

Someone gently tilted my leg from side to side as if examining it. "Not good, but I can see the healing process at work." The voice was soft-spoken and feminine.

"Is it moving, Zoya?" I recognized Tyler's voice this time.

I tried to blink and almost succeeded.

"That fucker is dead," the woman replied. I caught the sound of a hard kick. Zoya probably stabbed it a few times, too. "I always wondered what they looked like."

"Give me a nice, straight stick so I can secure her leg, please. We need to get it wrapped so I can carry her back to the car," Tyler said.

Finally, my eyes managed to open. Tyler leaned toward my face with a wide-eyed grin. The first light from the sun peeked from behind him through the pine trees. His blond hair had an ethereal glow to it. "Are there any other darklings around?" I mumbled.

"Don't worry," Luda said.

"It's good to see you, Natalya," he said.

"You look like shit," Zoya said, joining him.

I wanted to flip her off, but imagining myself doing so worked just as well.

"Good job on the darkling," she murmured. "Ugh, it stinks!"

The tugs on my leg grew uncomfortable, renewing the pain I'd been hiding from. Luda shifted me and removed the shirt tied around my thigh. She leaned in closer to the wound. "She smells strange."

I did? Was it the same scent Quinton caught?

"Maybe it's coming from this." Zoya pointed to the darkling.

"No, it's coming from here." Luda laid her hand on my stomach. Her palm warmed me. I'd briefly forgotten about the old magic spellcasters tucked inside me. "She's so cold here."

Tyler touched me, too. "It's hard for some reason." He glanced at Luda. "Is she…?"

"No, that's another smell entirely," she replied.

"Just get me out of here," I groaned. "I'll explain everything in a bit."

Tyler lifted me up in his arms and carried me to an SUV right off the road. I welcomed the warm air sputtering out of the vents. The leather seats were worn but toasty warm.

As everyone else piled inside, he said, "So what the hell happened to you back there?"

"It's a long story," I whispered.

Luda offered me a piece of fruit. It was the most gorgeous apple I'd seen in a long time. Screw manners or wiping it clean. I bit huge hunks out of it, not caring if I smacked my lips or opened my mouth while I ate.

While I inhaled the fruit, Tyler told me what happened to the three of them at Tamara's home. He sat in the front seat with Zoya while Luda tended to me in the back.

"She woke me up and told me to take the girls away somewhere safe," Tyler said. "I wanted to go with you and Thorn, but she told me she'd take care of you two." He sighed. "We left the house through the secret passage and ended up somewhere to the south. We went from town to town at first, catching rides where we could to add some distance."

"We had to get as far from the house as possible," Zoya said bitterly. "The darklings had our scent already, so it was in our best interest to scatter and go to my cousin's home a couple of hours from here."

Luda placed her palm along my cheek to check my temperature. "We were hiding at her home when Tyler told us you finally contacted him. We were so worried about you and Thorn."

"What about your grandma?" I asked.

Luda and Zoya exchanged a look. It was Luda who spoke. "We don't know what happened to her. We called the house, but the line came up as disconnected. A friend drove past the house and saw nothing but a smoldering ruin." Her voice drifted off and I sensed her pain.

"I'm sure she's still alive somewhere," I said.

"We can only hope," Tyler said. "So what happened to you?"

Where should I even begin? So much had happened over the past couple of days. Nearly a lifetime's worth of events. I recounted to them how Thorn and I escaped, how I left him behind with a pack in Finland, met the old magic acolytes and eventually set the old magic spellcasters free—into me—and how I'd run away, only to be cornered by a darkling.

"Holy fuck," Zoya blurted.

"Yep, that sounds about right," I said.

"You must be exhausted," Luda said as she hugged me.

"So what about the smell?" Zoya twisted in the seat to look at me. "That thing you have inside you. Is that why you smell the way you do?"

"I don't know," I murmured. "What do I smell like?" If I really took a whiff, all I caught was dirt, dirt, and maybe something in between like snowy, wet dirt.

"It's nothing I've ever smelled before," Luda said,

her gaze on the countryside as it zoomed by. "I'm surprised you can't catch it. It's almost like a blend of herbs, the smoke from a fire, and a bit of forest after a rainstorm."

"How poetic," Zoya said with a snort.

"I wonder if that means something. I don't know exactly what I have inside me—other than the essence of the twelve spellcasters who were trapped by some force centuries ago. I've wanted a moment to rest, catch my breath, and have the strength to set them free. I've yet to have that golden moment."

"You're going to get that rest whether you want it or not," Tyler said firmly. He gave me the eye through the driver's rear mirror. The dwarf's stern face told me he'd tie me down if necessary.

Other than the sound of the heater, no one spoke for a while. A question bubbled on my lips. "So where are we going now?"

"We need to get you patched up back at their cousin Oksana's farm," Tyler replied.

I held back a groan. "Does she live north or south from here?"

"You need to rest your leg," Luda chided. "Unless you'd like to hobble where you need to go on a bum leg."

"Those wizards have held out for a while now," Tyler said. "If they are competent spellcasters, they can wait a bit longer while you heal so you can help them."

With my luck, they were barely holding out.

I had no choice but to keep quiet, so I closed my eyes from the sun shining on my face as the old magic spellcasters circled my stomach, waiting impatiently to be set free.

Chapter 20

The trip to Oksana's house took forever. We had to be going north, though, as the sun was on my right.

Enduring pain for two hours with a bruised shoulder and a leg broken in multiple places made me one grumpy werewolf.

I closed my eyes most of the trip, but I had trouble finding sleep. After getting attacked so many times, slumber had trouble finding me. As much as I tried to find comfort, unease kept nipping at me.

Not that I felt alone or anything, Luda was the kindest soul. She checked on me now and then.

Her sister Zoya was far less concerned, every once in a while gazing at Tyler with admiration. My friend tried to keep his eye on the road, but I caught him looking at her once in a while.

When we finally reached Oksana's house, relief filled me when I saw the single story cottage with bright red shutters up ahead. But even the tranquil view of the pond right next to her house didn't calm my rising nerves. My body tried to heal itself, but there was far too much damage. I'd need time, something I didn't have much of, if I wanted to help those wizards.

A tall, blonde woman with glasses strolled to us from the pond near to the ivy-covered house. Before she walked up to the car, she shut the door to a nearby greenhouse.

Tyler carried me out of the SUV into the house. He tried his best to avoid my leg, but it hurt nonetheless.

"Sorry," he blurted.

"Don't worry about it. It doesn't hurt that bad." I had a broken leg. It hurt like nobody's business.

The sitting room off the mudroom was a mess and the house felt stuffy, as if someone had tried to keep the warm air trapped inside for too long. I was still grateful for the shelter.

The blonde woman, who had to be Oksana, followed us into the sitting room. In her hands, she carried a colorful flowerpot with a plant. She placed it on the fireplace mantle. It was rather hard to discern what type of plant, since it was a seedling. The flowerpot was actually one of many. About a hundred potted herbs filled every flat place in the room. From sage to watercress and even pansies.

This was an herbalist's home.

Tyler placed me on the sofa — one of the few free spots. A cloud of dust puffed up from where he placed me.

"Tyler?" I asked softly.

"That's the cleanest spot in the house," he said. "It really is."

"I just cleared off a bed for her," Oksana sang as she joined us. Her smile was welcoming and wide. As jovial as her bright orange dress that trailed along the floor. And that was when I noticed the hardwood, too. Not a single person had swept it.

Had Luda and Zoya sat on their butts their entire time at a relative's house and not bothered to offer a hand to pick up?

There was no way—without casting more spells to calm myself—that I could rest on a bed that most likely had enough dirt for a garden.

"I wouldn't want to put you out," I began. "Are there any inns nearby?"

"No, no, no," Oksana said in her sing-song voice. She leaned toward me, her brown eyes growing big behind her glasses. She was probably as blind as Grandma.

"I won't have you doing that," Oksana added. "The twins are family and anybody who is a friend of theirs is a friend of mine, too."

My eyes pleaded with Tyler, but he merely grinned and shrugged. He could've warned me.

Luda joined us. "How is your leg?"

"What happened to her?" Oksana asked.

"The monsters that kept attacking our house hurt her," Luda said.

"Hurt her?" Zoya laughed. "Not by much. She burned that fucker to a crisp."

"I see. I smell blood on her though, among other things." Oksana peered over Luda's shoulder while my friend pulled back the shirt she secured over my ripped pants.

Oksana described what she saw. I didn't wanna look. "There are so many puncture marks...The bleeding isn't as bad, but you've got extensive bruising and there are a few open wounds. Most likely from fractures. I'll make a poultice to encourage healing and keep infection away."

Now she had my attention. "What about gauze and alcohol? Boiling water?"

"Don't worry, dear. I've got everything covered." She looked to Tyler. "Will her leg need to be set?"

"No," we both said at the same time. The stick

Tyler had used to secure my leg made sure of that.

Oksana left us to go to her kitchen. The sounds of bottles jostling about reached my ears. As I lay there, the scents from what she prepared floated around the house: sharp apple cider vinegar, aromatic buds of Gilead, even black snakeroot. Her bubbling pot of ingredients made the place stink to high heaven. I ignored the pain and raised my head. I spotted her working in the kitchen while she steeped the ingredients like she was making tea. After some time, she used a pair of wooden tongs to place a white cloth into the brew. What she pulled out was the color of sour piss. *Ugh.* Not exactly something I wanted on my leg.

Oksana sang, "Not only will this heal your wounds, but it will cleanse your blood." She marched right up to me and, using Luda's assistance, applied the cloth over my wound. It took everything I had to look away and keep my mouth shut. I was in no position to refuse what was offered if I wanted to get out of here on two feet.

Oksana promptly returned to the kitchen and put the brackish fluid into a large mason jar. "This will be some good stuff," she declared. "We'll keep this to use on you later."

I wanted to ask her if she had a bottle of aspirin, but I wasn't in that much pain yet.

"So where did you learn all this?" I asked her to keep my mind off what was on my leg, what was flowing into my leg. Any distractions would work at this point.

"Old country healing from my dam and my sire. They took in any werewolf who needed help along the countryside. During that time, our packs used herbs after the hunt for fertility." Oksana giggled.

"We've heard tales for days about the olden ways,"

Zoya said dryly.

"It's rather fascinating," I had to admit.

Her enthusiasm was rather overpowering, so I tried to smile. I'd frowned enough for a while now.

"Oh, while I'm at the stove, I might as well cook that chicken for our guests. Zoya, how about you offer a hand instead of Luda for once."

Zoya rolled her eyes and joined her cousin.

The sounds of cooking kept coming from the kitchen while I rested.

An hour or so later, they checked on me again to replace the bloody gauze.

"How's the healing coming?" Oksana asked after she exposed my wounds. Luda acted as her assistant again.

It was weird sitting on the couch while they checked over me. I felt the strong urge to blink every time Oksana did. It was rather hard not to mimic her actions with the way her glasses magnified her eyes.

"There's something else," Oksana leaned in to sniff me.

"Oh, I bet she can smell *them*," Tyler said.

"The werewolf spellcasters?" Luda asked.

Luda explained what I told them in the car. That I'd taken a group of old magic spellcasters into my body and that I wanted to take them to Stolobny Island to help the wizards. She added I wanted them out as soon as I got some rest.

Oksana's mouth formed an "o" as Luda finished explaining.

"However did you do that?" the herbalist asked.

"Old magic," I said.

"That's very powerful magic, indeed. But that doesn't explain why you smell like clover, cinnamon, and bay leaves."

Interesting. "So that's what I smell like?"

"Your stomach does." She took my hand and smelled it up to my fingertips. "There's something else, too. It's everywhere though and it's sweet. It's an herbal scent I can't place since it's so faint."

"A necromancer said to me not too long ago that he smelled the same thing," I admitted. "Could it be a curse?"

"I don't think so, but I'm not sure. What plants have you come into contact with as of late? Are you carrying any herbs?"

That was an open question. "Since when?" I squeaked.

"Hmm, how about the past few months?"

Wow. It could be anything.

"My aunt Olga has an aloe vera plant." I shrugged. "There's a dead set of orchids at my mom's house she has yet to throw away. My husband Thorn wanted to buy me daisies but they were so expensive and out of season—"

"Yeah, that doesn't help," Oksana interjected.

She smelled my wrist. "So peculiar. But you're not *dead* or anything, so whatever it is, it isn't hurting you."

With that, she left me speechless.

A bit later, Zoya finished cooking dinner and brought me a plate. She had prepared crunchy chicken and hard peas, and I ate every bite of it to regain my strength.

Tyler ate at the dinner table with the twins. He shoveled in Zoya's food with gusto. He didn't say anything or look at her, but he appeared pleased with the hot food, scraping his plate to get every morsel into his mouth. "Is there any left?" he asked.

"Let me get you some more," Zoya said sweetly.

Nobody else asked for seconds.

Something had to be developing between those two.

While the others helped with the dishes, I checked the messages on my phone. I had a few from my relatives, most of them checking on me and berating me for not contacting them.

A message from Grandma touched my heart: *I'm so worried about you. Please come home.*

There were a few from Dad, Alex and even Mom. I replied to all of them and let them know that I was alive in Russia with Tyler, and that Thorn was in Finland.

Speaking of Thorn, I didn't have a single message from him. That pained me the most. I tried to call his cellphone, but the line quickly went to voicemail. I tried to think positive. Maybe in a village like Nuijamaa there wasn't a way for him to charge his phone?

I called again and left a message this time.

"Thorn, it's me, Nat. I'm so worried about you. Can you call me please? If I don't pick up, just leave me a text message." I sighed and tried to keep my voice steady. He had to be fine. "You're gonna piss me off if you don't send me something so I know you're okay. I don't care if it's by Pony Express, smoke signals, or anything." As much as I tried to sound stern, my voice began to break and my insides tightened. "You've always told me that you're always close by. Well, I know you can't manage too much in that department, but at least you can find the pack alpha and send me a message."

I sensed eyes on me, but I ignored them. I couldn't avoid them hearing me in this private moment.

"I need to hear you, okay —"

The phone beeped. I had used up my allotted time. I frowned, thinking that the last thing I said was "okay," instead of something beautiful like "I'm thinking of you" or "You're my everything." "Okay" was so simple and didn't express the depths of my longing for him.

Later Tyler offered to carry me to the bed, but I ended up sleeping on the couch. It was impossible to get comfortable though. As the night bled away, I noticed my stomach had hardened further. I couldn't even turn over to sleep on it. It was next to impossible with this full feeling that never went away.

As we were eating breakfast, I told Tyler what needed to be done. "You need to take me to Ostahkov today." Ostahkov was the nearest town to Stolobny Island.

Frustration lined his handsome features. "I said you needed to rest, Nat."

"I don't have time for that anymore." Casting modesty aside, I raised my shirt to reveal a new development. The pale skin on my stomach had changed, going from milky to less opaque. You could see my veins and arteries along with the hint of my internal organs.

"What is happening to you?" He sucked in a gasp.

I shrugged. I'd about shit myself that morning when I caught it. "I have a feeling it's an effect from the magic I'm using to keep them inside me."

"How do you feel right now?" he asked.

"Exhausted," I admitted. Beyond exhausted was a better term. I practically held my shirt up until Tyler gently pushed my hands down.

"Your eyes are bloodshot and your face is pale," he said.

"I can't stay here, Tyler. I need to release them."

He sighed. "Why can't we just release them right now, perhaps in the backyard?"

I held in a laugh. "I don't have enough strength to think straight."

"Then why should I take you right now?"

Ideas took a while to brew in my head, but eventually I thought of something, not the greatest idea, but I was willing to undertake it. "Talk to Oksana. Ask her to come up with a concoction to put me to sleep. When we reach Ostahkov, I should be rested enough to release the spellcasters."

His right eyebrow rose with doubt.

"You got a better idea?" I asked him.

"Not really." He patted my good shoulder. "Close your eyes for a bit while I talk to Oksana and the others."

The girls must've agreed to my plan, since Oksana showed up ten minutes later with a coffee cup in her hand.

"You asked for it." She pushed the hot drink into my hand.

"What is it?" With one whiff, I wanted to quash my bright idea. A green film sat on top of who knows what. The drink even smelled like a swamp.

"Well, since you asked, it's got—"

"I'm good. Denial is a beautiful place. You're gonna make me ill if I really know what's in it."

"But this is one of my best drinks! There's peppermint to soothe your stomach. Jerusalem oak for worms—"

"My leg is broken. That's it. I do not have worms."

"Werewolves can get it too, so hush. I even added…"

She went on and on, but I tuned her out as I gulped and gulped. It tasted so awful even with the peppermint, and it left a strange coating on my tongue. The heated drink warmed my throat all the way down to my stomach. From there the sensation swam around my midsection before it slammed into my head.

"What did you give me to make me tired?" My voice was already slurred.

Oksana's mouth moved, but I missed it. Her form blurred. I finally heard her say, "And that's about it. You wiped me clean for a few things, but that just gives me an excuse to plant more!"

As I drifted off to sleep, I wished I could've shared her enthusiasm.

Something pricked me again and again. From one moment to the next, I wondered when I'd wake up if what I was hearing or experiencing was a dream. I kept hearing Tyler, Luda, and Zoya. Yet they sounded far away, like they were on the other side of a huge room full of people and I was at a table all alone. The crowd contained my family and the whole South Toms River pack.

I was outside at a park somewhere.

I stood and everyone turned at the same time to look at me. They looked at me as if I should have something to say.

I searched my mind for why I was here and what I was supposed to do. But I couldn't think of anything. When I blinked again, I noticed I sat at a picnic table. Everyone else was at picnic tables, too. The sun shone outside and heated my shoulders. In the distance, families also sat underneath the protective cover of the shelter. I spotted my parents in their honorable spot near the pack leader Farley.

But Farley wasn't the pack leader anymore. Thorn was.

What kind of dream was this?

A hand touched my shoulder. It was my father. "It's time, Nat."

"Time for what?" My mouth moved on its own.

"It's time for you to accept your new life and cast your fears aside."

His grip was strong as he led me to where the

high-ranking families ate. The barbecue from their meals made my mouth water.

I spotted Grandma and wanted to call out to her, but I didn't.

Then I turned my head and saw the unexpected. It was Rex, standing in front of Farley.

No. Not again.

I tried to dig in my heels. To keep from replaying this nightmare. I didn't want to see the next sequence of events. To feel my heartbeat pick up. To feel my lungs close off as Farley and my father pushed me on Rex again. To relive the shame my family would experience when I lost my marbles in front of everyone.

"Are you ready to take Rex as your mate, Nat?" Farley looked like he always did. An older, paler version of Thorn with hard hazel eyes.

My dad continued to hold my arm, everyone looking at me expectantly. I waited for the panic to come like it always did in my nightmares, for the unease to overwhelm me.

When nothing happened, I yanked my arm away from Dad. I turned to Farley and said something I'd been waiting five years to do.

"That piece of shit bastard can rot in hell."

Farley stared at me. Rex, who had been smiling at me, went agape.

"I'm the South Toms River alpha female," I spat. "You're a royal asshole and you're not the leader anymore." My attention went to Rex. "And you don't intimidate me anymore." I closed in on him with a sharp growl. "You're most likely a shriveled up dickhead who needs to belittle others to compensate for your self-doubt." I couldn't stop myself from stabbing at him with my index finger. "As much as you enjoy trying to drive me into the mud and smear my nose in it, I'm a pack member. I deserve dignity and respect. And when I get back to the U.S., I'm gonna kick your ass up and down the Garden State Parkway until I run through five pairs of heels. Got it, pal?"

The only sound around me was my quickened breaths from speaking for so long, until my father placed his hand on my back and chuckled. "That's my Nat."

"*Nat?*" Someone called my name. The picnic tables around me faded as if my vision had been smeared with grease. Then they faded to black.

"Nat!" A hand cupped my face, tapping it a bit.

When I blinked and opened my eyes, I found Luda next to me, a look of concern on her face. When I glanced behind her, I gasped.

We'd reached the small town of Ostahkov.

Soon enough I'd see Stolobny Island.

Chapter 21

The late night view of Lake Seliger beyond the car window reflected my mood. It was clear and refreshing. Even with the chill in the air, Luda rolled down the window a bit and I reveled in the fresh air.

The lake was quite large, extending into the distance to the north. Just a few miles north of here was the island. We drove west along the main road, heading deeper into the touristy town.

"How are you feeling?" Tyler asked from the front seat.

"Much better, thank you."

"We were afraid you wouldn't wake up after Oksana dosed you," Luda chirped.

"Yeah, Tyler took a sip after you downed the stuff and he was high for about a half hour," Zoya said.

Tyler flashed Zoya a dark looked but his expression didn't last long before he grinned. "It wasn't that long. Dwarves can handle drinks just fine."

"There wasn't a drop of liquor in that stuff. What she put in there could take out a herd of horses. Or one of them, anyway."

After sleeping for so long, my mind was clear. Just looking out the window and seeing the town made me feel normal for once.

The spellcasters still stirred inside of me, but after so many days of pain and stress, I was ready to face what I had to do.

"Where are we going?" I asked.

Tyler said, "Zoya's been checking out the area on the maps and there's a forest to the west of here that's used for camping and such. It would be a great place to release your friends."

I nodded.

"Are you ready to free them?" Luda asked me softly. She handed me an apple, as large as the one I'd eaten before and something came to mind I'd completely forgotten. Did I even remember the chant to release them that Blazh had worked so hard over the years to memorize? He'd been at my side, the one to take the lead.

Worry snuck up on me and my fists clenched. There had been so many phrases. It wasn't just a simple, "Come on out, guys."

I faced away from Luda.

"I'll be fine," I whispered. The apple remained in my hands. My appetite had left me.

The town disappeared and pine trees began to take over the landscape. The sky overhead was overcast, threatening to rain as we ventured deeper into the forest. Soon enough, we reached a parking lot full of camping vehicles. Since it was so late in the night, no one stirred about.

"This is the place," Tyler declared. "Are you excited?"

"Of course. But I wonder why we haven't seen any warlocks or wizards yet."

Tyler sighed. "I wondered about that, too. Could

they be farther north? Maybe closer to the island?"

"Maybe," I said. "They're probably under a mask of some kind. Dr. Frank said they should be swarming all over the place around here. We need to be careful."

"Then I'll go out first and look around. I'll be back soon to get you three."

Tyler left the car. Luda took my hand as I looked around out the window. "Don't worry so much, Nat. You always take the burden of the world on your shoulders."

"Worrying has kept me alive so far."

"It might have, but that doesn't mean you have to let it constantly eat away at you."

I wished I could've explained to Luda what it meant to have an anxiety disorder, how I couldn't turn it off even if I wanted to. My medication, which I hadn't taken since I'd left home, only did so much. I'd never be normal, and, in a way, I'd come to accept that. It was making others accept it that was far more difficult.

Tyler returned soon. "The coast looks clear for now. I did see a warlock, but he was alone and he drove away."

"A warlock drove away?" Zoya glanced in the direction he pointed. "Why not just disappear like they always do?"

"I dunno. I guess he wanted to get some *beers* or something." Tyler opened my door so I could get out. "Next time he shows up, I'll ask him why he's driving a human's car."

Zoya rolled her eyes and got out. She took a long sniff in the air. "Seems clear so far."

We slowly walked past the cars into the forest. The pine and spruce trees hugged us, their scent pouring through me and satisfying the wolf. Whatever Oksana had given me, I needed it.

"How is your stomach?" Tyler asked me. "Is it still?"

"I don't know. I haven't looked since we left and I don't want to see if it's gotten worse." The army weighed hard on me. My shirt had a slight protrusion that brushed against my jacket. While I got out of the car, I felt it shift inside me. My leg was much better. Thanks to Oksana, my body had healed most of the minor fractures, but I still winced when I tried to put weight on the leg. I ignored the pain as Luda lent a hand.

"Just use me as a crutch, Nat."

After less than a mile of walking along a trail, we decided to jump off it and go deeper into the forest.

"How far should we go?" Luda asked. We'd taken a spot at the rear. "Nat shouldn't walk too much on her leg."

I couldn't help smiling at her. She was so sweet and kind. I wish I had a sister like her back at home.

"How's this, Nat?" Tyler yelled back at me.

We hadn't gone too far, but it would have to make do. Most of the night had been eaten away. The darkness settled into me and I was wary. I reached down and touched the ground. Not that I wanted to teleport, but I was curious about something. There was a pull to the left, to the north, indicating a great deal of magic at work there. It pulled at everything here and disjointed the space. Hopefully, it wouldn't bring the warlocks here and interfere with my spellcasting. The thought hadn't occurred to me before that such magic would draw the darklings and the warlocks, but this time, I wasn't so foolish.

Nick was able to do something he called masking. Where his magic could be hidden from others. I didn't know how he did it, though. My guess was that he thought or, I should say, he believed that others wouldn't see what he didn't want them to see. Nick was a pro at that. He'd hidden his feelings from me for years.

I sighed, thinking of my friend and hoping he was well.

"Are you ready, Nat?" Tyler asked.

"Yeah, as much as I'll ever be." I handed Tyler my backpack, and, with Luda's help, I headed toward a circle of trees. Judging their distance to be wide enough to accommodate the party, I headed to the edge and sat down like Blazh did near the field.

I closed my eyes, trying to imagine him sitting beside me. His burly bulk would be in a heap as he tried to sit cross-legged and wasn't able. His wavy, amber-colored hair would be reflected in the moonlight and he smiled at me. "You can do this, Nat."

Sadness touched me. I couldn't find the words. Blazh was dead and all I had left was his memory. Our friendship had been too brief.

With a sigh, I tried to chant the words. But I knew they were wrong. It didn't feel as smooth or as well as Blazh did it.

A palm touched my forehead. Someone leaned in to whisper in my ear. "You're doing great, Nat. Slow down."

Luda's hands touched my shoulders and rubbed them with encouragement.

I opened my mouth, but the words didn't come out. I had to remember or I'd be trapped with these people until they killed me. I had to remember or those wizards would die.

I had to remember or the love of my life would die, too.

No pressure, right?

I closed my eyes and tried to remember the last couple of days. Beyond the trip here from *Troyebortnoye* beyond the fight in the forest with the darkling. All the way back to when Blazh told me he was letting go of the old magic spellcasters. It was that moment, that physical memory that I remembered the most. I'll never forget the look on his face when he told me he was sacrificing himself for me.

My heart clenched in my chest. I fought hard to remember that moment. Remember that span of time. Seeing the old magic spellcasters as they approached me. Farther back until they had first appeared. From there, I was sitting on the ground with Blazh and he was opening his mouth to speak first. I was hesitant, but the way he spoke was so deep, so sure of himself, he'd practiced for years and whenever he spoke the first syllable of "*Ndinae*," it was spoken with pride.

With that first word, I had it. I lowered my tone and imitated Blazh. I tapped my knees like he did, settling into a rhythm, letting the words flow with me as I recited them.

A tug in my midsection expanded until it felt like someone was twisting my insides. I hunched over a bit, but I kept chanting.

"Nat?" It was Tyler.

"Don't interrupt her," Zoya snapped.

With each repetition of the spell, I took deep breaths and kept going. Oksana had prepared me for this. I could do it. I believed I could do it, so I kept at it. At my side, I sensed someone else was tapping. Tyler and Zoya clapped not far from me. With my eyes closed, I couldn't see much, but from behind my eyelids, I noticed something begin to glow. A light shone in the darkness of the night. I couldn't break my concentration, so I kept my eyes shut and focused. I was almost there. I could almost feel the strands connecting me to the group inside me pulling away, like a mother giving birth to a child.

The clapping and the tapping near me seemed to fade, as if they were backing away from me.

A feeling of euphoria drenched me, a haze of happiness only comparable to the night I first saw Thorn after he'd returned to town.

Then the glow behind my eyes faded and I dropped like a hard sack of dog kibbles onto the ground.

Ouch.

I expected to blackout, maybe even faint a bit, but I was face down in the pine-needle-covered dirt, breathing in and out, as a pine needle jabbed me in the nose.

"Nat! Are you okay?" Luda's strong arms pulled me up.

"She's weakened by the spell," Zoya said.

Zoya and Tyler leaned over me with concern.

Beyond them, my vision swam, but I caught the most beautiful sight. Twelve people, dressed in medieval garb, standing in the circle of trees. The range of emotions on their faces went from horror to pure anger.

Then twelve turned to eleven as one of them vanished in a flash of light.

Chapter 22

Chaos broke out in the small clearing. Eleven people in front of Tyler, Zoya, Luda, and me ran around like clucking hens. A few of them pulled out swords and pointed them at us. One of them shouted obscenities at their friends, and the only woman among the group screamed in anger.

"Silence!" The tallest man among them roared. Even the birds were silenced.

He had the widest dark purple eyes I'd ever seen, a strange purple that glowed like two setting suns. As he turned to look at everyone, his thick wavy brown hair partially masked his face. "All of you brats need to calm yourself or, by God's blood, I will cut all of you to pieces."

Zoya clutched Tyler, who had somehow pulled out his battle axe, while Luda remained frozen behind all of us.

"First things first." He glanced at each of them as if to do a headcount. "Where is Elric?" He stormed toward the group and searched through them. "Where is that Satan's whoreson?" he spat.

The others looked around them, too.

"What are they saying?" Tyler asked. Zoya translated into his ear what they were talking about.

"He's gone," the woman murmured.

"I don't see him either, Royse," another man said.

The tall man stormed across the clearing and roared at us. "Are you the magician who set us free?"

"I think so." Saying anything else seemed kinda dumb.

"Why did you keep us there?" he asked with a hard edge as he pointed to my stomach with a sword.

"I barely saved you," I mumbled. The weakness in my limbs clung to me. I couldn't even stand.

Behind him, the woman the man called Royse looked up at the night sky. She walked a bit forward and her mouth opened wide. "Oh, no. It's been so long, Vasili."

"What are you saying?"

"It's not cold anymore. And the stars have moved. At least four moon cycles. What happened to Kyjev?"

My heart dropped for them—even if they did point their weapons at us. "It's been longer than that. It's been over seven centuries," I said.

"Centuries?" For a werewolf, she was a strange sight. She had Russian features, yet a smattering of Asian ones. Her eyes were light blue, almost white. But her most striking feature was her thick black hair that had been piled on top of her head in a haphazard fashion.

"Many, many moon cycles." I did the math for her. "Thirteen moon cycles equals one year. Seven hundred seventy-four years is over ten thousand moon cycles."

One of the men sank to his knees. His narrow gray eyes honed in on me. He rubbed his hand from his nose to his prominent cheekbones with sadness. "Then we have lost much more than Ulricslav. What of

Kyjev?"

Tyler and the twins remained silent. So I choose to speak. Hopefully, they understood enough of my words. "Batu-Khan took Kiev in 1240. He massacred nearly everyone and continued east to kill more people."

Vasili swore again.

I think they got it.

"But you have a chance to help again. The wizards who needed your help before need it again. The warlocks have made war with them. A much bigger fight than the fights they had before. They have surrounded wizards north of here because those men have found a way to turn the tide for the war."

Vasili glanced at Royse, and she turned away.

"Seven hundred seventy-four years and the world looks just like we left it," one of the men said.

"Shut up, Tomislav," Royse said, not appreciating his sardonic humor.

"We shouldn't stay here or help those wizards," Vasili snapped. "We need to find Elric and avenge our families for his treachery."

"What did Elric do? Was he the man who disappeared after I set you free?" I asked.

Vasili harrumphed. He glanced at Tomislav, the quiet one who appeared to be the lowest ranking member. "Track him now. Find his trail and come back when you have his position."

Tomislav nodded. He scanned the ground and then sprinted east. As to how he caught a trail by scent or sight, I was curious.

"Who is Elric?" I asked again.

Vasili ignored me. He went from person to person, whispering to them to ask of their health and wellbeing. I'd guess shocked would be the perfect answer for all of them.

It was Royse who finally answered me. "We were on our way to Kyjev through the snow. While we were camping, one of the men overhead Elric speaking to a rock. He was telling the rock that he would fulfill his obligations to the warlocks and poison us to prevent us from reaching Kyjev."

My eyebrow rose. A rock, huh?

"His treachery ran deep and our suspicions were confirmed when he prepared dinner that night. He made us a strange stew, but no one ate it." She took a step closer to me. Up close, I could make out her cream-colored skin and her graceful build. "When our leader Ulricslav confronted him about it, he tried to attack us with a death spell." Her eyes glazed over a bit and I sensed her anguish. "If it wasn't for Ulricslav, we all would've died. He sacrificed himself, throwing his son out of the way, and trapped us in that horrible place. A place where apparently there is no time."

"So the man who disappeared was working for the warlocks?" I asked.

She nodded.

Tomislav appeared in the middle of the field like a whisper. One minute he wasn't there and the next he was. These werewolves were amazing. Did they possess the same powers as wizards?

"Elric went north," he gasped, appearing a bit out of breath as if he ran. "I followed him until I spotted warlock troops hiding among the trees. There are hundreds of them along the lake shoreline toward an island."

"Stolobny Island," I whispered. Elric had gone straight to the enemy.

"Is this the place you speak of where the wizards are trapped?" Vasili asked me.

"Yes, they've trapped the wizards there for the past week. They need your help."

"So you set us free just to help them?" His right eyebrow rose to mock me.

"I didn't know you existed before then. I didn't even know how to get you out without the help..."

Luda stepped forward. "Leave her alone. She's trying to do the right thing to save these people. She has repeatedly sacrificed her life to protect your people and get you here. The least you can do is listen to her and not turn on her for the mistakes someone else made. If you want to get mad, then go north, find Elric, and kick his ass."

Wow. Luda had a mouth on her when she wanted to speak up.

Even Royse smiled a bit.

"Why should we help them?" one man asked quietly.

"Let me think, you fool." Vasili stood there for a moment and I wondered if he was about to tell us all to go to hell and tell his friends to go their own way. "We can't go after him, yet, Gostislav. We need to be smart about this, since we're in foreign territory. We don't know the terrain or what we're dealing with, but I want revenge."

"I agree," Gostislav said.

He turned to me. "What's your name, girl?"

Now we were getting somewhere. "I'm Natalya Stravinsky, daughter of Fyodor Stravinsky."

Before we went anywhere, Zoya produced her map so the group could get their bearings. They weren't too keen on just following us anywhere.

Tyler suggested that Luda go into town to find a house off the lake for everyone to stay for a short period while they planned. In the meantime, Gostislav gathered wood and created a fire as the chill from the early morning hours set in. Royse, Vasili, and I looked over the map.

"So much has changed," their leader said stiffly.

"Yes, cousin," Royse said. "All these new settlements that never existed before."

"The scale here is different." He stared at the map as if memorizing it. "You said 5,280 of my feet equal a mile?"

I nodded. The dude had pretty big feet, so the scale worked.

He sighed. "We still have conflicts to face. I thought the day we'd be freed, I'd be able to keep the promise I made to myself to find you a good husband so I could travel the world."

Royse chuckled. "How do you know I didn't plan to find you a good wife and then see for myself what lies beyond the rising sun?"

His shoulders shook with laughter. "And that is why we follow the same path."

The two continued to discuss the map while I rested. The others sat around the fire, adjusting to their new circumstances. Seeing these amazing people filled me with hope. Just thinking of what their deceased leader Ulricslav did to save them meant they had potential.

Luda returned soon with a place for us to stay not far from the camping site. We trekked on through the night to a small cottage not far from the shoreline. The spellcasters approached the house with curiosity.

"Now this is a curious structure," Royse observed. "Look at those lanterns. And not a single candle. Far brighter than many fires."

"Those are lights," Luda said softly.

Royse approached the taller twin. "You're a curious sight. How long have you been like that?"

Like what?

Luda's smile faded and she took a step away from

Royse. "A while—please come inside."

I was on my way into the cottage, but grabbed Luda instead. "Is everything all right?"

"Just fine." She shrugged off my worry and tugged me inside.

The look of concern on Royse's face was obvious, but, based on how Luda turned her back on me, she had no plans to reveal what Royse saw.

I even tried a few times, but she clammed up.

Once inside, it was strange to see the spellcasters poking around everything. One man broke a picture frame and I moved to intervene. They were gonna trash the place.

"Just leave them alone," Tyler remarked as he added some food into the fridge. "They're going to need to explore. They've been through a great deal. I'd want to keep moving and learning the ropes."

So I turned on the radio. There weren't many stations and I avoided the ones with pop music or anything modern. A Russian folk station seemed appropriate.

"Are there spirits trapped in there?" Vasili asked about the radio.

"No, it's a device that captures signals in the air created by machines." I went on to explain how over the centuries, people had gone from wagons to machines that use chemicals and complex gear structures to take them from place to place. It was technology and not magic that made all this happen.

"Fascinating." Out of the group, Vasili assimilated everything the fastest. He made a natural leader.

A wonderful smell filled the air as Tyler grilled burgers and sausages. A few men hovered around him, eager to offer a hand like any hungry werewolf would.

But it was a knock on the door that startled everyone in the sitting room.

"Did you hear or smell anyone?" Vasili asked Royse.

"No, I didn't, cousin," Royse said. She pulled a knife from a sheath along her leg.

"Let me answer the door," I offered. If it were a poor human asking for sugar or milk, it would be really awkward to have them gutted by twelfth-century werewolves on the attack.

I didn't expect to find Dr. Frank. The bearded, white-haired wizard grinned down at me. "You made it, Natalya."

"Dr. Frank," I whispered.

Vasili and Gostislav peered behind me. Their eyes full of suspicion.

"We're good," I told them. "This is a wizard friend of mine named Dr. Frank."

Dr. Frank gave a curt bow of his head and then he spoke in flawless Russian. Hints of old Slavic touched his words. "I am Gustav Frankenstein. I am pleased to make your acquaintance."

Vasili visibly swallowed. "Greetings to you, wizard."

"May I come in?" Dr. Frank was always polite. "I'd prefer not to have our conversation out in the open."

"Please. Please." I got out of the way and the men behind me followed suit.

"Oh, wait." He turned behind him. "I found some friends along the way and they're catching up, since I walk a bit fast." He gave me a wink.

My eyes widened to see three men walk up to the house: the acolytes.

"Oh, God!" I left the house and limped to meet them. Leg be damned. "You made it."

The boys appeared worse for wear, but just seeing them, filled me with hope.

"I didn't know if Cato Fillian...killed you," I said.

Chestibor made a rude noise. "He barely escaped *us*."

Dragomir cocked a grin at Chestibor. "So you're going to leave out the fact that you told us to retreat?"

"She doesn't need to know that," Chestibor said, brushing past us toward the house. "Do I smell a feast cooking?"

The three acolytes ran into Vasili first. With eyes averted, they approached him and introduced themselves. The old magic leader nodded with approval and everyone went inside.

Our little gathering had grown in size. Who stood out the most was Dr. Frank dressed in a dark gray suit. It was almost as if the folks in regular clothing were the strange ones.

A werewolf offered Dr. Frank a spot in one of the chairs. Others took a seat on the floor.

Vasili remained standing. His cousin hovered near him, looking Dr. Frank over.

"I'm so proud of what Natalya has accomplished. Setting you free was one of the hardest things she has ever done." Dr. Frank glanced at me, and I blushed.

"How does she know you?" Vasili asked.

Now that question took me aback.

"I'm her mentor...of sorts," Dr. Frank replied. "Over the years, I've come to offer guidance during her times of trouble."

Dr. Frank would never outright say I had OCD, but every time I gave in to my compulsions, I hoped I didn't stand out. None of the werewolves had complained when I kept cleaning after them, and they probably assumed I was subservient to Luda, Tyler, and Zoya.

Vasili nodded, accepting the explanation. "And what brings you here—other than to bring these acolytes?"

"I'm sure you're aware of what has happened on Stolobny Island." Dr. Frank went into detail on the last couple of months of the war between the warlock and the wizards. How the warlocks had finally found a way to poison wizard weapons and render them ineffective. "We've tried again and again to clean up their messes, but their thirst for domination has no end."

"Those swag-bellied little prick bastards haven't changed one bit." Vasili spat on the carpet. Instead of losing my damn mind, I chose not to so much as twitch. Dr. Frank appeared proud.

"First, they helped that swine Batu-Khan and now you're telling me they want the world." Vasili appeared thoughtful.

Zoya kept Tyler in the loop by translating everyone's words. He finally spoke up. "Once the wizards are taken down, it will be dwarves and elves next. The fairy folk will hide like they always do, but some of my brothers might make a stand."

Gostislav made a snorting noise. "The wizards have always been the ones to make a stand. There's no way the wizards would stand a chance without a united front. The supernaturals bicker among themselves as it is."

"Maybe times have changed," Royse said.

"Not really," Zoya and I said at the same time.

I'd met too many goblins, brownies, and fairies to know they didn't give a rat's ass about each other. It was an each-supernatural-for-themselves kinda deal.

"So why are you here?" Vasili always got to the point.

"You and your men—and woman—are needed north of here to get onto the island to help our brothers who have uncovered how to help the wizards turn the tide. Any wizard who gets too close will have his weapons rendered useless. We will need your help to get on the island first."

"You need us to clear the path," Vasili said. "To take the first arrows up the ass."

"In a way, you could say that," Dr. Frank said.

"What do you think, cousin?" Royse asked Vasili.

Before he could answer, someone knocked on the door again.

Chapter 23

"Who the hell is at the door now?" Vasili shouted.

"There went the element of surprise," I said with a sigh.

I went to the door again, but Tyler slowed me down. "Be careful."

"Don't worry," Dr. Frank said. "They're not here to harm you."

He must've known who was coming. I opened the door, and a familiar scent came to me.

It was Tamara.

"Hello, Natalya," she said with a smirk.

For once, I was happy to see her.

"You made it," I said.

"So did you."

From behind me, the twins shoved me out of the way to reach their grandmother. She hugged them as they surrounded her with affection.

"Why didn't you answer us when we tried to call you, Grandma?" Luda chided.

"I had to add some distance to protect everyone. And I can see you did just fine without me." When she said, "did just fine without me," she was looking at me, though.

She gave me a short assessment, and, in return, I gave her a short nod. I got out of the way to extend my hand to let her in.

"How did you know we were here?" I asked her.

"Let's just say I have my ways to keep track of my young ones. Keeping track of you isn't possible, but when I noticed they were so close to where the wizards were trapped, I wondered what was happening, so I came to investigate."

"And here we are," Zoya said.

"Yes, here you are," their grandmother said softly.

Once we joined the others in the living room, Dr. Frank gave her a respectful nod.

He even got up to offer her a seat.

"Thank you." She sat.

"Do you know each other?" I finally asked him.

"It was a long time ago, but yes, we have met," he replied.

Tamara chuckled. "You're not going to tell them how we know each other, Gustav?"

So Tamara even knew his first name. How many folks knew him on a first name basis?

"That's was another time, another place, Anastasia," he replied.

Another set of looks passed between them.

"Either way, I'm here now for the twins," Tamara said. "I might as well stay and offer my help in your cause."

"Speaking of the wizards, have you decided?" Royse asked Vasili again. "I wanted to know before we were interrupted."

Vasili ran his fingers through his wavy hair and his face formed a hard edge. "Ulrichslav, our alpha, was betrayed. We must avenge him for our honor. Elric must be found and killed for his actions."

Royse nodded as well as the other old magic spellcasters and the acolytes, who appeared eager to please.

"If he hid among the scum to the north, we need to find his hiding spot among the ticks and pluck him out," Vasili said with a sneer.

The others agreed with shouts and encouragement.

"Kill the bastard!" one shouted.

"So when do we make our move?" Royse asked.

"We'll approach from the water instead of going by land. From there, we clear the path and destroy anything in our way."

He looked to each of the old magic spellcasters.

"For the honor!" he shouted.

From her spot, Tamara whispered, "To the end."

Before we embarked on our trip north, we ate. And ate. And ate.

The hamburgers and brats Tyler made was the *first* course.

"You couldn't feed a pup with those things," Gostislav barked.

So thanks to Dr. Frank's help, more food was brought in. "It's the least the wizards can do for your assistance," he said as local men delivered a supply of food.

And when I say food, I mean Renaissance-Festival-holy-shit-that's-a-lot portions. Five roasted pigs, the meat from three whole cows, countless turkey legs, ten buckets of vegetable stew, and four barrels of ale to wash it all down.

By the second barrel, I wondered how all of them were still sober.

"How can you eat this much?" I asked Royse, my stomach full to the point of being painful. Not far from me, Vasili was tossing hamburger buns off his burgers so he could mash the meat into his stew.

"We must prepare for what is to come," Royse said as she ate next to me at the small kitchen table. "Like shifting, spellcasting is costly in terms of energy. We need to focus, and that focus requires food." She gave me a curious stare. "Did you eat before you released us from our prison?"

"Not exactly," I replied. "I drank some kind of potion from an herbalist. I was still weak afterward."

"A beginner, I see." She stuffed a piece of turkey leg into her mouth like a pro. Then like a lady, she wiped her mouth off. "Over time, you will learn from your master how to prepare for battle."

"She smelled new to me," Gostislav joked. "How much elk did we eat before we marched to Kyjev?"

"A whole herd, I believe," she replied.

Wow. Maybe that wasn't a small herd either.

The food kept coming. One of the old magic spellcasters even brought over another serving of food for Royse.

"I thought you'd like some while they were hot." The stack of five burgers made my heartburn flare up just looking at it.

Royse kept eating the food on her plate, not a bit amused.

"I'll leave it here in case you change your mind." The guy rained smiles and sunshine her way.

After her admirer was out of earshot, I leaned over to say, "He seems nice."

"I've lain with him before." She pushed her hair behind her ear. "He's much better at swinging a sword than wielding the blade in his trousers."

I about choked on my spit. "It can't all be about sex. What about Gostislav? He was nice to you today."

"He hasn't bathed properly since I met him. That

was fifteen years ago."

Eww. It had been much longer than fifteen years.

"And him?" I pointed to another one.

"I've met women who can hold my attention better. Some of them made better lovers, too."

We went through all the old magic spellcasters, except Vasili, and she rejected them all. But when I absentmindedly pointed to Radomir, her mood changed.

"Mmm...Pretty hair," she purred, taking in the long, thick braid down his back. "I like the strong and silent type."

"He's only an acolyte, but he's really nice," I said.

Her light blue eyes twinkled with mischief. "I like to teach."

We sat in silence after that, watching the others eat and joke around. Seeing them all eat together, it was amazing to observe and learn so much. Vasili went over advanced spellcasting. He spouted off long spells that rivaled what Blazh had to learn.

Not far from Vasili, the acolytes listened with rapt attention. Just seeing the eagerness on their faces, filled me with a yearning for knowledge.

And for only a brief moment, I wondered what it would be like to follow the old magic spellcasters as an acolyte.

Only a brief moment.

I smiled. There probably wouldn't be any spots free anyway. Already, Chestibor, Dragomir, and Radomir followed him around and sucked in everything he said.

The late night turned into day. From the day into the afternoon everyone rested where they could find free space. By the time the sun turned the clear lake waters into light purple, it was time for us to go.

Two pontoons waited for us at the nearest pier to

the rental house. A few other wizards conversed with Dr. Frank at the end of the dock. Once they finished, Dr. Frank approached Vasili, our designated leader for the assault. "Vasili, we will wait along the shore until we see an opportunity."

Vasili nodded. "If I don't see you again, it was a pleasure to share a meal with a wizard such as yourself."

"The pleasure was all mine."

Dr. Frank nodded to me, too, but not before Tyler tugged my arm. "Nat, you shouldn't go with them."

"Yes, I should." I smiled at him. My friends always tried to protect me. "I'm here to help Thorn. I have to go to that island because this might be my only chance to learn a cure for him."

"Do you know what's out there?" he whispered.

"Trouble? Death? I've met them a few times already."

He sighed. "As your friend, I want you to do the right thing."

"You're officially one of my best friends, too." We hugged each other.

He chuckled. Over his shoulder, I caught Zoya throwing daggers at us with her eyes.

Even though Zoya might be able to hear us, I still whispered to him. "So are things getting serious with you know who?"

"What are you talking about?"

"Oh, c'mon." I gave him my who-are-you-trying-to-con face.

"I don't know what I'm feeling," he finally admitted.

"Maybe you're feeling like you've closed yourself off for so long from women who like you for who you are and not for what you're *trying* to be for them."

He rolled his eyes.

"Live in Denialville all you want." I tapped his shoulder. "I've got lakefront property there."

"Uh huh." He threw me a sour look. "I'll see you when you get back, Natalya."

"Yes...Hopefully, you will."

I left his side and got on one of the pontoons. I left my backpack behind, but kept my jacket and the goblin blade. Both of them would be useful on this trip.

The two boats took off northward along the lake. The shoreline was dotted with houses and trees. The place was deceptively peaceful. My stomach, even though it was full, had nerves all over the place. We didn't have far to go, but every mile was agonizing. Every turn seemed too quiet. The sun was no more than a sliver in the sky and cast a pink edge when the island came into view.

Nothing still seemed ominous.

Until the waters stirred ahead.

Vasili chuckled. He was in the boat with Gostislav, Royse, Tamara, and me. "Looks like our enemies have finally come out to play. Ready yourselves, friends."

My heart sped up a thousand times. My palms turned sweaty. My hand reached for the seashell necklace along my neck but found nothing yet again.

As a whirlpool formed ahead of us, I tried to ignore the breeze, along with its gathering cinnamon scent and the nagging feeling my life might end right here and right now.

You faced the darkling alone. You can do this.

At my side, Tamara took my hand. "Remember what you've been taught. React instead of act now. Let the more experienced folks do the offensive."

The whirlpool shifted with the wind, spinning faster and faster until a wave crested in our direction. The trees and bushes along the shore bent with the gathering gust.

"Royse," Vasili commanded.

The wave approached faster and faster.

On the other side of the pontoon, Royse began to chant, her voice low and guttural. A putrid, pungent-like fog slithered around the boat. The water around us rose with the wave and as the tsunami passed us, we reached the other side safely.

Five dark shapes shot out of the circling vortex into the air. They careened into the darkening sky, whistling with a shriek as they came down.

"Stay sharp," Vasili snapped. He shoved anyone near the edges of the pontoon toward the center.

All around me the spellcasters spoke, each saying something different, but their melodious voices carried power. Gostislav commanded the wind to knock a few arrows out of the way. A few landed at the end of our boat, knocked out by the wind. Tamara set off bombs in the air and many disintegrated before they reached us.

From the whirlpool a dark black head rose. Its body was serpentine in shape with white pupiless eyes at the top. Two men in black capes stood on top of the head.

"Water demon riders," Tamara said.

"Let them come for us on their little worm," Vasili sneered. "I need fish bait."

Then everything happened too fast. The demon surged toward us. With nowhere to go, the pontoons split formation as the creature swam between us. The warlocks jumped off the head, soaring through the air toward the boats. A rain of fire and ash shot out of the staffs they held. The purplish-pink sky lit up as everyone scrambled to get out of the way.

The warlock in black came at Gostislav first. He bared his teeth and growled as the warlock swung at him, but Gostislav disappeared in a flash and rematerialized at the hull. Our attacker aimed at me next, and, like a fool, I just stood there. Something shoved me hard into the side of the pontoon and out of the way. My side hit the metal bar with a hard *thwack*. I glanced up to see Tamara knocked someone else away from danger with a gust of wind.

"Don't just wait to get hit," she yelled at me. "Defend yourself!"

Sizzling fireballs from the warlocks' first attack littered the pontoon floor and began to burn the seats and the floorboard. As much as I wanted to react, it was rather hard to concentrate, as harsh smoke burned the back of my throat.

At my side, the goblin blade glowed and vibrated against my hip. The wooden handle on the envelope-opener-sized knife extended until the wood portion covered the whole weapon. The goblin blade was now a beautiful golden wand. Not the box I'd seen before against a warlock.

So what the hell was I supposed to do with it?

The spellcasters surrounded the warlock, sending flames and blasts of ice on him. He warded off most of the blows with a swish of his glowing staff, but there were too many of them. He scowled from each burn. From the corner of my eye, I noticed the water demon's head slam into the front end of the other pontoon, smashing it into fiberglass and wood bits.

Gostislav leapt over to offer a hand.

The wand quaked in my hands. There was so much power here, waiting to be tapped. Combined with my own I could act. Could it do what I wanted it to do?

The water demon chased after Gostislav, and I aimed the wand and recited the words.

And believed them.

An arc of ice snaked up from the water and slowed the water demon down enough to give Gostislav time to get away.

The warlock on my boat had been burned to a crisp by the time the water demon smashed the boat to smithereens. Vasili made a move, but it was too late. Our boat was next. As the water demon swept in, an oh-shit moment blossomed in my head. The stars above disappeared as nothing but blackness hovered over us. Water rained from the head before the head shot down fast towards us. My eyes widened, watching the beast open its bright red mouth wide. The jagged teeth twitching. From the corner of my eye, a form trailed after the head, a fiery sword in his hands. Vasili reached the head first, plunging his blade into water demon's crown.

The serpent kept coming at us and crashed into the middle of the pontoon. Royse shoved me out of the way, but I still bore the brunt of it. The sounds of the wood breaking and glass shattering reached my ears followed by the immediate sound of water silencing everything.

In the black, cold water everything was still compared to the chaos above. Below me, there was nothing but darkness, yet above me, lights danced about. My final fireworks show. The wolf within nudged me into action. *Move, damn you, move!* But my body didn't respond as if my head wasn't attached to my body. My fingertips went numb. My lungs begged for me to open my mouth to breathe. The gutted beast sank past me along with the rest of the boat.

Something else hit the water above, but I didn't notice.

My grip on the goblin blade faltered and my hand relaxed. If it floated away to the bottom of the lake, at least I'd be free of it.

Two pairs of hands grabbed my jacket and then pulled me upward. I allowed them to tug me until we reached the surface. Once there, I took in a deep breath. The cold wind was welcomed.

Something coppery ran between my eyes and dripped off my chin. Blood. One of the old magic spellcasters draped his arm around my torso to keep me afloat. With a wide sweep of his arm, he pulled me along as he swam. Others splashed forward or treaded water beside us.

My eyes blinked as sleep tugged at me.

"Stay awake, girl," a man grunted to me. "You'll heal soon enough."

"This water is colder than the last woman I lay with," Gostislav spat.

Royse chanted not far from us.

"Royse what are you doing?" Vasili shouted.

A gust of wind ruffled the water behind us, building stronger and stronger until a powerful force pushed us from the water and catapulted us to the shore. We dropped out of the sky with a *gentle* plop on dry land.

Chapter 24

The landing wasn't as gentle as I described it. More like we rolled several times and a few folks crashed into the rocks along the shore.

"Royse…" Gostislav said with a groan. Using the back of his sleeve, he wiped away blood from a deep gash across his cheek. "You still haven't mastered how to control the wind yet."

As a reply, she threw a few insults at him from a few feet away. Something about him resembling warty masses on a mule's rear end. She added, "How about we toss you back into the water and I'll try again, ehh?"

I wanted to kick Gostislav, too. He was far too abrasive for his own good. An evening rain shower began, bringing more chill to the night. The temperatures here continued to drop. I slowly stood, my body heavy from wet clothes. My head pounded from hitting the rocks near the shore.

"How are you feeling, Natalya?" Royse asked me. She twisted the hem of her skirt to wring it out.

"I've had better days," I declared as I leaned

against a tree. I took in our destination. We'd reached Stolobny Island. The place wasn't that large compared to the map. Just about five miles wide with stone structures, trees, and paths. Not far from us, a set of three-story buildings extended toward the dark sky. The neoclassical architecture made me think of this place as more of a hideaway palace than the battleground between supernatural forces. Such care had been given to keep the island, with its beautiful canary yellow and white buildings in such pristine shape.

"Everyone regroup," Vasili shouted.

He glanced to each of us, checking for everyone. I spotted the old magic spellcasters coming to their feet. Far to our left, the acolytes dragged themselves out of the water, safe and sound. Dragomir, the tallest of the three, had a noticeable limp, but he didn't let it slow him down as he followed his brother and Chestibor to shore.

Vasili pointed to Gostislav and another werewolf. "You two scout ahead. Wide formation. Report back if we will run into problems on the way to the frontlines. No sound. No human interaction."

"Yes, Vasili." Gostislav nodded to the other man and they disappeared into trees not far from the complex.

Vasili looked to Royse and me. "You two will take high point. Find the highest place on the island and protect the others as needed. If you find the wizards, confer with them on our status."

"Understood," Royse said.

She took my arm and pulled me away.

"And cousin," Vasili whispered.

She turned back with a sweet smile as if expecting he'd have more to say.

"Don't kill too many people this time. Stay alive if

you can."

"I'd say the same thing about you." She gave him a curt nod.

I chuckled. There was nothing like family love on the battlefield.

Royse led the way into the complex in the direction Gostislav went.

"Did you memorize the map?" I asked. She couldn't have visited this place before. The first buildings had been built in the late 1500s.

"Of course," she replied with a grin. "The highest point on the island is the cathedral. We'll scale the side to the top."

"We will?" I mumbled. "And how are we supposed to not be seen? I know monks might go to bed early and all, but there might be human pilgrims and such roaming the grounds."

Case in point, we froze when a man in monk's garb about fifty feet away strolled from one building into the next.

"We need to mask ourselves, then," she said.

Now that's a new one. She made it seem as if I did it on a whim whenever I wanted.

"Do you know how to do it?" I asked.

"It's all about wind mastery," she instructed. "By bending the light, you can obscure what others see. The good spellcasters, like wizards, can do it without an afterthought. The lucky bastards. It's far harder for us, though."

"Manipulating light and wind…" I chewed on the idea.

Seemed damn near impossible if anyone asked me.

As we crept toward the cathedral, Royse began to chant softly. I listened in, catching a familiar phrase here and there. A cloud of ozone, bitter and hard to breathe, gathered at her feet. The light around her head grew opaque and hard to make out. The haze grew larger and larger until everything appeared the same, yet I sensed I was behind something so much more. I'd witnessed a masking spell firsthand.

Royse moved on, not noticing she'd gotten hurt. A trail of bright red blood flowed from her ear down her neck. Was this the sign of a poor exchange in flesh for magic?

"Royse?" I whispered. She touched her earlobe and then noticed the crimson stain on her fingertips.

"I'm getting sloppy," she remarked. "Need to focus next time."

She took a few breaths and the bleeding stopped. The process was that simple for us to move on. Pretty soon, we'd reach the cathedral, but I had something on my mind I needed to say.

"Why did you bleed?" I asked.

"That's what happens when you let the exchange dictate where the power is drawn from," she said with a sigh.

So I was right. So that was why my nose bled as I tried to set the old magic spellcasters free. I'd pulled from myself and suffered the consequences.

Scaling up the church wall wasn't too bad. With a quick jump, we clawed past the first floor, beyond the bell towers on the second and third floors until we reached the very top. From up here, the wind beat against our faces and the night sky opened up to madness.

"No..." Royse's voice trailed off.

To the south, from the shore where we'd landed, another sea demon had rolled onto land. The beast attacked those who had remained there to protect the rear: the acolytes and a handful of the old magic spellcasters. While on the other side of the island, a great flash of light lit up the line of trees to the north. A full mile was bathed in brilliant light.

My mouth dropped open to see the frontline. A large cluster of wizards, most likely about twenty-five of them or so, formed a single line. Shoulder to shoulder they didn't move as unimaginable creatures slammed into a great wall of light. The red-orange beam radiated warmth that extended hundreds of feet into the night sky. None of the humans who walked along the grounds reacted to it at all. It was rather unsettling to see a grotesque monster, the size of an office building, mashing its gaping teeth-filled mouth against the wall of light, slamming into it again and again. Birds with feathers lit as if on fire, swooped in again and again into the quivering wall.

Both parties' collective power was a sight to behold.

"Good God, what happens if that wall falls?" I whispered.

"I don't want to find out." She peered beyond the wall of wizards and saw what I saw, far more warlocks concentrating their power on taking out their enemies, standing in loose formations near the monastery on the bridge to the island.

"Why aren't they using hand-to-hand combat?" I asked.

"The wizards will hold them back until that's necessary. There's far less bloodshed using that method."

I nodded, unease growing inside me. "How the hell are they holding up?"

"Sheer will. But they can't keep that up forever. Sooner or later they will run out of weapons."

"A source to draw from."

"Precisely. That's why most wizards lose when in battle like this. Either they lose in face-to-face combat or groups like this one run out of power. We need to help them."

"How do we do that?"

Royse turned and we watched the water demon go down with a final slash of Vasili's blade of fire. Flashes of light pulsed around him as wizards materialized from the far shore. That must have been the final barrier, keeping the wizards from reaching the island via the lake.

"Our army has arrived!" She turned to the frontlines. "Are you ready to show them how fierce the ladies can fight?" She took a piece of twine from a pocket on her leather belt. She wrapped it around her left wrist and then extended her left arm. While her left hand formed a fist, she used her right hand to pull the string away from her wrist. All the while, she spoke a spell. The string began to glow a golden hue and formed a beautiful bow of light.

"Let's see what you can do with your little twig, young wolf," she said with a sly grin.

I glanced at the goblin blade on my hand. The weapon had stuck with me until the very end. It still had the form of a wand. I pointed it toward the frontlines.

"So what do I hit?" I felt like a damn fool for asking, but what the hell, might as well ask.

"If it's not defending the frontline, take it out. The wizards won't harm the warlocks unless they have to do it, but we don't have to follow such rules."

"What about the wall?"

"The wall is to keep *them* out. Not us."

From the corner of my eye, I spotted Vasili, the other spellcasters, and a growing number of wizards, including Dr. Frank closing in from the rear. Like Royse advised, I tapped into what worked the best. Fire. While mumbling my spell, I prayed for success. A swirling arc of fire materialized in front of us and shot straight in the air.

"Control it, Natalya," Royse commanded as she shot arrow after arrow in quick succession. "Fire with control."

"I know," I blurted. "I'm not done yet." The fireball continued to head skyward, then shot down like a bat out of hell and rained down flames on the warlock frontline. Bursts of red-orange heat swept across the horizon, slamming into the warlocks who concentrated on breaking the wizards' frontline. Many fell off the bridge while others deflected the blow with a sweep of their arms.

The wall of light grew brighter as more wizards joined their brothers. The light intensified until it frothed and bubbled with power. So bright even Royse and I had to shield our eyes. The wall became a tsunami, surging forward and sucking in everything in its path: the warlocks on the bridge and the monstrous demons, who began to head back.

At my side, Royse shouted, "Time to leave this post for some fun."

She couldn't be serious. She wanted us to go to the frontlines.

"But I was enjoying the view…"

"Do you want to live forever, Natalya?" For some reason, a particular movie came to mind with that line, but I shrugged it off. This was real life and real people died down there.

"Do I have a choice?"

With a wink, Royse said, "We always do."

As the wave of light receded, not as many warlocks remained in the aftermath. The men left standing turned in the direction of the line of wizards and roared. As the warlocks ran for the frontline, wizards pulled out glowing white staffs and wands. The time for the final fight had come. But the warlocks didn't come unaided. Cyclops and trolls lumbered forward with clubs and maces. Dragons carried warlocks on their backs. Even worse, a handful of darklings sought out targets. The crimson glow from their eyes was easy to make out. A shock of red next to a cluster of darklings caught my eye. Cato.

We brought up the rear behind the old magic spellcasters, the acolytes, and Dr. Frank's wizards.

My heart pounded faster with each step. Through the monastery. Past the trees toward the bridge.

As my legs propelled me toward the fray, my fear subsided, only to be replaced with a growing craving in my stomach. A hunger to hunt. To tear apart anyone who tried to come for me. This cause was bigger than Thorn now. I was doing it for me, too.

Flashes of white and purple exploded across the bridge as combat began. It was so painfully bright. At my side, Royse fired at warlocks and ran at the same time.

Under the command of a warlock, a cyclops swung at Gostislav. The nimble werewolf leapt out of the way, then spun with blinding speed holding a serrated blade. The weapon sliced through the cyclops with ease. The creature groaned and fell hard with a thud.

Not far from us, Vasili ran into the first darkling. Royse's cousin appeared all too eager, the hints of his wolf touched his features. His bright purple eyes gleamed and he bared his teeth before he jumped onto the darkling and plunged his flaming sword into the darkling's tentacle covered back.

A fog of scents blanketed the land. Ozone and cinnamon, the aftermath of spellcasting, blended together with blood and sweat. The stench was so strong I tasted it on my tongue.

Light erupted to my left. I'd been distracted too long. A warlock dived off a darkling and aimed his marbled staff toward a monstrous furry creature that made me stop dead in my sprint. It was that thing from my nightmares. That towering creature with a gaping mouth filled with jagged teeth that Grandma Lasovskaya had transformed into to save my life when the Long Island Pack's flunkies cornered us. It had to be Tamara; my grandma was back home safe. The hair was different, a dark brown compared to my grandma's white hair.

The darkling tackled Tamara, wrapping its tentacles around her body. Her massive clawed hands snatched its snapping mouth to keep it from biting her. They wrestled across the ground, running into a tree with a shudder.

"Tamara…" I whispered. The wand tingled in my hand. How the hell could I help? They were too close together.

Two of the darkling's tentacles wrapped around her right arm. Snaking faster about the limb. With a vicious yank, it ripped her arm off at the shoulder. Blood sprayed the trees above.

"No!" I screamed. I glanced about, then up at the tree next to them. The ancient words Tamara taught me came fast. The wand responded in kind, channeling my fury into action.

Burn, baby, burn.

A limb exploded and fell across the darkling's back. The creature hissed. The distraction was just enough for Tamara to open her mouth wide and rip out the darkling's throat.

With a roar, Tamara tossed the carcass off and stormed away from me, right toward Cato, who had just taken down a wizard.

Cato laughed when he saw her coming. "Come for me, you old bitch!" I expected fire, ice, or any other form of magic, but when he aimed to fire, a golden arrow pierced his shoulder from behind.

A hundred paces away, I caught Royse, and, in a flash, she was on the next target. With another opportunity in place, Tamara swooped in for the kill. She only had one arm, but that hand had enough strength to wrench his staff away and hold him down. The cursing warlock wasn't totally unarmed though. A hand snaked out with a wicked blade. He stabbed it into her side again and again.

There was no way in hell I was gonna let this guy go without getting a taste of the action.

I jumped in, not caring what came at my back. His upper body was exposed, and that was just enough room for me to step in before Tamara had to let him go.

I swung my arms high with the wand pointed downward. I could have burned him. Froze the sneer on his face, but swinging the wand into his chest was all the more satisfying after he'd attacked my friends.

The wand cut into him as smooth as any blade. When he snarled, I gave the wand a hard twist to the right. "That's for burning down a perfectly good house," I growled.

Cato twitched and then with eyes still open he died. Tamara rolled off him. When I reached for her, her wide mouth opened, and she hissed at me.

The pain was there in her eyes, swimming through her so deep. I was better off leaving her to limp off the battlefield to a quiet corner.

When I looked up, not as much fighting was taking place. More fighters on our side stood than those on the opposing side.

Holy shit, we'd won.

Long hours in the night passed and I spent most of them walking along the bridge to Stolobny Island to check on prisoners and help the wounded wizards. Those who appeared hurt needed to be guided to one of the wizards who arrived for healing. With so many people roaming the monastery, it took a while to sort everything out.

I found Dr. Frank and told him Tamara was hurt, but we never found her. Her scent disappeared at the water's edge. Hopefully, she made it out of here alive.

Elric, the man who had betrayed the trapped werewolf spellcasters, also was never found, much to Vasili's disgust. Gostislav reported seeing him escape to the north with a few of the warlocks who went deeper into the forests. My heart hurt for the old magic spellcasters who wanted revenge.

By the time the light of day arrived, not a single supernatural creature dwelled on the island.

I was beyond eager to ask the wizards for answers on how to save Thorn, but Royse convinced me to rest for a few hours.

Chapter 25

I woke up a few hours after I collapsed into a bed at the lake house. The sounds of snoring came from every corner. On the other side of the queen-sized bed, Royse had claimed a spot. While I had curled in comfortably on my side, she had spread out with limbs extended in all directions. I couldn't help smiling as I took her palm off the side of my face. She stirred a bit and turned on her right side.

What I didn't expect to see when I got up was someone blocking the doorway. I almost gasped, but then had to keep myself from laughing out loud. Vasili had taken a spot on the cold wooden floor, his head on one of the pillows he must have stolen from the bed.

Royse's cousin was no doubt protecting our purity by keeping the upstarts out of the room.

So how the hell could I get out? I checked the window. It opened with a loud yawn, but Royse and Vasili didn't move. Man, they were out. Even the cool breeze in the room didn't stop Royse from snoring her heart out. After putting on my shoes, I climbed out and leapt to the ground.

I wanted my backpack. So, I went back inside to find quite the sight: a cluster of werewolves sleeping on the floor in the middle of the sitting room. The couches had been pushed to the wall along with any end tables and the space had turned into a communal sleeping area. My backpack had been used as a pillow, too.

With a few gentle yanks, I managed to get Gostislav to give it up. With a sigh, I left the lake house and made my way down the road toward town.

Before I'd fallen into a tired stupor, Royse had told me to go to a small restaurant at mid-day in Ostahkov. A place called Minas.

The walk into town was nice. Ostahkov felt like a small lake town you'd find in Minnesota or Wisconsin. I strolled along the never-ending road through town and welcomed the time alone to gather my thoughts after such a crazy night. A crisp, yet pleasant breeze from the lake flowed through my hair. Eventually, I reached a small mom-and-pop restaurant with a light blue sign labeled Minas.

An older woman greeted me at the door. "Are you Natalya?"

I nodded. "Something smells good."

The inside of the restaurant was well-cleaned with bright counters and personalized decorations.

"You have friends here." She led me to a private dining area full of people off the main dining room.

A single free seat must have been left for me. I immediately recognized Dr. Frank among the folks waiting. Most of them must've been wizards.

Tamara was here, too. She'd survived.

"You made it, Natalya," Dr. Frank said with a smile. "Are you hungry?"

No one had a plate in front of them. Only hot drinks. "I'm starving, but you know what I want. And I want that more than food right now."

Dr. Frank was the only man smiling at the table. Tamara had a slight smile, while Zoya, at her side, grinned brightly. Luda wasn't here though.

"I know what you want, Natalya," one man from the end of the table declared. "But we don't know if we should give it to you." He had a stern expression that didn't match his dark suit and short white hair. He had the kind of face I'd call handsome if he weren't frowning.

"Dr. Frank said your elders would consider it. Do you wizards have no honor? What about saving a life?" I asked him.

"There are always consequences to what we do, Natalya," Dr. Frank said softly. "To undo what others have done."

I fought the urge to stab my fingernails into my palms. "If I had to take down all of you at this table to find the answers, I would. I've fought a darkling, I've carried spellcasters in my body across hundreds of miles to help your cause, and I killed Cato. This is the final step, and whatever excuses you have frankly don't mean *shit* to me." On any other day, I would've kept my manners and refrained from swearing, but screw it. I'd been pushed into a corner, and I was damn tired.

"Gustav convinced us otherwise," the man said stiffly while looking in Dr. Frank's direction. "He said you've had a lot of personal growth on this journey. That you've done everything in your power, and, like any heroine, should receive a reward for your sacrifice."

My chest tightened and tears welled in my eyes. I wanted to look at my doctor, but I couldn't.

"How about we get to the secret then," the man in white began, a look of reluctance on his face.

"Wait! Shouldn't this be private?" I glanced at Tamara.

"We have other arrangements with her. She already knows the secret and has taken actions to help those in need in her family."

Tamara smiled, briefly touching the strawberry mark on her face wistfully. Had that mark been a curse of some kind? I still wondered about that. She appeared the same, though, yet at her side Zoya beamed. The young woman stole a glance at the man beside her. A man with black hair and brown eyes. They had similar facial features… The scent was different, yet the undertones the same.

My mouth dropped open wide when he blinked at me. "Luda?"

The man chuckled and I immediately recognized the grin. "Yes, Natalya, it's me."

"But how?"

"A few years ago, I was cursed," he replied. "All this time our grandmother has been working diligently to lift it."

My mouth bobbed up and down like a fool. So that was why Tamara wanted to learn how to remove curses. Maybe it was even the reason she wanted to tap into the magic of a captured fairy. "So why didn't you tell me you were a dude? Why didn't you tell Tyler?" *Awkward.*

"We were forbidden to talk about it or Lukas would've died," Zoya said. "Those were the terms of Cato's curse."

"All that time…" I managed. "He was behind it all."

"It's all right now," he said. It was rather hard to look at him now. I missed the sweet woman I thought of as a sister.

The wizard who must've been their leader, rose

from the end of the table. He walked up to me and leaned down. "Are you ready, Natalya?"

"I've been ready for so long." My heartbeat quickened as his breath fanned my neck and his sweet cinnamon-like scent filled the space around us.

He whispered into my ear and I burned every word into my mind. I tattooed and stamped it so that I'd never forget. When he finished, he rose with a smile and then every wizard vanished into light except Dr. Frank.

"Where did they go?" I asked.

"There is still business to handle in the area," Dr. Frank said. "It's also time for you to go, Nat."

I sighed. Thorn needed me now. "Do you know…" my breath caught in my throat. "If Thorn is still alive?"

He shook his head slowly. "No, I don't. You'll have to discover that on your own, but the least I can do is get you back to him quickly."

"Thank you." I stood, then turned to the three people still at the table.

"I'm sorry I can't stay and eat," I said. God knew I was ready to take down a deer.

"I'd be mad if you did stay," Zoya said, wiping away a tear that fell. "Hurry back to him."

"Is Tyler still here?" I asked her.

"We'll take good care of him," Lukas reassured me. He looked at his sister. "Or should I say my sister will take care of him?"

Zoya blushed before she ran to me to offer a hug. "Until we meet again."

"Until we meet again," I repeated. My gaze flicked to Tamara.

"I don't want any sad words, girl." She chaffed. "Our paths will cross again someday, whether we're exchanging spells or standing back-to-back in battle."

I nodded. "Please extend my apologies to the

acolytes, Royse, Vasili, and the others."

"No worries." The older woman sniffed but she didn't cry. "They have their own path to follow as well, their own journeys they must fulfill, as do you. Hurry to your mate."

I could have sworn, as Dr. Frank took my hand and we vanished into a blink of light, that a proud smile broke out on Tamara's face.

Chapter 26

Teleporting with an experienced wizard like Dr. Frank was a much smoother ride compared to other times. We materialized, on the ground like we should, in front of a small seafood restaurant in Finland.

"I thought wizards could only go so far?" I asked him.

He chuckled. "They can't, but a good friend loaned me a gift for such a purpose today."

By this point, I knew the power needed for such a jump of hundreds of miles. "Oh, thank you."

"It was my pleasure." He gave me a stern expression. "I expect you to contact Dr. Chainey while I'm away and make an appointment. You only have to share what you feel comfortable sharing, but I want you to do it. You've been through a lot since your last therapy session, a lot more than even most werewolves endure."

Reluctantly, I nodded. I'd have dreams for weeks about darklings, warlocks riding water demons, and the ravages of war. In particular, the dead. Having someone to talk to might be a good thing.

"Now you go find Thorn," he said. "I've kept you long enough."

"Thanks again, Dr. Frank."

"You're more than welcome. Good luck, Natalya."

And then I was alone again.

Finding Thorn shouldn't be too hard. I followed my nose through town until I returned to Jorge's house.

No one answered when I knocked, so I took a chance and the front door was unlocked.

"Thorn?" My stomach went queasy and I tried to quash the feeling. Any minute now, Thorn would show up and I'd feel stupid for getting worried.

The front porch appeared empty and beyond that all the bedrooms. All of the beds had been made and none of them smelled like my husband. My heart sank further and further as I went from room to room, hunting and searching. Drawing my nose along counters, checking light switches. The sob in the back of my throat turned to a whine.

I tried to call his number on my cellphone, but the line went directly to voice message.

Don't give up, yet. I went outside, not caring if I left the door open. One step onto the porch and I caught his faint scent from one of the cushioned seats. He'd sat there. I pressed my hands against the seat as if that would make him appear.

"Thorn, where are you?" A faint crunch when I pressed down drew my attention. Tucked between the seat and the cushion was a single piece of paper.

My hand shook as I read it.

A weak wolf never dies with the pack. Take heart in this decision, my love. Don't you dare let this bring you down. Protect the South Toms River Pack. I'll always love you.

And that was it.

He'd gone off to die alone.

The note floated out of my hand with the next cold breeze. My mouth hung open as my chest swelled with overwhelming pain. I couldn't stop the long moan from deep inside me.

My body collapsed on the wood floor. My eyes shut tight. So tight pain spread across my forehead until I gasped for breath. I couldn't breathe anymore.

What are you doing? Something whispered inside me.

Dying.

After everything you've been through, you're gonna just give up like this? Where is the woman who crossed thousands of miles?

Dying.

Where is the woman who fought for the rank of alpha female?

Dying.

What about the scent on the paper? How strong *was it?*

My head shot up and I opened my eyes. No more than ten feet away the note clung to one of the worn brown porch posts.

Strength surged through me and I ran to the piece of paper. I drew it to my face and inhaled. His scent was there. It hadn't been *days* since he wrote this. Maybe a day or even a few hours. The ink also wasn't light, but dark as if someone had recently written it.

I glanced around, managing to wipe the stream of tears from my face. There weren't any tracks in the ground. There had been rainfall recently, and any scents he had around the house had been washed away.

There had to be a way. Had to be.

I tried to figure out what to do. At my hip, I checked the goblin blade. It was silent. Nothing more than a piece of metal suitable for opening envelopes.

"C'mon," I begged it. "Don't you want to help me? For goodness sake, you fried darklings and fucking warlocks, but when I need to find *one* man you're just gonna sit there and do nothing?" I sighed. "My heart is what needs help this time."

The goblin blade still didn't move. Stupid blade.

I pressed my hand to the ground. There was nothing other than the faint pull from the jump point I discovered not long ago that took me to the acolytes. I didn't have the kind of spell to find Thorn. I was stuck. Anger welled inside me, pulsing through me, until my vision threatened to go red, but I managed to hold it in.

Think, damn it, think.

I stripped off my clothing. Not caring if a Finn saw me getting naked. I tucked my clothes into the backpack and left the pack on the porch. I didn't care if anyone found it.

Then I allowed the change to take me. It had been a while since I'd shifted. The last time had been the full moon at Tamara's farm. This time I hurried through the process, not suppressing the cry I made as my back snapped forward and my snout extended from my face. Rushing such a thing would be like trying to rush childbirth my grandma would say. Nature took the time it needed to take a caterpillar from a worm to a butterfly.

Pain pulsed through me, sparking every nerve-ending from my clawed fingertips to every hair follicle that sprouted dark hair on my limbs. But I rode through it, pushing the process harder. There was no time. No time left.

The world exploded with new sights and smells as I finished the transformation. I tried to run, but I collapsed on the ground not far from where I started. A few long minutes later, I got up and searched. Feeling exhausted could come later. I ran my nose along the note and circled the house twice.

On the third try, I caught the scent. It was so faint. A piece of him the rain couldn't wash away.

The trail led north. I sprinted into the forest as fast as my body could take it. Only stopping once in a while to check for the scent along the trail. I bounded around pine trees, jumping over dead trunks and rocks. For a moment, I lost his scent when I crossed a small brook, but footprints in the mud offered a new path. After a mile, snow began to patch the landscape, but a few places under the tall, thick trees offered shelter. A flash of red, his coat, up ahead made me race faster.

Thorn.

I ran to him, practically plowing into his body, but he didn't react. My nose touched his head, hoping and praying he wasn't dead and cold.

He had to be alive.

He had to hold on long enough for me to save him.

He was mine.

His chest rose slowly.

I licked his face with relief and whined.

"Damn you, woman," he whispered. His voice was faint. Even to my ears.

I licked him again and again. Taking in his scent as I covered him with my warm body. My fur tickled his face, and he laughed softly.

As much as I wanted to change back and do the spell, I needed a moment to rest first. Changing so quickly would leave me too weakened to help him. So I laid my head near his and continued to protect him. Every so often, I made sure he was breathing.

"I'm here." He reached out and pressed his hand against my flank.

Slowly, I let the change happen. With each breath, I

pushed again. First, my right leg. Then my left. My hands and then face. Never had I ever used such concentration to go from being a wolf to a human. It was freeing in a way. Most of the time, I let the wolf take over like it always wanted to do, but this time, I was in control.

I'd lost track of time, but when Thorn's now warm hand tucked my hip closer to his body, I sensed I was done. He opened his coat and drew my naked body toward his.

It was time.

"Don't move," I whispered.

I took his face between my palms. His eyes blinked as if sleep tugged at him.

The words burned into my mind came smoothly. Unlike when I had to free the old magic spellcasters, there was no doubt in my mind this time. My heart swelled as the power pumped through me, and death's dark hue around him was exposed to me as I spoke. It was dark gray and slithered around him like spreading ink in water. I continued to speak, feeling the magic tug at the blackness around him, slowly plucking it away. The curse retreated and turned from black into an opaque white that disappeared.

By the time my skin chilled from the cold and the sun sat on the horizon, the darkness was gone.

My beloved was free.

"Home?" he murmured finally.

"Definitely. As soon as possible."

"So how are we getting there?" he asked weakly.

"Ha!" I couldn't help laughing. "First I need some clothes. Then you and I are getting passports, and we are getting on a plane and flying like normal people. I don't care how much it costs. No more teleporting. No more casting spells. I want to have a normal life — as normal as I can — for at least the next decade."

He kissed my neck. "Normal sex, too?"

"Boring, normal sex. Dry humping if necessary."

He smiled sweetly at me. "I can work with that."

"So much has happened to us and I'd rather face our issues back home than what we've gone through. I'm about to get royally chewed out when I get back, but a new Natalya Stravinsky is ready to make her mark on South Toms River."

Chapter 27

Our flight back to the U.S. was the smoothest experience I'd ever had. Even the drive from the airport in Newark to South Toms River had gone off without a hitch.

The multiple plane rides had taken nearly a day to complete, but with Thorn at my side, everything was damn near perfect. Even the mystery salmon dish for the airline meal didn't taste that bad.

But as we approached my parents' house that evening, my heartbeat sped up and my grip on Thorn's hand tightened.

"Don't be scared," he said.

"I'm not."

"Then how come I feel like you're about to break my hand?"

"We have been apart for a while. I'm catching up..."

"Mmm-hmmm." He gave me a side glance that told me I wasn't fooling anyone.

After Thorn pulled into the driveway, I took a moment to breathe and wipe the sweat off my palms.

Then I opened the car door. *Might as well get it done and over with.* I walked with Thorn up to the house. Someone must have heard the car, the door was open and my mother waited behind it. Her grip on the door tightened and her blue eyes widened as she took me in.

Almost as if she didn't expect to see me.

I caught the scent of dinner through the door. Mom had prepared fried duck for Dad and Grandma.

Dad joined Mom at the door. They didn't say a word, merely getting out of the way as Thorn led us inside.

We stood in the middle of the living room as Grandma entered from the dining room. At the sight of me, her eyes brightened. Then she caught the glare from my father.

"I brought her back, Fyodor," Thorn said. "Or, I should say, your daughter brought *me* back."

My dad didn't move. Besides the loud thumping of my heart, the only other sound that bled in was the bubbles from the soup cooking in the kitchen.

Suddenly my dad rushed in to hug Thorn. The big man practically smothered my husband then pulled him back to bring their foreheads together. "I didn't know if I'd ever see you again, boy. Things had been...grim for you."

My family continued to face Thorn and I waited for what was to come. Would my dad reach for me next? But my mother hugged Thorn instead, then my grandma got a chance. She kissed his cheeks and looked him over.

"I can see you're healing again like you should," she said softly to him.

"Yes, Mrs. Lasovskaya." He ran his fingers through his blond hair, the grays long gone.

"I told you to stop calling me that. You're my grandson now. Call me Grandma."

"I'll try to remember next time." Thorn took my hand and tugged me toward Grandma as if to say, "Your turn."

Dad stepped forward, avoiding Thorn's eyes out of respect. "Thorn, I need you to leave for a moment."

Thorn and I exchanged a glance. I knew this was coming, but I managed to remain steady. I was ready for whatever was to come.

"There are words that need to be said to my daughter," Dad said firmly. "Not to your mate."

Thorn didn't let go of me. "I want to shield her."

Dad sighed. "That doesn't matter right now."

A loud knock on the door interrupted the moment. Mom hurried to open it. I held back a groan as all my relatives in South Toms River bounded inside and filled the room.

I was so screwed. None of them looked happy. Aunt Vera scowled and Aunt Olga looked about ready to use the fancy pair of high heels she had on to knock me out. All my aunts and uncles, followed by the cousins and such found a place to stand in the living room. My brother and his wife, who held the baby, came in last. I'd hate to say it, but even Sveta didn't look pleased either.

"Five minutes," my father said. He coughed and looked at everyone else who didn't hide his or her displeasure. "Make that about ten."

Thorn looked to me and I jerked my head toward the door. *I got this*, my eyes said. He reluctantly left to wait on the lawn with his arms crossed.

And so the conveyor belt of castigating began. Mom got a piece of me first.

"Are you out of your mind, Natalya Stravinsky?" she barked in Russian.

Based on past experience, I knew silence was the key. My mouth threatened to open, but Grandma made a subtle motion, drawing her fingertip across her mouth. *Zip it, girl.*

"I worried about you for days after you left." She pointed to Grandma. "Your grandma couldn't sleep or eat properly while you were gone. And she's too old *not* to eat." By the time she finished, she was breathless, her face a deep red.

I expected her to even slap me, but she pulled me into a hug. Mom smelled so good—like a warm blanket you wrapped around yourself for protection on the darkest of days. The hug was so unexpected, it took my breath away. Then she released me and Aunt Vera closed in before my dad could step in. And so on and so on.

Even my younger cousins got to have a word or two.

But no one looked me in the eyes—which was rather amusing. I kept a straight face the whole time, listening to my punishment and accepting the embrace when it came.

And finally, my dad approached me. Big Fyodor Stravinsky who stood far taller than me with his imposing girth.

"My daughter is a fool." He was so close I could make out the stubble growing on his face. I could take in his familiar and comforting scent. "A brave fool."

I wanted to say, "I'm your brave fool, Papa," but I remained silent.

He took me into his arms and I didn't stop myself from sighing. I'd come so far since I'd been pushed out of the pack.

Grandma came last, walking silently across the floor. I waited for her words, but she reached up and cupped my face. Her hands were so soft. She gently kissed my cheeks again and again. "I can't be mad at you, *vnuchka*. Never. A granddaughter I'd never forsake."

She took me in, smiling with her soft brown eyes. "You did good, girl."

"Thank you, Grandma."

After that, I noticed a few family members had helped themselves to Mom's food and began to sit and eat. She always made too many servings so everyone would be fine. The visitors weren't done yet, though. Thorn came back inside to greet pack members. More werewolves from South Toms River came by, paid their respect to the returned alpha, and left again with bowed heads.

Even Rex came to the house towards the end.

"You look good, Thorn." He strolled up to Thorn, but left a healthy distance between them. Briefly, he looked in Thorn's eyes, but looked away just as quickly.

"Thanks. I appreciate you *taking* care of things while I was gone," Thorn said.

There was hidden meaning behind his words. Almost as if they had been carefully chosen. My husband rarely smirked at his friends, but I caught the hint of one in his face this time.

"As always," he replied. "I'd do it whenever needed."

"Hello, Rex." I looked at him this time, but he didn't look in my eyes either. Not once.

"Natalya, it's good to have you back."

"I'm glad to be back." I continued the conversation, waiting for him to say something, to bait me or make me feel beneath him, but he remained silent. And I remained strong.

Rex left a humble man.

I think I destroyed that wall, Aggie.

The night wore on and the celebration continued with wine. The one person I expected to see hadn't shown up yet.

"Dad, have you seen Aggie?" I asked him.

He shrugged. "I haven't seen her since you left. Thorn's brother Will has been out of town, too."

Thorn nodded at the news. "Maybe they decided to have some time alone?"

"I don't know. Maybe she left a note or message."

"We'll have to look when we get home," Thorn said.

Just hearing the word "home" made me smile. I hugged my husband and pulled him close to me. His firm chest was the perfect place for my head.

His eyes grew stormy as he kissed my nose. "It's time for us to go."

"Most definitely."

There wasn't a note or message from Aggie, but I didn't learn that until the next morning. I spent the night making love with Thorn like we were a bunch of horny newlyweds. He was definitely back to his old self.

Being at home with Thorn, with all our things together, brought me comfort. Not all my Christmas ornaments could fit in his house, but enough fit in the small spare bedroom to keep me happy.

I wanted to go back to my routine or at least try to pretend things were normal. And that meant seeing Bill and begging for my job. I usually got time off when I needed to go somewhere. This time I'd disappeared and left him high and dry, which was rare for me.

I'd probably been fired during my absence.

But there hadn't been any message from Bill on the answering machine. Just a few from the Home Shopping Network on new sales. Thorn had ignored them, thank goodness.

It was a Tuesday, and I could just as easily go in to

face the pesky goblin.

Thorn's hands circled my waist, drawing me out of my moment of reverie. "I know that face. What's on your mind?"

"I wonder what's going on at The Bends..."

"Well, the last time I passed it, they were selling antiques and the spring sale should be going on soon..."

"Stop it. I mean I wonder if I have a job anymore."

"Do you have to work there?" He grabbed my chin and rubbed his nose against mine. "You don't have to go back. There are other jobs."

"But not like that one. It's a good fit for me."

His hands drifted down my sides to my lower back where he kneaded the muscles there. He pulled me close to show me what he really wanted me to do instead of going to work.

"You could stay at home. I could stay with you, and we could reproduce. Breed. Make babies?"

I couldn't stop myself from laughing.

"I can do that—at night—and work somewhere else during the day." I escaped out of his arms. "Wait here. In bed. And I'll be back in an hour after I talk to Bill."

He offered a half-smile. "You're not going to be back in an hour."

"How do you know?"

"I know my wife." He took my hand and led me to the closet. From there, he picked out a blouse and a pencil skirt. "This gray skirt should fit just right," he said with his eyebrows wagging.

After he picked out my clothes, he laid down on the bed with his hands behind his head. "If you're gonna leave me I should at least get something nice to look at while you're gone."

As I took off my nightgown, and then my bra, I

gave him a well-deserved show.

The Bends was relatively busy for a Tuesday morning. There still weren't any spellcasters, but the cashiers appeared to be rushing to keep up with helping customers and ringing up purchases. I itched to step in and help, but I kept on walking to the business office instead, my heels clicking on the floor. Quinton lumbered out of the dock and waved my way.

"Hey, Nat." The Bends's janitor appeared a bit less pale today.

"Quinton."

"Good to see you at work," he said.

"Thanks."

He almost turned to leave, but stopped mid-stride. "The smell is gone." His facial expression turned apologetic. "And I'm sorry, but I haven't found the time to do research for you."

"I don't need to know what it is — it's okay. You're busy with a new girlfriend and she should have your spare time."

After my chat with Quinton, I found Bill in the office going over invoices. He grumbled under his breath, even more so after I walked through the door.

"Hello, Bill," I said softly.

He grunted.

"I know what you're thinking," I began. "And I wanted to say outright that I'm sorry."

He grunted again.

"If you don't want me to come back after an unexcused —"

He pushed up his glasses and snorted.

" — lengthy absence, I understand," I finished.

He finally looked up at me. "After you left, that fire witch finally set the counter on fire."

I cringed, not wanting to look behind the counter if

I ever saw it again.

"Also that harpy, you know the one who tried to swindle us for that scratched up vase? That crazy bird came back and tried to do it again."

"She was rather—"

"And the new girl I hired to manage the invoices after you disappeared has messed up everything in your system." He made another rude noise. "She said she went to some fancy business school. Business school, my ass. Back in my day, we learned in the field. You took a few blows in the crotch, you bent over and recovered, and then you picked yourself up by the britches and you learned. This girl has a brain the size of a smashed walnut."

"I'm sorry." There was a new scent here—a perfume I'd smelled before.

The door swung open behind me, and a blonde woman walked in. Erica Holden. She stopped in her tracks when she saw me.

"Nat, you're back." Her gaze switched to the floor and then she adjusted her clothes with twitchy fingers. Her cotton-candy sweater still clung to her boobs and hung on for dear life. Be that as it may, out of all the women in town, I still believed Erica was one of the most beautiful ones. Too bad she had a past history of being a major bitch.

"Hello, Erica." I tried to hold her gaze, but she wouldn't look at me, which was as it should be, since I had a role to play as alpha female.

The goblin coughed to get his new worker's attention. "Erica, I don't know if you're just too smart for the software, but you managed to change half the ID numbers on past orders."

Now, *that* made me shudder. The only way to do that was if someone had *really* messed with my work.

Bill got up from the desk and Erica took his place.

"Fix it," he ordered.

"Of, course. I'll get right on that."

"Nat, go to the dock, I want to talk to you."

The woman who had walked past me and sat down didn't exude spite or smugness. Her scent came off as calm and submissive. Apparently, I wasn't the only one who the new spring season had changed.

I extended an olive branch to show there were no hard feelings between us. "Once I talk to Bill, I can offer you a hand if you'd like?"

"I'd appreciate that," she said softly.

I followed Bill out to the dock. My boss walked up to the edge but didn't fall over. "I've already hired someone else," he said with finality.

"I know and I'm okay with that." I kinda wasn't, but Bill didn't need to know that.

Bill cleared his throat. "She's wet behind the ears and stuck up, though. She could use someone to train her."

I hid a smile. Bill rarely outright said when he needed help. Ordering folks was ten times easier.

"Yes," I folded my arms and joined him. "She could use a hand to get her on track."

"With her business degree, she'd make great manager material."

"Maybe." I wouldn't let him take it that far.

He coughed again. "So did it help you in Russia?"

"Did what help me?" Color me confused at this point.

"The blade." So he meant the goblin blade.

"Yeah, it did."

The smile on his face widened and even his eyes brightened. A rare sight for Bill unless he held some cash in his hands. As he stole a glance at me, a thought came to mind.

"So it was yours all this time?" I asked. "The

knife?"

My boss's right eyebrow rose over his glasses. "Not really."

"Okay, now I'm lost."

"That's not unexpected." He sighed. "You gave it to me when you asked if I knew the owner."

"I handed it to you to show you—"

"You *never* hand something like that to someone like me." He chaffed. "Remember that...okay."

I nodded. A bit touched. *A little bit.*

"When you put it in my hand, it became mine. When I *reluctantly* gave it back to you, I guess I left it with some operating instructions."

Ah, so that was what Tamara had noticed. The secrets the blade had kept.

"Anyway, times a wasting, and Erica is probably in there tossing my money down the drain. Offer her a hand, will ya."

"Sure." I wanted to ask why he'd hired her of all people, but even Erica needed a job. Her dad was one of the wealthiest guys in South Toms River so something must have gone down between the two to where she felt compelled to work.

How things had changed.

I had worked a full and rewarding day.

My husband knew me all too well.

As I walked into our home, dinner's rich aroma and a clean house greeted me. As I shrugged off my jacket, I smiled. That smile ended when I looked at the coat. It had tears in a few places and the zipper didn't go all the way up. A thorough dry cleaning and some mending would do it some good.

Maybe I should buy a new one.

"You ready to eat, wifey?" Thorn called out. "I burned some soup for you, sweetheart." He laughed, enjoying his joke. My husband was actually a pretty good cook.

"Sounds wonderful." I cleaned out the pockets so I wouldn't forget to take care of it tomorrow morning. What I plucked from the recesses of one pocket made me pause. Two petals. I'd gotten them from Nick. A few months ago, they'd been vibrant and red, but now they were now black and withered. What happened to them?

My mind flashed to when he'd first given me a rose:

"Plant it at the perimeter of your property. Water it with frankincense and the flower will protect you from those who mean you harm."

I laughed to myself remembering that day. I'd been reluctant to part with just one of my Christmas ornaments, and he didn't want to give me his flower.

Eventually I'd given him his flower back, but on the day of my trials around New Year's he'd given me the most wonderful gift.

He reached into his pocket and palmed something I couldn't see. Then slowly he opened my hand and placed rose petals there. Bright red and freshly plucked. My skin tingled from where they lay.

With my right hand, I traced along the edge of the two petals. "Is this from the rose you gave me? The one to protect my property?"

"Yeah. Magic still lingers there." Our gazes locked briefly. "It'll always be there."

He never fully explained what powers the rose held, but since I'd received them, they had been tucked away in my pocket.

Realization sucker-punched me in the gut.

Every time I cast a spell, I had to draw from a source. Each time it should have been from *me*. A few times it must've been, but when I needed it, really needed it, a part of Nick had been there to shoulder the burden. My dear friend Nick had helped me save Thorn.

I was quiet during dinner that night, enjoying the soup and chicken dinner with Thorn in front of the TV. After a few hours of mindless TV, Thorn dozed off, so I left him to prepare for bed. As I hung up my clothes and prepared my blouse and skirt for tomorrow, I noticed something shiny on my dresser.

Right there on my jewelry box was another unexpected gift: a pink seashell on a gold necklace with a note on it: *I didn't forget.*

I hurried to the window and found it cracked open. When I gazed outside, no one was there. My mermaid friend Heidi was long gone. With a barely contained giggle, I ran my hand over the beautiful shell. It warmed my palm.

When I put the necklace on, I breathed a sigh of relief and brushed my fingers along the ridges. Heidi had told me she used it as an anchor to keep her steady during the rough times. Its magic didn't work on werewolves, but for just a brief moment, I *believed* that it did.

And that was more than enough for me.

THE END

Did you love COMPELLED?

Wonder what happened to Aggie? Her adventures continue in BEST SERVED BITTER. But before that we got a sneak peek into her past with BITTER DISENCHANTMENT. Read on to check out the first chapter of Aggie McClure's first book called BITTER DISENCHANTMENT.

Available now from your favorite retailers.

Werewolf Natalya Stravinsky's outspoken sidekick, Aggie McClure, is featured in this prequel novella. Before Agatha set foot in South Toms River, New Jersey, she had the fight of her life to face. Destined to be the alpha female over her Manhattan pack, Aggie was fully prepared to take on her role until her father arranges a marriage without her consent. She wants out–but the only way is with money–something her new controlling husband won't give her to escape. But such odds never kept a wolf like Aggie down. To sever the twisted tie, she finds herself pitted against raging wood nymphs and backstabbing brownies in an underground supernatural fighting ring. With every victory, the sweet taste of freedom is closer, but her husband isn't willing to let her go that easily. Until the very end, Aggie must fight for the one thing she's never had: a choice.

BITTER DISENCHANTMENT
BOOK 1: AGGIE MCCLURE

You can't run away from your family forever, Agatha.

For the last hour, I sat at a bus stop bench, no more than two blocks from home: my family's penthouse. My dad's words bounced around my head, and all I could do was think about the shit I had to face tonight. A few steps away, Park Avenue was busy, but that was no surprise, it was practically rush hour in New York City. No one paid me any attention. At first, a man slowed down with an interested smile, but one look from my slitted eyes sent him on his way. This wasn't the day to fuck with me.

"Agatha, there's a woman I'd like for you to meet when you come home," my father had said over the phone this morning. "Don't be late today."

A sour feeling crept into my stomach and twisted it into wicked knots as I stood. If I'd been in wolf-form, I would've been circling the streets without a sense of direction or destination. Instead of spending my time walking, I merely warmed the park bench.

Reluctantly, I walked home. Each step closer to my building weighed me down. My leather boots felt impossibly heavy. Even the collar of my shirt seemed to tighten around my neck. I didn't want to live in my skin right now. Tonight my family would change — in a way I didn't want.

Eventually, I reached my building. The doorman, who'd known my family for the last twenty years, opened the glass doors with a smile. It faded when he saw my face, but it wasn't his job to ask so he put on a chipper mask. "Good evening, Miss McClure. Hope you had a good evening."

"Thank you, Burt," I murmured. It was more than what most of my family said to him.

The elevator trip up to the twentieth floor was just as somber as my walk had been. Once I arrived, our guards, who protected our household, merely nodded my way heads bowed. They were large men, burly in stature, but they paid respect to the daughter of a pack leader, the Midtown werewolf pack leader to be exact.

A white-haired human butler waited at the door. I had nothing for him to carry or put away so he merely mimicked the guards.

"You're late," he chided gently.

"I would've been later, Helms, given the circumstances," I said.

"I understand — but you know Mr. McClure. He prefers punctuality."

I frowned at the bruise on the side of his neck. My dad, Desmond McClure, had most likely taken out his frustration for my tardiness on Helms. The poor human was paid well, but that didn't mean he deserved to be treated like a slave. Life in my world wasn't pretty if you sat on the lower rungs. Everyone had a price they were willing to pay in exchange for closeness to wealth and power, both of which my dad had far too much.

Right before I'd left for college at New York University, I'd said to Helms, "If you want to leave, I'll find a way to protect you."

At the time, he shrugged and gave me a wise smile that touched the wrinkles around his eyes. "A member of the Helms family has taken care of the McClure family since my grandfather immigrated from England. It's a tradition I'm meant to bear." Even though his family had adopted him, he took his service seriously.

At the time, I acquiesced, but now I'd rather just kick Helms out of this house with a generous check in hand. As difficult as the circumstances were for him, at least he was here by choice. I was trapped by birth.

Helms followed me from the foyer to the sitting room. I didn't need to be told to go there. My nose was sufficient enough to follow the trail of cigar smoke. My dad loved to smoke exotic ones — rich and thick, a blend of cedar and walnut. When I was a child, they reminded me of warm hugs from my dad. Now they made me feel nothing but contempt.

Two people waited in our sitting room. The tall windows gave a beautiful view of Central Park and the lit skyline of NYC. I expected the grand fireplace to be lit, like it always was in the evening, but it wasn't. The place felt as cold and empty as my heart.

When I sat on the Queen Anne couch opposite my dad and the woman he'd mentioned on the phone, Helms offered me a drink.

"No, thank you." I kept my gaze focused on a beautiful set of hydrangeas in a thin glass vase. A fresh set of flowers every day of the year. Barely perceptible with all the damn cigar smoke.

The grandfather clock on the other side of the room ticked with every swing of the pendulum. The ever faint sounds of the evening traffic bled through the windows and touched my inner ears. Yet no one said a single word for several minutes — until Dad spoke. "You didn't come home when you were supposed to."

"An hour or two doesn't change anything," I replied.

The tall, blonde woman shifted her legs. Her perfume was expensive and floral. Not a personal favorite to be honest. I could've looked up and greeted her, but if my assumptions were right, this guest wasn't someone who wanted to be my new BFF.

"Agatha, I'd like for you to meet Kelly."

Before my common sense kicked in, my mouth moved. "So you're the woman who's replacing my mother."

Kelly's smile twitched, but she held it nonetheless.

"Agatha," Father warned. A subtle growl rumbled in his chest.

"Kelly, have you met my mother to discuss this matter?" I asked her.

"Another remark, Agatha and your position in the pack will be lowered." Dad's warning had a bite this time so I crossed my arms and turned away from them.

Kelly didn't speak, but I could practically detect the smugness. A rich musk that deepened her perfume. Our eyes met and I wished she would've challenged my gaze, but she looked away.

4

Under most circumstances, Kelly couldn't slide in as my dad's new consort. Since Morwyn McClure was alive and well, she'd have to fight Mom for the job. Alpha females were very possessive when it came to their mates. They had to be since other women lined up to take their place. In my pack, no one had *ever* challenged Mom. She dominated other females without even trying.

My father had simply cut off their marriage ties as if their bond had meant *nothing*.

My hand gripped the side of my chair tight enough for the fabric to cry out from a tear.

Kelly switched her legs again, smoothing over her skirt. She maintained her silence. I wondered what she'd do if my mother walked through the door right at that moment. Once Mom got word of Kelly's attempt to usurp her position in the pack, Mom would challenge. Would Kelly accept, or would she fall to the floor quivering like a pup? Mom was the alpha female, and the only wolf she had above her was the alpha male. Unfortunately, that alpha was my father, and I was sure he'd find a way to prevent Mom from exerting her rights.

I bit my tongue as the sour words I wanted to say tainted my mouth. Oh, how I wanted to say how I really felt. How I wanted things to go back to the way they were even if that meant I lived in a household where my mother and father lived apart.

Helms entered the fog of our *tête-á-tête*. He flicked a glance my way and gave me an expression I remembered from my youth. *Back down, Agatha*, his brown eyes said. *Choose another day to fight.* As much as I wanted to knock this chick across the room, it wouldn't happen today. So I sighed and did nothing to hide that I was sulking.

"Dinner is served," he announced.

Dad got up first, with Kelly not far behind him.

When he noticed I hadn't moved, Dad checked behind him. I reluctantly followed. He had no right to assume I'd accept this. Other packs didn't operate this way. Just a few like ours who swayed from the Code, or the code of ethics for werewolves. According to the Code, the strong led the pack and the weak were cast aside. Mom was strong enough to lead. It was in other pack matters where she wasn't good enough for him.

For the most part, the dinner service in our formal dining room was like any other. Dad sat at the head of the table, but I wanted to snarl at the sight of Kelly sitting to his right. I shouldn't be surprised, after entering the room, to see someone else had taken my mother's place. The urge to take the spot was strong, and I could've stared her down until she gave it up. Instead, I sat in my usual place. Right next to Kelly. She squirmed beside me, and I grinned.

"Kelly, sit up straight," Dad chided. "I won't have my only daughter intimidate my future mate."

I raised my eyebrow at my dad's frown. What would he do if I said the impossible? Right here, right now. The wolf in me grinned, ready and eager to strike. I took a deep breath. "Kelly, on my honor, I challenge—"

"Don't you dare!" In an instant, Dad's arm stretched across the table, his hand slapping down between the place settings. The table shuddered as fine china rattled and glasses of water spilled. "This is your final warning, Agatha. This isn't the time or the place to go against me."

Kelly and I froze under his glare while the servants rushed to clean up the water. His face hardened, every muscle tightened like a stretched bow. He slowly picked up an upright wine glass and gulped.

I kept my gaze on my plate. All the while, Dad chuckled. "That's my Aggie. If only you'd been born a man, you would've made a fine pack leader."

To keep myself from laughing at his condescending, sexist garbage, I focused on the shiny reflections in the plate. I counted every curve, even the minute nicks beyond a human eye's capability to see. Anything to escape the very thought that my life in my pack could end up in the very manner my mother's had: abandoned by my mate who no longer saw me as the woman he chose as his life partner. No more than ten feet beyond the doorway to this penthouse, my mother had been relegated to a one-bedroom apartment. All alone.

My trance ended when the staff brought our food. Almost as if to calm me, Helms served me first after my father. He gave me a knowing look and gently squeezed my shoulder as he filled my bowl with soup. He pushed the spoon closer to me.

Eat. He tilted his head toward the food.

I picked up the spoon. As the food slid down my throat, my anger dissipated a bit. How well Helms knew me. My pesky, yet persistent, habit. Just the thought of eating — the very act of chewing — brought a deep comfort. Something that could only be compared to the satisfying feeling you'd have when you scratched an itch that never went away. The servants added two rolls to my bread plate where others had one. An extra serving of baked chicken when my plate quickly emptied. As I gave into the place where happiness resided, a place with a fork in my hand, I sensed Kelly's eyes on my food. Most werewolves ate a lot to keep up with our advanced metabolisms, but I had just eaten my fourth serving. Far more than usual, even for a werewolf.

Naturally, my dad had to interrupt my blissful moment with a word or two.

"Since we're dealing out all the cards tonight," he said, "I thought you'd like to know I arranged your engagement not too long ago."

"Excuse me?" I said between bites. "How *long* ago?"

Our eyes met. His blue eyes to my blue eyes. A slight grin etched into his cheek. "Three or four years ago..."

I chortled a bit. Matchmaking among the packs wasn't new. But over the past year, I'd made an organized effort to reach out to other single pack leaders or males who would inherit the position, meeting and talking to them — on my terms. No hiding in the dark with secrets or deals under the table. I wanted to choose a good man for myself, not stew in the situation where I was now.

"You promised," I said crisply. The food in my stomach turned heavy as iron.

"That was five years ago, Agatha."

"You promised," I repeated.

"I have your best interests in mind."

"So how much am I worth to you? A hotel? Land?" I tried to distract myself with my meal again and managed to take a bite of the custard pie one of the servants hurried to place in front of me. Their attempt to calm my anger was touching, but far too late a gesture. At the moment, disgust clawed through me like razor-laden ice, slicing across every inch of me. So I filled my belly, cramming in every bit in hopes I'd think of something else. Unfortunately, my grip on my fork tightened again and again. Until the fucking metal bent.

Dad wasn't far from me. Just five feet away. I could imagine myself flying across the table to tackle him with my butter knife. Not exactly the best blade to do the job—but it was the feeling that counted. The muscles in my legs clenched, ready to jump, but I took a few cleansing breaths and focused on my reflection in the glass of water.

Stay calm. You know how this game is played. This wasn't the right time to fight. My father was far too strong and fast for someone my age to challenge. I was only twenty-four. Still a pup by an elder's standards.

Helms entered the room and announced a guest. Not far behind him, a stranger waltzed in. I could smell him at first: a thick ass fog of Brut. An overpowering choice in cologne—but his appearance was another story. He had an angular face, with a wide back and narrow hips. Black hair and eyes. Not too shabby at all in the looks department. But he had one strike against him already that nothing— including a golden-tipped pecker—would make me agree to a relationship with him. His black eyes assessed me, perhaps waiting to see if I'd acquiesce on our first encounter.

Not gonna happen, pal.

He approached my father, shook hands with him, gave something to me, and then took a seat across from me. I refused to acknowledge him. Refused to see the bouquet of exotic flowers he'd left at my side. Even more, I refused to look at the tiny box he clutched in his palm. Tiny enough to fit an engagement ring. How *traditional* of him. Why even bother to bring it if they had planned to just *tell* me I was engaged?

8

My gaze flitted to the seat beside me where Kelly sat. I could almost hear my mom's words in my ear. *You're the daughter of a high-ranking female from the* Carreg *Pack in Wales. A lineage of strong women. Always display dignity, Agatha.*

Mom's refined breeding always battled with the one thing I inherited from Dad: a need for control. I should thank him for it—after I figured out how to get out of this mess. For both my mother and me.

My father spoke quietly with Victor Pershing, as he was introduced to us, about Dad's plans to claim Kelly as his mate during the next full moon. That was a few weeks away. An ideal time for our marriage to begin, Victor agreed. According to the Code, werewolves mated for life. Apparently, the exception to the case was women like my mother, women who no longer produced children.
No matter how hungry I was, I couldn't eat another bite. A strange thing for a compulsive overeater like me. My eyes met Dad's again before I turned away. I should've tried to take him out, but my time would come someday.

OTHER TITLES BY SHAWNTELLE MADISON

COVETED SERIES

Natalya Stravinsky:
Collected (Prequel Novella)
Coveted
Kept
Compelled

Aggie McClure:
Bitter Disenchantment
Best Served Bitter (Coming in 2014)

Tessa Dandridge:
Repossessed: The Warlock Repo Man Chronicles

HADLEY WEREWOLVES
Bitten by Deceit
Bitten by Treachery
Bitten by Vengeance (Coming in 2014)

ABOUT SHAWNTELLE MADISON

Shawntelle Madison is a Web developer who loves to weave words as well as code. She'd be reluctant to admit it, but if pressed, she'd say that she covets and collects source code. After losing her first summer job detasseling corn, Madison performed various jobs, from fast-food clerk to grunt programmer to university webmaster. Writing eccentric characters is her favorite job of all. On any given day when she's not surgically attached to her computer, she can be found watching cheesy horror movies or the latest action-packed anime. Shawntelle Madison lives in Missouri with her husband and children.

If you'd like to know when Shawntelle releases her next book, please sign up for her newsletter list. Visit her website and click on contact in her menu: shawntellemadison.com

You can also join Shawntelle's Facebook community to learn more about her books!

Find Shawntelle Madison online:
http://www.shawntellemadison.com
http://www.facebook.com/shawntellemadisonauthor
http://www.twitter.com/shawntelle

Made in the USA
Charleston, SC
26 June 2014